MW01282830

# CATWALK DEAD
## Book 2 in the Housekeeper Mystery Series

## F. Della Notte

**Catwalk Dead**

**Copyright** © by Francine Paino

All rights reserved.

**ISBN: 13:978-1-7326489-1-3**

**CATWALK DEAD**
Murder
in the Rue de L'Histoire Theatre

# 1920

The night sky over Austin was filled with a thousand stars, but it was black as ink inside the barn.

The knife-wielding watcher's pupils dilated to capture any particle of light; his ebony clothes were covered in dirt and grass from crawling through the field to confront his target. He moved in silence, melting into the dark interior, focused on his prey.

Sweaty from digging, dressed in dirty pants and a tee-shirt, the watcher's quarry had a gun tucked into his waistband. After unloading and hauling bottles, he pulled one last box from his wagon. Grunting from the effort, the man set the box down at the back of the barn and then mopped sweat from his face and neck with a bandana. Something moved behind him. He reached for his gun and swung around. Too late.

The knife-wielding watcher with coal-black eyes was on him in a flash. He sliced through his victim's stomach with surgical skill and up into the man's heart.

"Damn you and yours to hell!" the victim screamed as his dead body thudded onto the barn floor.

"I'll see you there," the watcher whispered, wiping the blade on the dead man's shirt. He stepped over to where his gutted enemy had been working. With his booted foot, he pushed the hay aside, ever mindful of snakes, and was stunned by the discovery.

There was a six-foot-by-six-foot hole with gold bars at the bottom. He looked at the last box his vanquished foe had carried in—more gold bars.

"You worked with foreigners. You should have worked with me. Now all of this is mine."

The distant hum of a motor penetrated the night; he listened. Through the spaces between the slats of the barn's siding, the truck's lights became visible, and its engine louder as it approached on the dirt road. He needed to hide what he'd done and what he'd found, and he didn't have much time.

First, he shoved the box of gold into the hole; he then dragged the body over and rolled it on top of the gold. Hastily, he filled the makeshift grave with dirt, tamped it down, and covered it with hay.

Returning to the kill spot, he scraped away blood from the packed dirt floor then slithered out the same way he'd come in through broken barn boards.

The truck was still a ways off, its headlights getting brighter as it came closer. He ran to the horse-drawn wagon in front of the barn, jumped into the seat, and snapped the reins. The horse clopped deep into the adjacent field, pulling the wagon as it bounced up and down on the uneven ground.

He left it there and returned to the barn on foot.

The truck had parked where the wagon had been.

Kneeling outside, he peered through the slats and listened.

The two men inside swept the interior with their flashlights. "Le bottiglie sono qui, ma dov'e lui?" said the first.

His partner answered in broken English. "Maybe he-s-a-done early, he go home. Let' s-a-load-a these up-a."

Dagos! He spit on the ground.

When the bottles were on board, one climbed into the cab, and the other gripped the iron rotator handle to crank-start the engine. The truck sputtered, backfired, and then departed.

He was sure they hadn't suspected anything.

While he watched them, he formulated a plan.

PRESENT

# CHAPTER 1

## APPROACHING DEATH

It was late afternoon, and the July sky was almost dark as night. Grey storm clouds overwhelmed all light, matching her bleak mood. She sat on the side of his bed and held his hand while he slept; her heart ached at the sight of his frail body, barely visible beneath the sheet.

Monitors kept a steady rhythm of beeps and hums, but death wasn't far off. She knew it. He knew it, too. Worn out by the stress of watching him die, the only person she truly loved and who truly loved her, she closed her eyes. When she opened them again, he was gazing at her.

"What is it, child?" he asked. She smiled at the endearment, even though she was in her thirties. "We've talked about this," he said, "and agreed there would be no tears. After all, how many people live to almost one-hundred?" The chuckle in his throat turned into a cough.

She waited. "Grandfather, we promised no lies between us." He squeezed her hand to give her confidence.

"Father had a heart attack. He's dead."

"When?"

"Yesterday."

"Who gets control?"

"I do."

"At least he did one smart thing in his life." Her grandfather's voice became surprisingly strong. Using his elbows, he pressed himself up. "What will you do?"

"I'm giving notice at the firm. I'll take control of the family's affairs. Dad and my darling brother have decimated the all our money between their flagrant lifestyles and bad investments."

Her grandfather nodded. "I know," he whispered, still calm, although her father was his son.

She continued. "I sold the History Street property for $750,000 to cover some of the debts." She didn't mention the cost of the nursing facility where he was passing the end of his life in as much comfort as she could provide.

"No!"

She was surprised by the power of his voice so close to death.

He struggled to sit up. His agitation made him cough again. When the coughing stopped, he continued. "I should have left you in control when I signed everything over. I'd hoped the responsibility would make your father grow up. Forgive me, my darling." He coughed and hacked up bloody spittle. "I should have told you years ago."

Nurse Walton came in to check on him. Her grandfather shooed her out. "Not now," he said. "I must talk to my granddaughter. Alone."

"Grandfather, please let the nurse…"

"Listen to me," he ordered. "Our name and your future must survive. I've waited too long. I didn't want you involved. My mistake," he panted. Using the side rail, he pulled himself up to a semi-sitting position.

By the end of the disturbing story, he was fighting for breath. The wheezing and rattling in his chest became louder, competing with the monitors tracking his heart and pulse.

He forced the words out. "Papers, maps, documents. All in the attic. My father's journals. They explain everything. You are more like him than you know; you will understand. Promise me..."

Spent, he flopped back on the pillows. His mouth moved; no words came out.

"Grandfather, I don't understand!" Again she shouted, "Grandfather!"

His eyes rolled up; the monitors became erratic.

In one final effort, he demanded, "Swear it! You must get it back. It's all—" A burst of air expelled from his mouth, and the monitors sent the alarm to the nurse's station; the lines went flat.

Nurse Walton ran in. She listened to his chest and felt for a pulse at his wrist and neck. "He's gone. I'll call for the doctor."

"No. Not yet!" she cried, almost incoherent.

"My dear, you know he signed a DNR," the nurse said.

Fighting to control her emotions, she nodded and looked down at her grandfather's lifeless body. "Give me a minute, please."

"Of course." Nurse Walton turned off the monitors and left the room.

The silence was both comforting and disturbing. Dry-eyed, she drew his hand to her lips and kissed it. The first blast of thunder drowned out her vow. "I promise. No, I swear—"

The rainstorm had passed on the east side of town by night, leaving the blank marquee dripping in front of the Rue de L'Histoire Theatre. Inside, only the soft creaks and moans of the building resetting itself after a day's work broke the silence.

Fly-wires squeaked as the backdrops held above the stage swayed; night creatures skittered across the floors unhampered by humans.

The fabric legs of the wings moved as if something brushed against them, and the ghost light stood erect on a long pole, casting its glow from center stage, and the theater held its breath.

# CHAPTER 2

## STRANGE CONFESSION

It was mid-September, and Austin hadn't seen rain for twenty days. The pastor of St. Francis de Sales Church, Father Melvyn Kronkey, sat on his side of the wood screen of the reconciliation room looking out the window opposite his chair, watching the leaves on trees and shrubs rustle in the hot breeze.

While he waited for someone, anyone, to come to confession, he thought about the changes in the confessional ritual. Gone were the days of the dark, three-part stalls where the priests sat in the center cubicle, and the penitents entered compartments on either side and waited for the screen in front of them to slide back before they began their confessions.

He looked at his wristwatch. Few were looking for forgiveness today. His mind wandered to guessing what his trusted housekeeper, Mrs. B., had on the menu, when the familiar creak of the kneeler on the other side of the screen refocused him on the work of saving souls.

"Bless me, Father, for I have sinned. My last confession was three months ago."

Father Melvyn made the sign of the cross and asked, "What sins have you to confess?"

Adam Leightman mumbled a few minor transgressions and paused, no longer sure that confession was a good idea.

"Go on," Father Melvyn said.

"I don't know if..." he paused."I have nowhere else to go."

"What's troubling you?"

Adam sighed, thinking that maybe he should walk away. Instead, in one breathy sentence, he blurted out, "I think a ghost is haunting the theater where I work."

Clearing his throat, the priest asked, "What makes you think that?"

Adam rushed into an explanation. "I'm a stage manager in a local theater, and at the end of the day, it's my job to be sure everything is in its proper place, tools, ropes, knives. That sort of thing. Over the past few weeks, I arrive in the morning and things are not as I'd left them the night before." Adam shifted on his knees again. "Then there's the ghost light," he whispered.

"What's that?"

Adam sighed. "It's an old theater tradition. After a show, or if there's no show, you will find a single bulb, illuminated on a light pole, somewhere on stage."

"Why is it called a ghost light?"

"Superstition. Many theater people believe that theaters are haunted. After all, is there a better place for ghosts other than a cemetery?"

"I don't understand."

"Actors strip away their own personalities to allow identities they are portraying to take over. It's like a shift or an exchange of energy." Adam adjusted his balance again. Kneeling was becoming uncomfortable.

"There are hundreds of theories, and over time it's become accepted that it's in the best interests of the theater to have a ghost light. One story is that it helps keep ghosts from bumping into things when they visit darkened or deserted theaters." The priest was silent.

Adam continued. "Others say that the ghost lights help ward off evil spirits by fooling them into thinking there are people in the building." Adam waited. The priest still didn't speak. "Are you there, Father? Are you appalled?"

"I'm here, I'm listening, and I'm not appalled. Go on."

"Superstitions aside, there's a practical purpose. Empty theaters are dark, very dark, and walking around without light can be risky. There are all sorts of things that can trip a person. Without any light, someone might misjudge the end of the stage and take a header into the orchestra pit. So, every night, before I leave, I turn on the ghost light. The next day, I'm the first one in, and I turn it off.

"Lately, I've been arriving, and the ghost light is off. I know I've left it on."

"Perhaps there is a short in the wire?"

"I checked everything: the wiring, the fixture, the bulb. I can't find anything to account for it."

"Do you believe these superstitions?"

Adam sighed. "I didn't, but I don't know anymore. When I mentioned it to Charlie, our oldest and long-time stagehands, turned custodian, he said, 'maybe someone from the beyond is sending a message.'" Adam tittered. "Frankly, I always thought these superstitions quaint, but now..."

"Because of Charlie's opinion?" Father Melvyn asked.

"No. Because strange things are happening."

"How long has this been going on?"

"About two months. It started after a ballet company bought the theater and renovated the audience section. They're scheduled to open this coming weekend."

"Have you spoken to anyone else other than Charlie?"

"No. I'm afraid they'll think I'm crazy, but I can tell you the crew is starting to notice, too. They're getting antsy."

"Any possibility that construction impacted other things? Sometimes, especially in old buildings, you fix one thing and inadvertently another breaks."

Adam thought for a minute. "Umm. Possible, but not probable."

"What theater did you say?" the priest asked.

"I didn't, but it's the old Rue de L'Histoire Theatre on the East Side."

"Ah yes, I saw a picture of it in the newspaper when it sold. Old place. It must need a good deal of work."

"It does," Adam answered. "The seats in the auditorium are new, plush, and comfortable, but the ballet company couldn't afford to renovate backstage. The equipment is still from the 80s."

"Could someone be coming in for any reason during the night and not telling you? Maybe someone is pranking you?"

"I didn't think of that," Adam blurted. Had the priest hit on a logical possibility that he'd missed?

Without waiting for absolution, Adam jumped up. "Thank you, Father. I know what I need to do." He flew out of the reconciliation room, his mind occupied with getting to the bottom of the strange events at the Rue de L'Histoire Theatre.

"No. Wait..." Father Melvyn called out, too late.

# CHAPTER 3

## "SOMETHING WICKED THIS WAY COMES."
### Shakespeare's Macbeth

Father Melvyn left the reconciliation room, crossed to the sacristy, and unlocked the door. Fighting off the distraction of the last penitent's abrupt departure, he forced his mind to stay on the prayers as he drew on his robes and prepared to say mass.

When he walked to the narthex, the mass assistant told the congregation to stand. Father Melvyn walked down the center aisle to the altar, turned, faced his flock, and began. "In the name of the Father, the Son, and the Holy Ghost."

After greeting some of his parishioners at the end of mass, Father Melvyn returned the vestments to the sacristy, locked up, then made his way back to the rectory through the covered passage, walking at his usual pace, just short of a jog.

Over six feet tall and a bit portly since Mrs. B. took over the rectory, Father Melvyn's full head of reddish-gold hair was streaked with grey, but the bushy mustache between his nose and upper lip remained pure. Behind his wire-rimmed glasses, warmth and intelligence radiated from his brown eyes, fringed by reddish-blond lashes. Father Melvyn was an intelligent, thoughtful man and a dedicated priest, but a bit stuffy, something he readily admitted.

He entered the rectory to the aroma of his favorite meal, and his associate pastor, Father Declan, crooning to their resident cat, in the bright kitchen, at the back of the old Victorian-style house, where LaLa sat on the counter next to the sink.

After her mistress's death, LaLa had come to live at St. Francis de Sales and promptly took over the rectory.

The pastor's eyes twinkled with mischief. "Feeding her on the countertop? Don't let the boss catch you," he said, crossing his arms and watching.

Father Declan laughed at the reference to their housekeeper. "Good evening, Melvyn," he said. The cat glanced back over her shoulder with her cat-smug look that said I won before turning back to her dish.

"Speaking of the boss," Father Melvyn continued, "is that Mrs. B.'s eggplant parmigiana I smell heating?"

"Yes. She left your favorite for dinner. The salad is in the fridge. Are you hungry? We can eat together tonight," the younger priest said. With their busy schedules, it was usually each man for himself, other than on Friday nights when they routinely shared dinner and drinks with Father Joe Russo, their resident professor of ethics and science at the university.

"No meeting tonight?" Father Melvyn asked.

"The teacher for the confirmation candidates needed to change the class to Thursday, so I'm free."

The two men sat at one end of the table, enjoying their dinner. LaLa sat on a chair with her head above the tabletop at the other end, watching them eat and talk.

Father Declan looked at the cat. "Do you suppose she'd tell Mrs. B. everything we say if she could?" He was only half kidding.

"Sometimes I think she does, and I think Mrs. B. is fluent in cat-speak," Father Melvyn answered, also only half kidding.

After dinner and the cleanup, Father Declan retired upstairs to his room, and Father Melvyn headed to the library. LaLa followed the pastor to his favorite place.

The library was a cozy spot between the dining room and the front offices. It was masculine but welcoming, with bookcases flanking the fireplace. There were two stuffed armchairs, a brown leather couch, and an assortment of nondescript side tables, and a coffee table providing plenty of surfaces to set down coffee mugs and teacups, as well as magazines and books. Suitable floor lamps, perfect for reading, were scattered around the room, with one next to the pastor's favorite chair adjacent to the window.

Once Father Melvyn had settled into the recliner, LaLa wasted no time; she jumped onto his lap. Absently, the priest stroked her as the incomplete confession he'd heard that afternoon returned to the forefront of his thoughts. "Ah LaLa, I wish that man hadn't run off. I'm worried that he will get himself into hot water."

LaLa mewed sympathetically, turned around a few times, and settled on his lap.

Mrs. B. rushed into her kitchen through the garage door, almost stumbling over Sasha and Ziggy. Both cats scampered away from her feet.

She smiled at the Caller ID. "Yes, John," she greeted him breathlessly.

"Bad time, Mom?" he asked. "You could have called me back."

Mrs. B. dropped her purse on the kitchen table. "No, Son. Not at all. How are rehearsals going? When do you go into the theater to rehearse?" Her questions gushed out as she swiped her unruly white curls back from her face, pulled off her big, round, blue-framed glasses, and rubbed her eyes.

"Things are going well. I'm leaving three tickets at will-call for Saturday night's opening and the gala."

"Wonderful. Thank you. My friend, Nancy Jenkins, the school principal, and my boss, Father Melvyn, are looking forward to this. They've never been to the ballet."

"Lisa and I are excited too," John said. "And Our partner, Chelly, is looking forward to meeting you."

Mrs. B. heard the anticipation in her son's voice. "I have high hopes for this company, Mom. We have technically strong, well-rounded dancers, and there's one in particular who will knock your socks off. I think you'll pick her out."

Mrs. B. knew that John had always Respected her knowledge of ballet and her eye for talent."

Sounds like a challenge," she answered.

John laughed. "I know better. Gotta go," he said. "Lots to do. On Thursday, we go into the theater for the tech and dress rehearsals."

"Love to Lisa," Mrs. B. said and hung up.

Soft fur brushed against her legs. She reached down to stroke her cats. Their bemused expressions said, *how could you not greet us when you came home?*

"Okay, kids, sorry," she said. "Let's get you fed." Sasha and Ziggy circled and rubbed her legs. *All was forgiven.* While she fed them, she thought about how life had changed since her son and daughter-in-law had moved to Austin.

John and Lisa had danced with a Dallas company for several years, and she'd always looked forward to their performances. Unbeknownst to her, when they had decided it was time to retire from the stage, they began a search for other avenues to earn a living and pursue their art.

In a dance publication, they saw an ad from the Bernardi Ballet Company in Austin, looking for expansion partners. They'd made contact. Without telling Mrs. B., John and Lisa had accepted the artistic director's invitation to come to Austin for an interview and conduct some masterclasses. It was a perfect fit, and voila, they were invited to buy-in.

Mrs. B. was still conflicted. She was thrilled when John told her about the offer but saddened that they would no longer dance.

The night of their farewell performance at the end of the Dallas company's season was a bittersweet affair; she'd cried.

"Oh, how short the stage life of ballet dancers. Twenty years of training for twenty years on stage...if that," she lamented while stroking her cats. "But I must admit having them here is a joy. And to make even sweeter, they are now partners in a company, renamed to include them."

The new Bernardi-Bono Ballet Company was in rehearsal for their premiere performance. Saturday night was going to be thrilling. She could hardly wait.

After dinner, she made her usual tour of the house, securing windows and doors. She activated the alarm then got out of her "harness," the special bra she wore for her breast prosthesis since her mastectomy a few years earlier. Checking her posture in the mirror, Mrs. B. made a conscious effort to suck in her stomach, press her shoulders back and down, and pull her neck up. "Stand up straight," she commanded the reflection in the mirror. "Ugh! Time to start sit-ups again," she mumbled, turning from side to side. Enough vanity for tonight!

She changed into pajamas and then returned to the kitchen and opened her menu book to plan the week's meals for the priests in her care.

Wednesday's and Thursday's menus were easy. "But what shall I cook for their Friday night dinner," she asked her cats, who sat beside her chair, paying rapt attention and wiggling in anticipation. They knew she'd give them a treat when she closed that book.

Friday nights were sacrosanct at St. Francis de Sales unless there was an emergency. She always prepared something special so that Father Melvyn, his associate pastor, Father Declan, and the professor, Father Joe Russo, could share their week's work, experiences, and problems, or just enjoy a good meal and general conversation.

"I know. A lovely roast chicken in lemon and garlic sauce, sautéed broccolini, roasted potatoes, and a mixed salad. That should keep them happy. And, if I have time, some of my almond biscotti cookies for dessert."

Satisfied, she closed her book. That was the signal. Sasha and Ziggy stood up on their hind legs and turned circles; Mrs. B. laughed with delight. "Dancing for your desserts?" she asked before giving them their favorite snacks.

With the day's work completed, she settled into bed with a book, but her mind returned to John and Lisa. They'd saved most of the money needed to buy in, but not all. She'd loaned them the difference.

"Look at me, darling." She directed her remarks to the ornate wooden box on the dresser that contained her late husband, John Senior's ashes. "I'm an impresario." She laughed. "A very little one, but an impresario all the same."

Flooded with contentment, she dozed. Her cats were curled up beside her on John's side of the bed.

*The soft strains of the Sugar Plum variation began The dancer moved forward on the dark stage as the music's volume increased. She wore a pink tutu, with rhinestones and pearls scattered over the stiff fabric.*

*Overhead, a silver thread snaked its way forward and down; its incandescent glow encircled the dancer.*

*Red dripped onto her tutu and coated the rhinestones and pearls, forming a puddle on the floor. The Sugar Plum continued to dance, but the music took a bizarre turn, its chords now dissonant. The tip of her pink pointe shoe dipped into the puddle on the floor; the red seeped up over her foot and up her leg; it soaked into the tutu. The circular motion of the incandescent thread became smaller, tighter, and it pulled her to the front of the stage until her head was the only visible part of her body. The music stopped. The Sugar Plum was faceless.*

Struggling to breathe, she thrashed and felt herself dropping from space. Mrs. B. opened her eyes, aware of her racing heart. The clock said 4:00 a.m. *Where did that come from?* She sat up and shivered as her sweat-soaked pajama top cooled in the night air.

"I never remember dreams, so why do I remember this one? It's too horrible. Go away," she commanded. Instead, it replayed in all its vivid detail. She looked over at her cats. Sasha and Ziggy slept soundly, curled up against each other.

Mrs. B. lay back on the pillow. Unexpected and unbidden, tears welled in her eyes.

*Maybe it's something I ate; perhaps it's too much excitement, too much joy that John and Lisa are here in their new careers.* Yes, that must be it, she thought, pushing back against the foreboding that gnawed at her bones.

# CHAPTER 4

## TO CATCH A GHOST

After his confession, Adam planned to spend as many nights as necessary hidden in the theater, but he failed to stay awake on the first night. At 5:00 a.m. on Wednesday, he sneaked out before daylight. When he returned at his regular time, nothing had changed.

Determined to catch whoever was pranking him, he let himself back into the theater again at 10:00 p.m. The ghost light was on, and everything looked normal, as normal as it can in the theater world of unreality.

He walked through the theater, checking equipment, doors, locks, levers, and hardware on both sides of the stage. All was as it should be.

Looking up into the blackness, the scenery elevated above the curtain line reflected bits of the ghost light's weak beam; the backdrops seemed to sway on their cables. He'd noticed it the night before. "Is it a natural air current moving them, or my imagination?" he muttered.

Back in his office, instead of sitting in his comfortable desk chair, he opened the door wide and placed a hard-backed chair and small table almost at the doorway to maximize his field of vision. The chilly air in the theater reached him. He took off his sweater and set his thermos of strong coffee on the table.

His eyes adjusted to the dim light field provided by the ghost lamp. Again, the creaks and groans of the empty, silent building unnerved him.

Despite the cool air, hard chair, and coffee, it wasn't long before his eyelids became heavy. "Stay awake!" he whispered. Stand up. Stretch your legs."

*Whoosh.*

His heart skipped a beat. Something was there that wasn't there a minute before. He strained his eyes. Goosebumps rose on his arms; the hairs at the back of his neck tingled. Had something moved across the stage?

A different sound pricked his ears, faint, almost indiscernible, not the creaks and groans of the theater. It took all of his resolve to move.

His sneakered feet were silent on the floor. Forcing one reluctant foot in front of the other, he crept out the door. There was a muffled patter above his head, moving away from him. He realized the sound came from a catwalk, but he couldn't see beyond the reach of the ghost light.

Adam backed up into his office. The skin on his arms tightened from the raised hairs. He vacilated between hiding and venturing out. Did something move at the edge of the ghost light? Sweat dripped into his eyes. He held his breath and remained still.

Then nothing.

He strained to pick up any unusual sounds. He had the notion that the theater held its breath, too. Blowing out one breath and sucking in another, he put one foot in front of the other and left the safety of his office.

Adam knew every inch of the place, and his feet found the path between objects without difficulty as he walked in the same direction he thought the movement had gone.

He stopped. There it is! A deeper, denser black form became apparent at the opposite side, beyond the stage. Soundless, it melded into the atmosphere. An elongated flash of light from inside the prop room froze him in place; then, it disappeared. "What the hell was that?" he mouthed, even though no sound came from his vocal cords.

Fear made his leg muscles quiver; he stood rooted to the floor. Throwing caution to the wind, Adam took out his cell phone and lit it, moving it from side to side. Nothing.

"This isn't possible," he whispered.

A frightening sensation gripped him and knotted his back muscles, it screamed danger. Adam spun around and dropped his phone.

It hit the floor like thunder, but not before its light shone into a pair of fierce and terrifying eyes that paralyzed him with fear.

The sledgehammer coming down was the last thing he saw.

# CHAPTER 5

## HE'S MISSING

Father Melvyn dashed from the carport to the kitchen door. Will it or won't it, he wondered. Big drops of water fell sporadically from the overcast sky and splashed to the ground. He entered the kitchen expecting food; instead, he found a power battle between his two favorite females, his trusted housekeeper and assistant, Mrs. B., and LaLa, the green-eyed feline with the shiny blue-grey coat.

"You really are naughty," Mrs. B. said, scooting LaLa off the kitchen table. Once the cat caught sight of Father Melvyn in the doorway, Mrs. B.'s authority evaporated. LaLa jumped back on the table and stared at the housekeeper. Her eyes said *I don't have to listen to you.*

Mrs. B. folded her arms across her chest and huffed. "You do spoil her. It's like I'm raising another teenager who knows how to play one adult off against the other."

"I wouldn't know about that." The priest chuckled. "I think she knows you don't mean it. Look at her sitting there staring at you, waiting for your next move."

"Stop laughing. You won't be amused when the bishop has dinner here after the Confirmation ceremony, and LaLa decides to sit on the table."

"She knows to stay off the dining room table. She only does this in the kitchen. Now, I'm headed over to the church," he said as the sky dropped buckets of rain.

Sally Leightman stared out the window, deep in thought, barely noting the sheets of water hitting the windows. She paced her living room for the tenth time, alternately tugging her short, spiky hair and running her fingers through it. He should have been home by now.

She knew what Adam was doing and why, but he'd sworn her to secrecy. Her thoughts flew in different directions. If he had an accident, someone would have called. He should have left the theater before daylight. Maybe he fell asleep in his office, she thought. His car wouldn't be in the theater parking lot because he didn't want anyone to know he was in the building. Maybe he stopped at the church on his way home. "Bet that's it. He fell asleep then stopped at church," she said aloud, giving herself hope and courage.

Not a regular churchgoer, Sally looked kindly on her husband's devoutness. He was a faithful and humble believer, but not a self-righteous, holier than thou prig. It was one of the things she loved best about him, even if she didn't have the same feelings about organized religion. She grabbed her car keys, confident that she'd find him at church.

The windshield wipers slapped back and forth like a metronome. Its rhythm whispered, *he's there.*

When Sally reached St. Francis, she circled both parking fields. No sign of him. Her heart banged in her chest. She parked and wiped away the tears falling on her cheeks. The rain had let up. "I guess a prayer can't hurt," she said, turned off her car, and dashed to the front door of the church. Sally grabbed the handle, but the door flew open, knocking her backward. "Yow!" she yelled. Two strong hands grabbed her shoulders and kept her upright.

"I am terribly sorry," a man's voice said, but Sally's tears were flowing again, accompanied by hiccupping sobs. All she was aware of was a massive black-clad body leading her to a bench inside.

She covered her face and continued to sob. A large hand appeared holding a wad of tissues. The man in black sat next to her and waited. When she quieted, he introduced himself.

"I'm Father Melvyn Kronkey, the pastor here. Can I help you?"

She wiped her eyes, took a deep, shuddering breath, and looked into the warmest brown eyes she'd ever seen. "My husband is missing…" was all she managed before sobs again constricted her throat. The priest waited until she regained control.

"Have you called the pol…"

"No. I came here looking for him; it was my last hope. I can't call the police. I promised him I wouldn't say a word." She sobbed again. "This is complicated. Oh, God, I don't know what to do." Sally sobbed.

Father Melvyn patted her arm. "Come with me. We'll go to the rectory. My housekeeper will bring you a cup of tea, and you will tell me what happened."

Sally regained her composure as they walked through the drizzle. Despite her fears and worries, her trained artist's eye noticed her surroundings.

Shrubs and trees marked the stone church's perimeter. The dove-gray rectory with white window shutters stood adjacent to the church with a narrow alley in between. They walked up a few steps to a broad, wrap-around porch and the front door.

"Mrs. B.," Father Melvyn called out when they entered.

The housekeeper appeared. "Yes, Father."

"Make some tea, please."

In front of him, LaLa sat like a sphinx on the staircase-landing in the center hall. Paws extended through the spindles and overlapped in the most ladylike fashion, ears erect, eyes-wide-open, nose pointing upward; she sniffed every person's scent when they entered. If she smelled trouble, she let everyone know it.

As soon as she sniffed the woman with Father Melvyn, LaLa's ears flattened. She opened her mouth and emitted a sound between a hiss and a growl, but she didn't move off the landing.

Father Melvyn ignored the cat. He settled the woman in the front office. "Be right back," he said, as the word *trouble* popped into his mind.

He dashed past LaLa. "I'll take that cup, Mrs. B. She's distraught. Seems her husband didn't come home."

Father Melvyn walked back into the office and handed the teacup to the woman. Sitting behind his desk, he studied her. She was disheveled with dark circles under her eyes; she hadn't slept much, and they were now red from crying. "What's your name?"

"Sally Leightman." Before he spoke again, she added, "But I promised my husband I wouldn't tell anyone what he was doing."

"If you think your husband is in danger, perhaps it's a promise you must break."

Sally nodded. "You're right," she said, and then the words tumbled out like water rushing over stones.

"Adam has been worried about strange Things going on at the theater where he's the stage manager." Sally sipped the tea. "He said he's been finding equipment left unsecured, ropes frayed, and a special light he leaves on every night turned off in the morning. He didn't want to alarm anyone, so Tuesday night, he decided to sneak back into the theater and spend the night to see if anything happened, but nothing did."

Sally took a break and drank more tea. "Last night," she continued, "he went back, but he didn't come home this morning." Immersed in the details of her story, she hadn't noticed that the priest paled while she spoke.

Father Melvyn waited for Sally to finish. "My dear," he said in his most comforting manner, "this is a terrible situation for you, and I understand your worries and fears, but I think you must call the police. Would you like to do it from here?"

Sally set her cup down and looked at her wristwatch. "I know you're right, Father, and thank you all the same, but I'll go home and call them."

"As you wish," he answered. "Here's my number." He wrote it on a piece of paper. "Call me any time, night or day. I'll pray that Adam gets back to you unharmed, and please let me know as soon as you have any information."

Sally took the paper and nodded. When she looked up, Father Melvyn saw a reserve in her eyes. "My Adam is a regular churchgoer. I'm not like him."

"Mrs. Leightman, Sally. May I call you Sally?" She nodded. "Our concern today is for Adam's safe return. Let's focus our thoughts and prayers on him."

Father Melvyn walked her to the front door. "Is there anyone you'd like me to call for you?"

"No, Father. Our only son lives in California, and I don't want to scare him."

"I understand, but is there anyone here I can call for you?" Again she shook her head.

"Mrs. B.," the priest called out. "Can you come here, please?" A tall woman with unruly white curls and large, blue-framed glasses walked toward them.

"Yes, Father?"

"This is Sally Leightman. Her husband, Adam, didn't return from work. She's going to call the police as soon as she gets home." Mrs. B. nodded but said nothing. "If Mrs. Leightman calls, please be sure to find me."

"Of course," Mrs. B. answered.

"Thank you." Sally moved to leave, then turned back and pointed at the cat, still sitting on the landing.

"Your cat seems upset."

Father Melvyn eyed Mrs. B. "She wants to eat," was all he could think to say. He couldn't explain to Sally that her presence upset had upset the cat.

After Sally left, Father Melvyn closed the door, turned to his housekeeper, and said, "Put up the coffee. We need to talk."

"I'm sure we do." Both of them looked at LaLa. The cat was already trotting to the kitchen.

While Mrs. B. got the coffee going, LaLa meowed, grumbled, and chirped. "Too early for food, LaLa," Mrs. B. said. The cat turned her charms on Father Melvyn.

"The boss says you have to wait," he whispered conspiratorially, lifting the cat to his lap and scratching her under her chin.

Mrs. B. set the steaming coffee cup in front of him and sat at the table with her own. "You never call me out that way to meet someone. What's the problem?"

"What's the name of the theater your son John's ballet company bought?"

"The Rue de L'Histoire Theatre, on the East Side," she said. "What does that have to do with..."

"The woman who just left?" He finished her sentence. "Sally Leightman's husband, Adam, is its stage manager. He's disappeared." Father Melvyn couldn't tell her that two days earlier, in confession, Adam had confided the strange problems at the theater.

Although Adam hadn't given his name, Father Melvyn reasoned that it had to be the same person. How many stage managers could there be at the Rue de L'Histoire Theatre?

"And?"

"I don't suppose you've heard anything from John."

"No. I don't expect to. I know the company will be in the theater tonight for a tech and dress rehearsal, and then tomorrow, they do a full-dress rehearsal for an audience of community groups. You, Nancy, and I are going to the opening on Saturday."

"Let me know if you hear anything," Father Melvyn said and abruptly changed the subject.

"I woke up at five this morning. My husband wasn't in bed," Sally said to the officer who answered the phone. "I tried his cell phone. He didn't answer. I've left three messages, but he hasn't called me back. I'm worried." Trying to be reasonable, Sally added, "I know he's not missing 24 hours yet."

"You did right to call. We don't have to wait 24 hours before gathering information, Mrs. Leightman. What time did you last see your husband, and did you know he was going out?"

Sally knew where he was going and why but already felt she'd betrayed Adam's confidence by telling the priest. She couldn't tell the police, too. "I saw him around ten. I was asleep when he left."

"Okay, Ma'am. I'll have someone from Missing Persons contact you. Meanwhile, call the hospitals and see if anyone matching his description was brought in. Try not to worry. These things usually turn out fine."

Sally hung up and took out Adam's list of the theater personnel's contact information. She began to dial Tony Volpe's cell but thought better of it. She set the phone down, realizing she couldn't tell anyone at the theater what he was doing. Instead, she followed the police officer's advice and called the local hospitals. No one fitting Adam's description had been admitted anywhere.

An hour later, two detectives from Missing Persons stood at her door. Detective Sonders, a big, burly man, and Detective Ramirez, shorter, trimmer, and younger. Both men held up their badges after ringing her bell. They spent an hour with her, taking information and a couple of recent photos.

After they left, the rest of the day stretched in front of her. The phone rang, making her heart leap in her chest. She grabbed it.

"Adam?"

"Sally, it's Tony Volpe. Where is Adam? Is he ill?"

She burst into tears. "He's missing."

Sally went through the same scenario she'd given the detectives. "When I woke up this morning, he wasn't in bed. I've called the police, and Missing Persons was here. They took some pictures, and they are filing a report."

"Adam, missing? I don't believe this. Have you tried the hospitals? What time did you see him last?" They rehashed all the steps she'd taken, but she left out her church visit and conversation with the priest. When they'd exhausted all that could be said, Tony told her, "Getting ready for the ballet company has stressed him these last few weeks. Their needs are a bit different from drama troupes. The flooring alone took a lot of work."

Sally didn't answer, worrying that if Tony knew the real reason Adam was stressed, he'd be shocked.

Tony sighed. "I'm sure he'll turn up. When you hear from him, tell him not to worry, I have everything here under control."

She set the phone down, feeling as if she'd lose her mind if she didn't get out of the house. There was an unfinished portrait waiting for her in the sunroom, but she knew she wouldn't be able to concentrate.

With her cell phone gripped in her hand, she drove to the nearest supermarket. She tried Adam's cell three more times, leaving frantic messages between pulling products off the shelves. Something's happened to him. The poisonous little voice in her head gave her no peace.

The two detectives from Missing Persons arrived at the Rue de L'Histoire Theatre and introduced themselves to Tony Volpe, the assistant stage manager.

"Is there somewhere we can talk privately?" Sonders asked. Volpe led them to his office. When they were seated, Volpe's eyes darted back and forth between them, and he ran his fingers through his thinning grey hair.

Detective Ramirez explained that they were looking into the disappearance of Adam Leightman. "You seem rather agitated, Mr. Volpe. Is something troubling you?"

"Frankly, yes. Adam Leightman is a reliable and hands-on manager. This is very unusual for him. He's a precise and careful man."

"Is that a nice way of saying he's overbearing?" Detective Sonders asked.

"No, not at all! Adam is well respected and takes nothing for granted, even though we are all experienced and know the drill. But there is extra pressure right now."

"What kind of extra pressure?" Detective Sonders asked. The detectives watched Volpe's expressions as he spoke and occasionally wrote in their notepads, as he explained.

"Tonight, the ballet company comes in here for their tech and dress rehearsal. Tomorrow night is their full dress. It's a rehearsal but in front of an audience. They bring in community groups for free, like seniors. Saturday is their official opening and gala. Since this is their first performance here, Adam has been working closely with the artistic directors to be sure everything goes smoothly."

Tony tapped his pencil on the desk. "I want to be all the help I can, but there's too much to do for me to sit here talking." Volpe sighed. "Sorry. I don't mean to be rude. It's just that..."

"When was the last time you saw Adam?" Detective Ramirez asked, moving the interview along.

"Yesterday. We left together around eight last night. Adam said everything looked good, but he was worried about the flooring."

"The flooring?" Detective Ramirez echoed.

"It's a special floor laid down for dancers, so they don't slip. It needs time to settle."

"Other than that, was he worried about anything else? Does he go off on occasional benders? Is there anything you can remember that might shed some light on why he'd take off?"

"No. Adam is the most dependable and dedicated man you'll ever meet. He wouldn't take off on a bender and abandon the theater at such a crucial time."

"Any other time?" Detective Ramirez asked.

"Again, no!" Volpe's answer was terse. "I have work to do. Can I go?"

Detective Sonders stood up. "We'll come out with you. We need to talk to the crew. Sorry about the delay it's causing, but we want to find Mr. Leightman."

An hour later, the detectives walked out of the theater into the bright sunlight. "Leightman sounds like a pretty normal person, but who knows," Sonders said.

"Not much to go on from here, but something's off," Ramirez replied.

"Starting with Volpe," Sonders said. "But they all seemed edgy, nervous. Almost like they weren't saying something, even though they gave great detail about what Leightman was doing over the last week and how reliable he is—was."

"Well, if he doesn't show up by midnight tonight, this will become an all-out search. At least we've done the preliminary due diligence," said Detective Ramirez, sliding his notepad into his jacket pocket.

# CHAPTER 6

## TECH, DRESS AND DEATH

On Thursday afternoon, the dancers of the Bernardi-Bono Ballet Company assembled on the stage of the Rue de L'Histoire Theatre.

New to the company, Isabel Sanchez Reardon was giddy with excitement. She'd had professional experience dancing with some of the pick-up companies in New York and New Jersey, but this was her first full-time contract with an established professional company.

She'd seen the audition notice in a trade magazine and took the chance. The memory of that day still thrilled her. As soon as the audition had ended, the artistic director called her aside and offered her a contract. She'd jumped at it.

Isabel was so excited that her feet barely touched the ground. In record time, she covered the five New York City blocks uptown and two avenues from west to east.

"Mom, Dad, the artistic director, hired me. I was the only dancer in the class offered a contract immediately. I'm going to dance with the Bernardi Ballet in Austin, Texas."

A dish fell from her mother's hand and crashed on the floor. "No!" her mother shouted. "Not Austin. Turn it down!"

Isabel felt as if she'd been hit with a bucket of cold water.

"Liz!" Isabel's father spoke up. "This is a wonderful opportunity for her."

"She knows the stories," her mother yelled. "My father filled her head with them for years. We escaped from Austin and those people when we moved here to New York."

Despite her mother's arguments, her dad stood firmly on Isabel's side, with one condition. "You must promise to let sleeping dogs lie. Focus on your big chance and let the dead stay buried."

Isabel promised. She would have agreed to anything to end her mother's objections, but her mother's distraught face made her feel guilty. She was, after all, their miracle baby, and her mother was too protective. "Mamá. Don't worry. Nothing bad will happen."

"From your mouth to God's ears," her mother answered and left the room in tears but made no further objection to Isabel taking the job in Austin.

Now, here she was, three months later, getting ready for her first performance with the Bernardi-Bono Ballet Company. She sent a silent thank you to her father.

Isabel smiled, rechecked her pointe shoes, and took her place at one of the portable barres already on stage. She stretched and prepared for the warm-up class.

"It's really chilly in here," Janet, one of the younger, less experienced dancers complained, pulling on leg warmers and a shrug.

"You'll get used to it," said Orlando, a veteran of the company. "Most theaters, especially the old ones, are drafty and chilly. Once the class starts, you'll be warm as toast in a few minutes."

"I hope so. I hate being cold," Janet whined.

Orlando looked at Isabel and rolled his eyes knowingly.

Isabel changed the subject to distract the whining Janet. "Isn't this a beautiful theater with its turn of the 20th-century Italian Baroque architecture, and ornate and opulent interior?"

"Attention, please." Chelly Bernardi, the artistic director, clapped her hands and stepped up with her partners, John and Lisa Bono.

John addressed the dancers. "Before we begin, I've examined the floor. It looks good. It's smooth, and the gaffing tape is secure. No edges poking up. If during class or the walkthrough you notice any problems, bring them to me immediately. Understand?" The dancers nodded in agreement, placed their left hands on the barres, pulled themselves erect, and were ready.

Chelly gave the combination: "First position, two demi-pliés two counts each, one grand-plié four counts, repeat in second, port-de-bras to the barre, then away." Chelly nodded to the pianist. The music began, and the warm-up class was underway.

Isabel focused on every part of her body, from the top of her head to the tips of her toes. As she worked, she noticed some of the stage crew standing on the sides watching. Another man came along and waved them back to work before making his way over to John and Lisa.

"Isabel, shoulders down," Chelly said, walking alongside the dancers at the barre. The correction pulled Isabel's attention back to her technique.

Volpe shooed the crew back to work, then made his way over to the artistic directors. He stayed close, watching them. In the hollow space of the stage, sound carried well.

When he thought it appropriate, he made his way to Lisa and John. "I'm Tony Volpe, stepping in for Adam Leightman," he whispered. "Can I see you for a minute?" The three walked to the side.

Keeping his voice low, Tony lied. Rather than tell them that Adam had disappeared, he said Adam was ill. "The timing is unfortunate, so I want to double-check the list to be sure we have everything right." He paused. "Can I go over this with you, or do I need to wait for her?" he asked, looking in Chelly's direction.

"Sorry to hear about Adam," John said. "We haven't met him, but Chelly speaks highly of him. Hope he recovers fast. Yes. We can go over everything with you."

"Good. I assure you, we will be ready for all performances and the gala on Saturday night. For tonight, we'd like to leave the lighting cues to the end," Volpe told them.

"During the full run-through?" John asked.

Tony nodded. "That shouldn't be a problem."

Volpe nodded. "Thanks," he said and made a note on his clipboard.

"By the way," Lisa said before Tony walked away. "We noticed the stage left prop room is locked. Can someone unlock it? We need to get in there."

"I'll do it now," Volpe answered. Rather than walk across the stage where the dancers warmed up, he made a big loop around the back of the open area to the opposite side and unlocked the prop room door. He remained there, in the offstage area, watching, while the electricians, sound techs, and stage crew prepared for the rehearsal.

When the warm-up ended, at Tony's direction, several men removed the barres from the stage, while he listened to Lisa Bono direct the dancers.

"Let's start with La Vivandiere," she said. Tony noted that the first piece used six dancers. Lisa had them walk through it, marking the stage at different points in the ballet. "Good," she said. "Take fifteen."

After the break, clipboard in hand, Tony came back to the stage area with the dancers. Chelly called the next group forward for *Capriccio Maestoso*; this piece used eight dancers. After they'd completed their walkthrough, they were given another short water break.

Volpe noticed that the dancers didn't waste time. They grabbed their water bottles, rehydrated, shook out arms and legs, and prepared to walk through the last piece on the program.

John Bono assembled the cast for the final ballet on the program, *Salute to America*. When the walkthrough was complete and the stage marked, he said, "Good work. You all look comfortable in the space. Pay attention to those around you." The dancers nodded. "Okay, we resume at seven, full out with partial costumes." He turned away, then back. "A reminder. Tomorrow's rehearsal is a full dress, with the orchestra, and we will be performing for some of the underserved of our city. They and we expect your best."

Tony liked what he heard and saw; he felt good about this company's professionalism. He walked away to give instructions to his crew.

From the stage left wing, Tony watched the dancers gather again after their break.

Lisa asked, "Where's Isabel?"

"Probably in the ladies' room. There was a line," Janet answered.

A loud whistle from above got everyone's attention. A mechanical click engaged a mechanism and kicked off a whirring sound. Lisa and the dancers stepped toward the back of the stage. The light bridge above the proscenium arch, hidden by the border curtain, came down slow and steady.

Two spotlight operators stood nearby, chatting, while the apparatus descended.

"What's that thing coming down?" Janet asked, stepping forward. Tony saw Lisa put a hand on Janet's arm. Good, he thought. We don't need an accident. He heard Lisa explain.

"Don't walk over there." Lisa pointed to the two people dressed in black. "They are the lighting techs who will be raised up on the light-bridge to work the spots."

"They stay up there through the entire show?" Janet asked.

Lisa chuckled. "Sometimes, they can't even get a bathroom break. It used to freak me out during my dancing days. Something about the crew suspended on a metal bridge, working spots above my head felt weird, but I got over it. You will too."

Tony smiled at Lisa's explanation and turned to go to his office when a dancer running forward collided with him.

"Excuse me," she said, heading to the dancers clustered on stage.

The light bridge was barely ten feet off the stage.

The thud was loud, sickening. Something hit the floor right in front of her. The dancer screamed, staggered back, colliding with Tony again, then dropped to her knees and covered her face with both hands.

Someone hit the stop button, leaving the light bridge suspended. Other workers and technicians ran forward to see what had happened.

Everyone stared then there was a collective gasp. It was a body, with its arms and legs at unnatural angles and its head a horrible mess.

"What the hell?" Volpe pushed past the Dancer kneeling on the floor, covering her eyes.

"Everyone, stay back," he ordered.

The stagehands pushed the dancers to the far end of the area, where they turned away from the grisly sight and clustered in groups.

One of the lighting technicians, slated to work a spotlight on the bridge, rushed forward. When she got close, she muttered, "Ugh," covered her mouth and nose, and stepped away.

Tony ran over. Bile rose in his throat from the odor. He pulled on his work gloves, covered his mouth with a handkerchief, kneeled and stared at the corpse.

Its face was swollen, caked with clotted blood and bits of brain matter that had spilled out of the shattered skull. Recognition dawned. He gagged.

The pulp that had fallen from the light bridge was none other than Adam Leightman.

The doorbell rang. Filled with hope, Sally yanked it open. Adam's name died in her throat. Two solemn-looking men she didn't know held badges up for her to see.

"Mrs. Leightman?" asked the taller man with iron-grey hair and black-rimmed glasses. She nodded.

"I'm Detective Jake Zayas. This is my partner, Marv Clingman," he said, referring to the younger, sandy-haired man wearing jeans and a blue pullover. "May we come in?"

Without speaking, she opened the door wide for them to enter. Detective Zayas took her arm and led her to a chair. She placed her hands over her ears. "No," she whispered.

Gently, he took her hands away from her head and held them in his own. "Mrs. Leightman, I'm sorry."

"NO!" she screamed. Sally pulled her hands away and grabbed her short, spikey hair; her breath coming in short bursts. She squeezed her eyes shut. The other detective was suddenly in front of her with a glass of water.

"Mrs. Leightman. Can we call someone for you?"

She sipped the water. "How do you know it's my Adam?" she demanded.

"He's been identified."

Sally jumped up from the chair. "Identified? By whom?"

"His body was found in the Rue de L'Histoire Theatre tonight. A man named Tony Volpe identified him."

All the strength went out of her. Strong arms guided her back to the couch and laid her down. "Is there someone who can stay with you?" The question sounded far away.

Unaware of time passing, Sally suddenly noticed a uniformed policewoman sitting on a chair facing her. She sat up and whispered, "I must call my son, Adam, Jr."

"Does he live nearby?" the officer asked.

"No. He lives in San Diego." Sally tried to control her emotions. She took the phone from the officer's hand and dialed it. When her son picked up, she could barely say hello, and dissolved into tears once again.

"Mom? Mom!" The man's voice was frantic.

The officer took the phone from her hand. "Mr. Adam Leightman, Jr.?"

"Yes. Who is this? What's wrong with my mother?"

"Mr. Leightman, I'm officer Janell of the Austin Police Department. I'm so sorry to tell you this on the phone, but there's been an accident. Your father has been killed."

"What? NO! Who are you? Put my mother on the phone."

Sally took the phone. "It's true." Her voice wobbled. "Dad was found dead in the theater where he works." Once again, Sally dissolved into tears and dropped the phone.

The officer picked it up and explained the situation to Adam Leightman, Jr.

"Let me speak to my mother, please."

Sniffling, Sally took the phone. "How soon can you get here, son?" Her voice was hoarse from crying.

"I'll get on the first possible flight, but you can't stay alone. Call Marina or another friend?"

Sally was crying again. "I will," she said and hung up.

Half an hour later, Officer Janell opened the door to Marina Conny. The policewoman beckoned her to the kitchen and told her that Adam was dead.

"Her son is coming on the first flight he can get. Can you stay with her until then?"

"Yes, of course, but if I can persuade her to come home with me, will that be okay?"

The officer nodded. "Let the police know where she is." Lowering her voice, she said, "It's a homicide investigation now."

"This is terrible. I can't believe it," Marina Conny whispered.

Janell nodded sympathetically, returned to Sally, and put an arm around the grieving widow. "I'm going to leave now. Your friend will stay with you. Can I do anything else for you before I go?"

Sally sobbed and shook her head.

"I'm so sorry for your loss," Officer Janell said.

# CHAPTER 7

## THE SHOW MUST GO ON

Mrs. B.'s emotions were in turmoil as she, Nancy Jenkins, and her boss, Father Melvyn, slid into their seats. Her stomach quivered. John and Lisa would not be dancing, but tonight was the next step in their careers. It was the premiere of the Bernardi-Bono Ballet Company.

"Excited?" Nancy asked.

"Yes, and nervous, too," she whispered. The house lights went down. Please, God. Let this go well, she prayed. Nancy squeezed her hand.

When the ballet ended, the audience was on its feet, and the applause went on for a long while. The dancers walked forward a second time, the soloists and principals bowed again; the conductor walked out of the wings and was drawn to center stage by the leading female. He took his bow and gestured for the orchestra to stand, and the applause increased with shouts of "Bravo. Bravi."

Mrs. B. couldn't hide her joy and pride when Chelly Bernardi, the founding artistic director, came forward and presented her new partners, John and Lisa Bono.

The curtain descended for the last time; Nancy and Father Melvyn both kissed Mrs. B.'s cheek.

"Congratulations," they whispered as they moved out of the row and headed toward the backstage door where guests gathered for the company's party.

Waiting for the door to open, people chatted about everything from the mundane to the performance they'd just seen and then to the tragic discovery of Adam Leightman's body two nights earlier. Mrs. B., the priest, and Nancy heard murmurs of "Shocking," "Terrible," "Bizarre." There was a disdainful quality to the conversations, and yet, here they were.

Before coming to the theater, Mrs. B. had told Father Melvyn and Nancy that after the murder hit the newspapers, the show, already selling well, suddenly sold out. Father Melvyn shook his head and grimaced.

"I'm saying Adam's funeral mass on Tuesday," he whispered.

For a short while, the thrill of performance lifted the dark cloud that had hovered over the company. The opening performance had gone off without a hitch, and the horror of the backstage death, while not forgotten, was set aside.

Isabel had forced the image of Adam Leightman's crushed skull from her mind, well aware of the first commandment of theater: The show must go on. Her heart was still racing from the adrenalin rush when the curtain came down for the last time.

She and Orlando high-fived; Isabel hoped that she'd be paired with him often. He was strong and had a gift for anticipating his partner's movements.

While the dancers milled about, the catering company set up drink stations and tables for the finger foods. The party guests would be admitted backstage shortly.

Chelly's voice rang out. "Quickly now, dancers, get out of your costumes and back on stage. No Jeans." Isabel heard the annoyed twitters around her. Chelly continued. "The entire board is here tonight, and we have many important guests. No alcohol. Technically, you will still be working. We need you sharp, alert, and circulating." Chelly smiled. "Show everyone how wonderful you are, even out of your dance shoes."

The dancers were about to move toward the dressing rooms. "One more thing," Chelly said. "I'll let the party get started; then I'll introduce the board members and then John and Lisa, and I want all of you on stage for these introductions. So, no dallying."

The guests entered, oohing, ahhing over the conversion of the stage to a party venue. Mrs. B. smiled, watching her friends take in this new world—new for them.

Congratulations were offered to people whom Mrs. B. couldn't identify. Looking around, she saw John. "There he is," she said, pointing. They walked over. Mrs. B. hugged and kissed him.

John shook hands with Father Melvyn. "Did you enjoy your first ballet, Father?"

The priest not only said "yes," but he also identified the parts he liked best and his impressions of how the movements related to the music.

"Excellent observations. That's very good, Father. Not a small thing for a first-time ballet goer," John said, smiling from ear to ear. Father Melvyn nodded at the compliment. Nancy added her congratulations.

Lisa joined them. Gathering her daughter-in-law in her arms, Mrs. B. said, "My dear, you look lovely." John and Lisa thanked them for coming, then excused themselves to circulate among the guests. It wasn't long before the dancers joined the party.

"Even in street clothes, you can tell who they are," Nancy said, sotto voce. "It's the posture. A dead give-away." She paused. "Bad choice of words," she added sheepishly.

Chelly Bernardi called for quiet. "Ladies and gentlemen," she began. "Thank you all for your support. We couldn't have done this without you." More applause. "Tonight, before we talk about the new Bernardi-Bono Ballet Company, there is another important matter to address." Everyone was quiet, waiting expectantly.

"We don't usually talk about the men and women of the stage crew, but without them, performances would not be possible." There was a smattering of applause. "I know you've all heard of the terrible death of Adam Leightman, the stage manager of the Rue de L'Histoire Theatre. Let's have a moment of silence." All murmuring stopped; heads bowed. No one spoke until Chelly lifted her head and resumed her speech.

"This was our inaugural performance. Please give a nice round of applause to the wonderful dancers of the Bernardi-Bono Ballet Company. Dancers, please step up." Applause and whistles greeted them.

Mrs. B., sandwiched between Father Melvyn and Nancy, nudged each of them. While her hands clapped, her chin jutted in the direction of a tall, statuesque dancer with long flowing brown hair. "I think that's the girl John mentioned."

Nancy leaned in and said, "I think we all noticed her on stage. She's something." Father Melvyn nodded.

When the applause died down, Chelly introduced John and Lisa. They, too, received an enthusiastic ovation. She then went on to the board of directors, starting with the president and finishing with a special introduction.

"We are so pleased to have everyone here as we welcome our newest board member. Victoria, please step forward." More hand-clapping.

"Victoria's family has supported the Bernardi Ballet Academy for years, and now, we are honored that they've become company donors. We are especially pleased to welcome Victoria Asturias to our board of directors."

After waiting an appropriate amount of time to let the applause die down, she raised her hands. "Lastly, before we party, I want to tell you the schedule for this season. The first weekend of November, we will premiere a new ballet. It will be our own John Bono's *Macbeth*." There were some murmurings of surprise and more applause. Mrs. B. thought her heart would burst with joy for her son.

"Of course, *Nutcracker* will follow." There were some whoops and laughter. "And in late January, we will present our own *Giselle*." Everyone cheered. "The season will close with *Taming of the Shrew,* one of Shakespeare's great comedies." More applause. "Now, on behalf of the dancers and staff, thank you all for your support, and please enjoy the party."

After the last round of cheers, well-wishers surrounded Chelly, John, and Lisa.

Mrs. B., Father Melvyn, and Nancy stood to one side of the stage, holding their drinks and watching the interactions between board members, guests, and dancers. Groups formed and dissolved, and new groups came together.

Mrs. B's attention was again captured by Isabel Sanchez-Reardon. Even in civilian clothes, she was a standout. Isabel's ready smile lit her face and reached her beautiful hazel eyes. Her long hair, loose and straight, was a rich chestnut brown, and the most alluring widow's peak created a heart shape on her forehead.

"Even off stage in street clothes, she has more than a dancer's posture. She has a presence that separates her from the rest," Nancy observed.

"And that's a quality that can't be taught," Mrs. B. added.

Father Melvyn nudged her. "Speaking of presence, isn't she the new board member?" he asked, gesturing toward the woman striding toward The Reardon girl.

Victoria Asturias was strikingly beautiful, with her jet-black hair pulled back in a chignon at the nape of her neck. Petite. Even in high heels, she couldn't have been more than five-and-a-half feet tall.

"Her posture is almost as erect as a dancer's," Mrs. B. said.

"Whom are we talking about?" Nancy asked.

Using the pinky she'd taken off her glass, Mrs. B. pointed. "The new board member. She's going over to the Reardon girl."

"Odd," Nancy said. "She didn't approach anyone other than Chelly Bernardi, not even John, and Lisa, or any of the principal dancers."

Nancy's, Mrs. B.'s, and Father Melvyn's attentions were riveted on Victoria as she reached Isabel.

Father Melvyn, who stood a head above the women, still took a step forward. "Is it my imagination, or is there tension between them?" He watched the shorter, more mature, and commanding woman confront the taller, younger, wary dancer. They couldn't see Asturias's face, but the Reardon girl looked hostile even from a distance.

Mrs. B. and Nancy jockeyed about, leaning from left to right, not wishing to be obvious but wanting to see the interaction between the new board member and the new dancer.

Asturias extended her hand. The dancer said something, and to their surprise, she pushed past the board member and walked away. Asturias turned and stared. Her dark eyes glittered with anger and locked onto Isabel Sanchez-Reardon's back as the dancer crossed the stage.

"There's a story there," Mrs. B. said.

## CHAPTER 8

## A BAD OMEN

Sunday morning, Isabel woke up with a broad smile creasing her face as she basked in the memory of the show and the attention she'd received. It validated her decision to accept the offer to dance with Bernardi-Bono Company. Sunlight spilled through her bedroom window. Isabel stretched and smiled, confident she'd found her artistic home.

The digital clock said 9 a.m., but she knew it was 10 in New York. Her phone rang. Caller ID showed a picture of her mother, Salvata-Lizabetta Sanchez-Reardon.

"Good morning, Mamá. I was just about to call you. Telepathy, I think."

"Are you still in bed, sleepy-head? Dad went to the gym, so I thought it would be a good time for us to talk."

Isabel threw back the covers, held the phone to her ear, and made her way to the kitchen, where she flicked the lever on the coffee pot. "No, I'm not in bed. Just making coffee," she answered, opening the blinds to let the day in.

"So, tell me. How did the opening go?" Isabel heard the edge in her mother's voice.

Isabel started her recitation, working backward from the gala party after the performance. She told her mother about the congratulations they'd all received and the many compliments from people who said that they'd spotted her on stage and couldn't take their eyes from her.

Her mother laughed. "I'm not surprised. I know you have that indefinable quality. I think it's called charisma, or is it stage presence?"

"Oh, Mamá, you're just prejudiced."

"Yes, and so I should be," her mother laughed. "But that doesn't mean I don't know what's good. After all, I've been watching ballet for as long as you've been dancing. How long is that? Why I'm a professional audience of one." They both laughed.

Isabel took a breath. She had to tell her mother about the bizarre murder because it might be reported in other Texas newspapers. If her cousins or her Aunt Marie in San Angelo read about it, they'd tell, and that would be worse. "We were sold out," Isabel said.

"That's great." Isabel didn't answer. "Isn't it?" her mother asked.

"It is, but not entirely for the reason you think." Isabel stirred cream and sugar into her coffee. "Unfortunately, two nights before the opening, the stage manager was found murdered. His skull was crushed."

"Why would it affect ticket sales?" Isabel was

silent. "Isabel," her mother said, "what's going on?"

"He was found murdered in the theater. His body dropped from the light bridge during the tech rehearsal." Her next words tumbled out in a rush. "And I was the first one to see it."

It was her mother's turn to be silent.

"Mamá?" Isabel held her breath.

"Why were you first to see it?" her mother asked in her most professional nurse's voice.

"I was coming back on stage after a break, and the light bridge was lowered directly in my line of sight."

"Oh, Lord. This is too awful. Are you okay?" Salvata-Lizabetta, Liz to friends and family, asked.

"Don't be upset," Isabel said. "I was shocked, as you can imagine, but I'm fine. The police questioned everyone in the theater: stagehands, dancers, all of us. It's an ongoing murder investigation, but it spooked a lot of the dancers. You know how superstitious we tend to be. No one is talking about it, but everyone is a little nervous. It's a bad omen."

"Isabel, don't fall into that kind of thinking. To me, it sounds like a very human crime." Her mother quickly changed the subject. "What's next this season?"

"*Macbeth*. One of the new partners, John Bono, is choreographing it."

"Sounds exciting. What are the dates? Maybe Dad and I will come. We can visit my sister in San Angelo and then come to Austin for the performance."

"I'd love that, Mamá. The cast list goes up on Tuesday. I'll let you know what I'll dance. There aren't a lot of women's roles, other than Lady Macbeth and the witches, so I doubt I'll get anything special, but it will be fun, and I'd love for you and Dad to come." Isabel refilled her coffee cup. "Austin has changed so much since you last visited. It's a beautiful city. Lots of transplants, like me," she joked. "I think visiting, seeing where I live, and work will do a lot to relieve your anxieties."

Isabel and her mother agreed to talk again on Tuesday night. "Tell Dad he'd better be home." They laughed together. "Love you, Mamá."

"I love you too."

Isabel hung up, not having mentioned anything about the Asturias family. She knew better. The memory of her mother's words the day she'd auditioned for the company rang in her brain. *We escaped Austin and those people.*

Isabel's guilt stirred. She'd broken her promise not to go reviving old stories, but once she'd settled in Austin, she began her research, determined to find out what had happened to her great-grandfather, Rafael, who had disappeared in 1920.

To his dying day, her beloved grandfather, Oratio, believed that his father, Rafael, had been the victim of foul play at the hands of one Victor Asturias.

Two weeks ago, she'd gotten a lot of information from the Travis County appraisal office, but it wasn't what she'd needed. The woman there who'd helped her was sympathetic, but Isabel would have to research other sources at other locations to trace the land information further back. Sill, once the ballet company was in production mode, there was no extra time for research.

Looking down at the folder, she considered doing more research immediately but changed her mind. The sun was shining; the day was too beautiful to spend cooped up in the library. "I'll spend the afternoon on the boardwalk at Lady Bird Lake."

She rationalized that the fresh air would do her good, and the company was off on Mondays. She would go to the library then, but a new worry nagged her.

The day she'd visited the Travis County office, she'd lost track of time. Rushing out, afraid she'd be late for rehearsal, she collided with another woman. The stranger's purse and the papers in her own hands fell to the ground.

Isabel had tried to apologize but was frozen by the flash of anger in the woman's eyes.

"Watch where you're going," the stranger had snapped before disappearing into the building.

She hadn't given the incident another thought—not until last night. When the newest board member was introduced, Isabel's stomach dropped. Victoria Asturias was the woman she'd crashed into on the stops of the appraisal office and a descendant of *those people*, the family whose history was entangled with hers. And now, another Asturias was involved with the ballet company.

Isabel hadn't thought about how she'd react if she met an Asturias. She'd hoped not to be discovered by any of them for months, maybe never. Well, that's moot, she thought bitterly, more than a little worried. Isabel wondered how much Asturias knew about their families' past connections.

A bluebird flew onto the rail of her balcony and began to chirp. Its song sounded like *get dressed and go outside*. It lifted her spirits. Isabel got dressed and left her apartment for a day in the sunshine.

A couple of miles from Isabel's apartment, Mrs. B., her son John and his wife Lisa sat on Mrs. B's shaded deck outside the kitchen, sipping wine and enjoying a perfect Austin day.

Mrs. B. half-listened to her son's talk about the business side of dance. She was comparing him to his father. His tall, trim frame was folded into the deck chair. He's so handsome, she thought. His features were sharp, like his father's, and like his father's, his wavy black hair showed some gray at the temples.

She still missed her late husband, John Buonofigliuola, Sr., a problematic name even for some Italian-Americans. Hence, John Jr. shortened it to Bono. He continued to talk, and she continued to compare him to his father. He, too, had a way with words and could make any story exciting and amusing.

John's wife, Lisa, sat beside him. Long blond hair hanging loose, she was still thin, but no longer dancer thin. Lisa reached across her husband to take another of the little toasts. John stopped talking and knowingly smiled at his wife.

"I promise, I won't eat them all," Lisa said sheepishly. "Mom," she said to Mrs. B. "these are so good. I try to make them, but somehow they don't taste the same." Lisa popped another bruschetta into her mouth. "I do the same things. I toast the bread rounds, rub them with some olive oil and fresh garlic, and then top them with the chopped tomato and mozzarella. What's missing?"

"Nothing's missing, love," John said to his wife, giving her a quick peck on the tip of her nose. "You need a few more years of cooking. The flavors can't be duplicated because they've permeated my mother's fingertips. She seasons everything she touches."

Mrs. B. smiled. "I know you love them. I have more in the fridge. You can take them home if you like."

"Thank you, I will," Lisa said, taking another.

Sitting on the inside of the screened kitchen door, Sasha and Ziggy sat upright, watching their humans.

"Do you ever let those cats out?" John asked.

"No, son. There are coyotes and grey foxes around here. Too dangerous for them."

As soon as Mrs. B. spoke, the cats lay down and curled their front paws under them. They sniffed as if to say, *Those cats? We have names, and just you try to get us outside!*

Sasha's and Ziggy's eyes moved back and forth from one person to the other as the conversation centered on the Bernardi-Bono Ballet Company's performance the night before.

"Mom, you have a great eye, and you understand the physics behind the craft. What did you think?"

"I'm impressed. And your *Macbeth* is next. Have you been working on it long?"

"On and off for a few years. When I told Chelly, she jumped at it, and the dancers in this company are strong enough to do it."

"Speaking of the dancers," Mrs. B. said. "Who is that tall, statuesque girl? The one with the widow's peak and long, chestnut hair. Father Melvyn, Nancy, and I couldn't keep our eyes off her."

Lisa answered. "Isabel Sanchez-Reardon."

"That's the one," Mrs. B. said. "Great stage presence."

"We do have high hopes for her," John added.

Mrs. B. was about to describe the troubling encounter she'd observed backstage between the new dancer and the new board member when John stood up.

"How about the spaghetti and meatballs you promised. We are starving. Let's eat before Lisa bites off her arm from hunger," he said, winking at his wife.

"Yes, of course, son," Mrs. B. answered, deciding not to mar the happy calm of the day. It could wait. Probably nothing, anyway, she thought. "Let's get these glasses inside. It won't take a minute to finish dinner."

# CHAPTER 9

## GRIEF

Father Melvyn looked around the restaurant crowded with mourners after the Leightman funeral Mass and burial. He circulated among the guests, stopping to chat with a few whom he knew and noticed a man shifting from foot to foot, holding a drink, and looking uncomfortable. When it was time to depart, Father Melvyn stood behind this same stranger, waiting to say goodbye to Sally Leightman, and overheard their conversation.

"Sally, I need to get back to the theater. Please call me if there's anything I can do to help you."

Sally nodded. Her son answered, "Thank you for coming, Tony. I'm sure the theater will be in good hands under your management."

Father Melvyn stepped up to Adam's widow. His heart ached for her. She wasn't just sad. She looked defeated, lost. Her son stood beside her. Father Melvyn extended his hand to Adam Junior and again expressed his condolences. He then took both of Sally's hands in his own. "What can I do to help you through this?" he asked.

"Thank you, Father, but I'm leaving Austin in a few days. My son is taking me to California to be near him."

Adam Junior placed a comforting arm around his mother's shoulders. "I've taken care of everything. The movers will pack up the house, and I have a real estate agent ready to sell it. I want my mother with me. The police assure me that they will keep us posted on the progress of the investigation—although, thus far, it's gone nowhere." Adam Junior sounded angry.

At the mention of the investigation, Sally's eyes welled with tears. "I should have done something to stop him," she said, her voice clogged with emotion.

"My dear, don't take that on yourself. What happened is not your fault," the priest said. Her shoulders shook with sobs. Feeling sad and helpless, Father Melvyn added, "I wish you both the best, and if ever I can be of help, even long distance, please don't hesitate to call me."

LaLa lounged on the desk and watched Mrs. B. filing baptism certificates. Periodically, the cat swatted at the papers in her hand.

"You want to know when he's coming back, don't you?" Mrs. B. asked. Abruptly, LaLa sat up straight, tilted her head, listening. She then jumped off the desk and galloped into the hallway before the doorbell rang.

"Hello, Jake," Mrs. B. said, opening the door. "What brings you here today?"

"Is the padre around?"

"He's at the Leightman funeral luncheon. Should be back any minute. Come in. I'll get you a cup of coffee."

"I see your guard cat is watching," he said, half-smiling.

"Yes. LaLa has become an addition to the staff at St. Francis de Sales." Mrs. B. laughed as they walked to the kitchen. "What can I help you with, while we wait for Father Melvyn?"

"It's you I want to talk to."

Mrs. B.'s eyebrows popped up. "Me? Why?"

"Because your son is part owner of the ballet company that owns the Rue de L'Histoire Theatre, and we are getting peculiar vibes from both the crew and the dancers."

"What are you talking about?"

"Let me be blunt. We've heard too much about ghosts and curses. What's that about?"

"Ah," she said, understanding the detective's confusion. "Theatre people are a superstitious lot. John told me that.

"Adam's death is looked upon as a bad omen, especially since this was the company's first-ever performance in that theater."

"Well, certainly not an auspicious beginning," Jake responded, somewhat amazed, "but do they think there is a supernatural explanation for this? Does John?"

Mrs. B. shrugged. "I don't think John does, but dancers tend to the dramatic, as do most performers. Think about it, Jake. To portray others with depth and feeling, performers empty themselves psychologically and emotionally. I think that makes them susceptible."

"Susceptible! To what?"

"Psychic Impressions. Different energies."

She watched Jake's face as he considered what she was saying. He looked doubtful. He'd opened the door with his questions, so she decided to ask her own.

"How is the investigation going? Any leads? Anything new?"

Before he could say, *I can't discuss an ongoing investigation*, the back door opened, and in strode Father Melvyn.

"Jake. Good to see you," the priest said, extending his hand.

"And you, padr… uh, Father Melvyn."

"Anything I can help you with?"

"Not really. Just talking to my friend here. Picking her brain about theater superstitions." Without pausing, Jake drained his coffee cup and excused himself. "Thanks for the coffee, Sammi. I'll be on my way. Give Terri a call," he said, referring to his wife. "Let's have dinner."

Jake waved at the priest. "Take care, Father," he said and walked out of the kitchen to the front hall.

*M-e-e-o-o-w.* LaLa sat on the landing staring at the detective. Jake didn't speak; he gave her a crisp salute and let himself out.

As soon as the detective was out the door, Father Melvyn pulled off his clerical collar and shrugged out of his jacket.

"How about a cup of that coffee. I suspect the investigation is stalling if Jake is here asking questions about theater superstitions."

# CHAPTER 10

## GHOSTS AND CURSES

In the Bernardi-Bono Ballet Studio's spacious foyer, Mrs. B. was greeted by the bright-eyed receptionist, Laurel Minton, whose desk faced the front door. Laurel welcomed her and brought her to John's office. Passing the first studio, Mrs. B. caught a glimpse of her son teaching a class.

"He'll be done in a few minutes," Laurel said. "Can I get you a cup of tea or coffee while you wait?"

"Thank you, no, Laurel. I'm fine." Mrs. B. sat in a chair facing the desk.

"Would you like some company while you wait?" Laurel asked.

"My dear, I wouldn't want to keep you from your job. John will blame me if you're not at your desk."

Laurel smiled and hovered for a few minutes. "I suppose you're right, but if there's anything you need, just give a shout," she said and left.

Mrs. B. didn't often visit John and Lisa at work, but she was always happy when she had an opportunity. The stately old house, located in an older section of the city, had been converted into dance studios and was now the home of the Bernardi-Bono Ballet Company. This was a special place where dreams were made. She understood those dreams.

As soon as Laurel closed the door, Mrs. B. stood up and circled the room, looking at the framed pictures of John on stage. Her favorite was the one of him in the air. Head back, arms out to the side with his legs out behind him, ankles crossed, feet pointed. He looked as if he was flying. She smiled at the memories the photographs evoked.

She edged her way around the room and glanced at the papers on the desk. It was a cast list. The names meant nothing to her until she saw Isabel Sanchez-Reardon written beside the Weird Sisters, the three witches of Macbeth. Voices outside the door cued her to hurry back around the desk and sit down.

"Hi, Mom." He pecked her cheek when he walked in. "What brings you here this afternoon?" "Didn't you get my message?"

"Yes. I did. That's why Laurel brought you to my office. I'm happy to see you; it's just unexpected."

"I was going home and thought I'd stop by for a quick chat. Can't I visit my son at the end of his workday? I didn't think I'd be interrupting or intruding," she said, smiling.

"You know you aren't," John answered. "Actually, Lisa is working late. Why don't I buy you dinner, and we can talk."

"That would be lovely, but I should go home to feed Sasha and Ziggy."

John sighed. "Mother, the cats won't die if they have to wait an hour longer. C'mon. We'll walk over to Congress and grab a bite at the corner Italian. It's pretty good, and it won't be crowded this early. We can have a nice chat."

At the restaurant, John was greeted warmly. "Hello, Mr. Bono," a middle-aged man said when they entered.

He must eat here often, Mrs. B. thought. They were shown to a table. After they were seated, they ordered wine and their dinner. John excused himself.
"Be right back," he said and winked.

She watched him walk away. *One might think there was a metal rod from the base of his skull down his spinal column, holding him beautifully erect.* She knew it was a result of years of ballet training.

When he returned, their wines were served, and they ordered dinner.

John sipped his glass of Chianti and stared straight at her; the question was in his eyes.

Just like his father, she thought. He's not fooled, she thought. "Okay, son. Here it is." Mrs. B. put down her glass. "While Father Melvyn was at the funeral luncheon today, Jake stopped by to see me. Did you tell him that some dancers see the Leightman murder as a bad omen?"

John didn't answer while the waiter set down their piping hot dishes of penne arrabbiata. Mrs. B. closed her eyes and enjoyed the aroma of the spicy red sauce. They thanked the waiter, raised their glasses, and chorused, "Cin-Cin."

"This smells heavenly," Mrs. B. said. For a few minutes, they enjoyed their pasta without speaking.

"Like it, Mom?"

"Oh, yes. It is delicious."

Referring to her question, John said, "When Jake asked me about how the company viewed Leightman's death, I did tell him that."

"Do you believe it?"

"Honestly, I'm not sure what I believe. Do I think a ghost or some paranormal activity killed Adam? No, but it is disconcerting to start the company in its new theater this way."

Mrs. B. didn't respond. For a while, they ate in silence, each deep in thought.

John asked. "You're friends with Jake and his wife, Terri, right?" Mrs. B. nodded. "Why do you suppose he wanted to ask you that? What does theater superstition have to do with the murder investigation?"

"Jake isn't the sort to allow something like theater lore cloud his reason. Father Melvyn and I suspect the investigation is stalling, and he's just gathering information, developing other ideas, and seeking new leads."

"FYI," John said. "Lisa, Chelly, and I have discussed these notions. We are setting *Macbeth*, which carries its own sack of superstitious bricks. We don't need the dancers worked up into a spooked frenzy before we even get it into the theater." He sighed. "I hope Jake solves this soon."

"Me too," she said and sipped her wine. Then asked, "Macbeth superstitions?"

John smiled. "Ahh. The Scottish curse. It's Shakespearean theater and taken very seriously. Of late, even ballet companies give it deference. Why take chances, right?"

"Son, I don't know what you're talking about."

John smiled at his mother's quizzical look. "Since its first performance, hundreds of years ago, there have been accidents and tragedies associated with the play." John put down his fork. "Some say it's because Shakespeare used real incantations for the three prophetic witches." He raised both hands beside his head and vibrated them. "OOOHH," he pretended to make ghostly sounds. "Good Halloween stuff."

Mrs. B. laughed.

"Look it up when you have time. You'll enjoy the stories, but there is one hard, fast rule: you never mention that play's name when you are in the theater. Everyone calls it 'that play,' or the 'Scottish play.'"

After dinner, they walked back to the studios where she'd left her car. John kissed his mother goodbye.

"Give my love to Lisa," she said and drove off as dusk turned to night.

# CHAPTER 11

## I'M A WITCH!

Isabel hurried home. The cast list had been posted, and she couldn't wait to call her mother. She dialed. "Mamá, great news."

"What is it?" asked her mother.

"I'm a witch!" she blurted. When her mother didn't react immediately, she said, "Mamá, I'm one of the three witches in Macbeth."

"Congratulations, my darling. You're new to the company, and that's an important part." Her father picked up the phone to congratulate her. Her parents were pleased. "I spoke to Aunt Marie today," her mother told her. "She said if Dad and I come for the ballet, she and her boys will drive in from San Angelo."

Isabel's heart thudded in her chest. In her excitement about her role, she'd forgotten about the Asturias family. Her zeal cooled. Using her most enthusiastic voice, she answered,

"That would be great. We'll talk more about it on Sunday, okay?"

"Are you in a hurry?" her mother asked.

"Yes. Lot's to do tonight, but I wanted you to know. Love you guys. We'll talk again on Sunday," she repeated, anxious to get off the phone.

Isabel hung up. She still hadn't told her mother that *those people* were involved in the ballet company. How was she to explain why she'd broken her promise not to go dredging up the past? And it wasn't a matter of *if* her mother found out. It was a question of *when.*

Unlike most people, Isabel's mother read everything in the ballet program: ads, names of musicians, the lists of donors. Isabel knew her mother would be furious when she saw the name that was anathema to her family on the board of directors.

"Think, Isabel," she commanded. She knew there was little time to finish her search. *And if I prove what grandfather always told me, then what? Why am I doing this?* but she knew why.

She'd adored her grandfather. It always hurt her when he'd get that pained, haunted look. Oh, grandfather. I miss you so, she thought, and breathed in, trying to recapture the smell of his pipe, an aroma she'd always loved, but it wouldn't come. "If nothing else, grandfather, they will know for sure that you were telling the truth," she said.

Looking up, she blew a kiss toward heaven.

# CHAPTER 12

## A LOVE HATE RELATIONSHIP

Victoria Asturias stormed out of the lawyer's office on 6th Street. Emerging from the shaded doorway, the September sun hit her in the face like a hot iron. She stopped long enough to get her sunglasses on and realized that some shitty paparazzo was snapping away.

"C'mon, sis," Nando's voice came from behind. "So what? We'll sell the house. We don't need it," he said in his flippant, partially intoxicated way. "Why are you rattling around in that big old barn all by yourself?"

Victoria grabbed his shirtsleeve and tugged him in the direction of her car. "What's wrong with you? Don't you see the creep with the camera?" Nando opened his mouth to answer. "Shut up," she snapped and pulled her brother along. He panted to keep up with her slender, well-exercised body.

In the car, Victoria opened up. "You fool. We have been one of the stellar families in Austin since the 1930s. I can't believe how you and Father have decimated the business in a generation with your drinking, whoring, and bad investments."

Nando laughed. "Well, he's dead now, so you have one less to worry about. And, Miss Perfect, who are you to criticize? You've had your share of affairs and peccadillos. Dad paid off your men when you went through your slut days."

Victoria had all she could do to focus on driving in the late afternoon traffic. Between clenched teeth, she snarled, "Yes, but eventually, I grew up. Something I cannot say for you or Father."

"Don't speak ill of the dead." Nando snapped and reached for the flask in his pocket.

"Besides, we've been over all of this before. Didn't we sell some property? That should keep us in the chips for a few months while we get the mansion fixed up and on the market."

"Are you deaf along with being stupid and half-drunk?" she shouted and slammed the brake to avoid hitting another car. Taking a breath, grateful not to have an accident and another Asturias scandal on her hands, she said, "Be quiet. Stop drinking, and let's get home."

"Well, you're driving, bitch."

Her insides boiled. If she wasn't driving, and if they were at home, she might have killed him. At that moment, she hated her brother.

She resumed the conversation as

soon as they entered the house. "I've cut your allowance, and I'm not reinstating it until we have the entire estate settled."

"What happened to the money from the sale?" Nando demanded.

"It went to pay off debts. We got a measly $750,000.00, which saved us for a short time. We are on the verge of bankruptcy."

Nando walked to the bar to pour a drink.

"Do not drink. I'm talking to you," Victoria shouted.

Slamming the crystal top back on the decanter, Nando turned to Victoria. "I'm sick of you. Either you reinstate my allowance, or I'm going to get a lawyer and take you to court. What a lovely scandal that would be to tarnish the illustrious Asturias name."

She knew he'd do it. Folding her arms across her chest and controlling her voice, she answered. "Okay. I'll reinstate the allowance for three months, on one condition."

"And that is?" he asked, gloating.

She itched to slap his smug face. "Get out of Austin for a few weeks until I get further along." Her heart sank; she realized her mistake.

"Further along in what?" Nando asked.

"In restructuring the business and paying off creditors." She had an idea. "Nando, you've made it clear that you have no interest in anything Asturias, other than the advantages of name and money. If you want your allowance to continue beyond the next three months, do as I ask." She paused and waited until he was paying close attention.

"Go to one of your friends in Dallas or Houston. I'll get everything settled, and you'll have your trust fund refinanced." She stuck out her hand. "Deal?" she asked.

He didn't take it. "Hmmm. You're up to something. I'll think about it after you up the allowance again," he said and walked out the front door.

Victoria heard the loud rev of his sports car as he flew out of the driveway. "I can't think like this," she muttered. Rage and frustration turned her cheeks red. She decided on a strenuous workout to relieve the stress.

An hour and a half later, she peeled off her sweat-soaked exercise clothes, showered, and put on jeans and a tee.

Taking a glass of Pino Noir, she sat at her desk and thought about how her life had changed.

She'd set aside her regret that the engineering career for which she'd fought so hard had to be abandoned, but she'd sworn a deathbed oath to her dying grandfather that she'd save the family fortune and reputation.

Frowning, she sipped her wine and revisited conversations she'd had with their lawyer, Tom Smithson. More than once, he'd outlined the seriousness of their financial situation. She'd allowed the sale of the History Street property, which helped buy more time, but Smithson was firm. Selling the family home would be necessary. It was worth at least five million, and she'd have to cut back on support for charities.

Since her grandfather's death, she'd combed the house for the materials he'd sworn were hidden.

She thought about the day her grandfather died. He'd become so agitated when he learned she'd sold that property, struggling to tell her something more, but what? In the attic, she'd found his journals and what a surprise they'd held, but no explanations. She needed her great-grandfather Victor's notes. Victoria held her head in her hands. There were tough times ahead, and Nando didn't care.

# CHAPTER 13

## MAINTAIN CONTROL!

"Révérence." The company assembled in the center of the floor to begin the last exercise, a formalized series of bows and curtsies.

After the last note, Lisa said, "Thank you, class." The dancers clapped in a show of respect for the teacher and the pianist.

Lisa addressed the company. "Dancers, you have the rest of the day off." She smiled at the surprised murmurs. "We have a special board meeting, so enjoy the sunshine, and we'll see you in the morning."

The dancers exited the studio, chatting about what to do with this surprise, but Isabel knew what she was going to do. After a quick change, she headed to the front door and noticed Tony Volpe, the new stage manager, waiting at the reception desk.

Anxious to continue her research, Isabel slipped on her sunglasses, jumped in her car, and headed to the driveway. A Mercedes swung in and blocked her exit. *Asturias!*

Isabel pretended not to see her. "What the hell is she doing here?" Isabel muttered through tight lips; then, she remembered the board meeting.

The sight of Victoria made Isabel more anxious about her search to prove her grandfather's belief that the family's land and legacy had been stolen.

Once the Mercedes moved past her, Isabel turned her car in the direction of the public library where the Sanborn Map Collection was located.

Victoria recognized Isabel Sanchez-Reardon driving out. She was impressed with the dancer's cool pretense not to see her as she left the parking lot. She'd have to be dealt with, but the business at hand took over Victoria's thoughts. She was ready for the upcoming meeting with the artistic directors, Chelly Bernardi, John and Lisa Bono, the new stage manager, Tony Volpe, and several other board members.

Even though she didn't have money to waste, she was prepared to underwrite the production of *Macbeth* as a necessary investment. She needed free access to the theater without raising suspicions. Hence, she needed good reasons to be there. Smoothing her already perfect hair, Victoria entered the Bernardi-Bono Ballet studios, ready to make her case.

Two hours later, Victoria recapped the meeting. "The designs have been accepted by the artistic directors, and even though the sets, scenery, and costumes are minimalist, combined with the costs of special effects and props, and the usual operating costs and salaries, the estimate for this production is $475,000.00." She paused. "The staging and technical needs have been mapped out, and Tony," she said, looking directly at the stage manager, "you've detailed the problems in a theater equipped only with 1980s technologies."

Tony Volpe interjected, "I feel it's my responsibility to suggest that we put *Macbeth* off until some backstage renovations can be done. This is a demanding production."

"Do you not feel up to the task?" Victoria asked sweetly.

Volpe's face turned red. "No. I'm just pointing out that while you've recapped the costs very well, there are going to be hidden expenses triggered when the crew begins to prepare for this production."

John sighed. "It's my ballet, and much as I hate to consider not doing it, I think Tony is making points that need consideration."

*Maintain control!* Victoria nodded, staying calm. "True," she answered. "But, it's not a good strategy for a company to announce a program then back away from it at the last minute. Even though it's eight weeks away, this, in theater, is the last minute." She looked around the table. She had their attention. "Cancellations can make a company, especially a new company, seem weak, incompetent, even." She waited, allowing her words to sink in. "I'd hate to see the Bernardi-Bono Ballet Company suffer a setback, so here is what I'm prepared to do." She paused. All eyes were on her.

"Tony, I have great faith in your abilities and knowledge. If problems arise, please bring them to me. If, ladies and gentlemen, the operating budget is too tight, I will cover any additional costs." Everyone gasped.

Chelly recovered first. "Victoria, your family, has always been generous to the arts, but this is above and beyond anything we expected. How can we thank you?"

"My thanks will be the successful season and the growth potential we have." Her smile softened the hard lines of her face. "I've always had a special place in my heart for ballet. Let's get this done."

Tony remained professional, but quiet.

Victoria knew she'd cut him with her question. She went over to him and, in her most soothing voice, said, "Keep me posted, Tony. If there are technical problems, let me know. I am an engineer, and while that's not the same as stagecraft, I do have some expertise in the mechanics of how things work. Please let me help."

Back in his office at the Rue de L'Histoire Theatre, Tony was pensive. He spread the worksheets across his desk and studied the technical requirements for this Macbeth. He'd done his best to convince the company to put it off, but who could argue with the Asturias woman, especially since she'd offered to cover additional costs and overruns?

"Careful, Tony," he whispered to himself. "When you tried to talk them out of it, the first thing Asturias questioned was your capability." Tony gathered up the papers and put them in the file cabinet.

He was worried. When he arrived first thing in the morning, set pieces had been moved and the ghost lamp was off. He'd checked the wiring and the bulb once again. Nothing was wrong. Had the light been turned off, or had he forgotten to turn it on?

Tony was reluctant to question the crew since his appointment as stage manager was new, and Asturias's question at the board meeting still stung, but he was concerned.

Tony shrugged off the stories of the *Macbeth* curse, despite his disquiet. He had always been a level-headed guy, except for one time. And he'd paid a high price for that mistake.

An idea surfaced. Before leaving the theater he'd take phone pictures of everything and compare them to what he found the following day.

That would show him if anything had changed or if he was losing his mind.

# CHAPTER 14

## LET THE DEAD STAY BURIED

Disappointed and tired, Isabel left the Sanborn Map Collection at the Public library. The librarian had suggested that she visit the Travis County clerk's office, out on Airport Boulevard. Deeds from 1910-1920 would be there on microfiche. It was already after four, traffic was heavy, and there would be little time for research if she went to the clerk's office. She headed home, hoping she could find more online.

Sitting in traffic, not in the mood for the radio, her grandfather's stories swirled in her head. They kept her company.

At home, she first took care of the mundane chores of life: listening to phone messages, sorting bills, preparing dinner, and getting organized for the next day. Then, after two hours of online searching, she'd found nothing new. Isabel had no choice. She'd have to go to the clerk's office. She sighed. There wouldn't be time for that until at least next week. Her rehearsal schedule was full.

From the box where she kept her grandfather's papers, Isabel took out the fragile piece of yellowed paper. Rafael's deed.

The first time her beloved grandad, Oratio, showed it to her, it was already fragile and faded with age. The delicate paper was tearing, and some of the print and official stamps were difficult to read. She'd made copies and protected the original in a clear plastic sleeve. Since moving to

Austin, more than ever, something about her family's history felt off incomplete.

Through the years, Isabel had tried asking her mother about the land, but her mother became agitated and dismissive.

"Even if it's true, there's nothing we can do almost one hundred years later. *Those people* have caused us enough pain," her mother had said, repeatedly, and again she'd recap the family misfortunes.

"After my grandfather disappeared, my family lost everything. Their house burned down, and Grandmother moved to San Angelo with her children, said her mother. "The story ends there."

Isabel's heart squeezed. She felt the heartbreak afresh, remembering the pain in her grandfather's eyes whenever he'd spoken of his family's tragedies. Isabel took out the photos of her great-grandfather, Rafael Sanchez.

The faded sepia tones of the snapshots did nothing to detract from Rafael's handsome face. Her favorite was the one of him in a suit and tie, a cigarette in his hand, and a distinctive ring on his right ring finger.

In the other photo, he posed with his son, her grandfather, Oratio. The close-up showed Rafael with his right hand on Oratio's shoulder. Again, the distinctive ring was spectacular.

When she'd asked her grandfather about it, he said that his father always wore it.

"The picture doesn't show it, my darling, but the ring had markings like the seal of Peter," he'd told her.

"Really? Where did it come from?"

"I don't know."

When her mother heard him talking, she'd interrupt, her tone frigid. "We have a new life here, Papa, far away from Texas."

Her grandfather would smile, but his eyes always remained sad. He'd wink and say, "Okay, Isabel. We'll put these dusty old pictures away. Let's go outside and do something."

Even at a very young age, Isabel felt confused and intimidated by her mother's coldness. I love my mother, Isabel thought, but she prefers to forget or hide from the past.

"Don't go stirring up old ghosts. Let the dead stay buried," was her mother's final warning.

Victoria's face flashed in front of her. "I can't let it die," she whispered. *This story isn't finished.*

Satisfied with the results of the board meeting, Victoria returned home. Now she had to find more money for the company. "It's an investment," she reminded herself.

After a taxing workout, she had a quick dinner, then took a cup of coffee and went into her attic office. She'd transferred checkbooks, bills, legal notices, and everything else up there and kept it all under lock and key, away from her brother's prying eyes away.

I'm probably giving him too much credit, she thought, but right now, I need to decide where I'll get at least a hundred grand immediately.

Victoria's desktop was loaded with bills. She reached for the stacks waiting for her attention. They were sorted alphabetically separated into two groups. The least pressing bills were in one, and those needing immediate attention in the other. She lifted the stack that needed immediate attention. The top invoice was out of alphabetical order; she was puzzled. That wasn't like her.

Nando's face popped into her head. Could he? No, he couldn't, she thought. He doesn't have a key to get up here or the ability to pick the lock. I made a mistake, is all; she smiled at the thought.

Victoria made a mental note to call Tom Smithson, her lawyer, in the morning. She'd tell him what she wanted. *I'm walking a tightrope, and Smithson won't be happy, but he'll get over it.*

When she left the office and went downstairs, she waited in the hall to hear the new lock catch after she'd closed the door. Victoria walked away, then turned back and bent over to look for scratches around the keyhole.

She was being neurotic because Nando had moved back in. He'd said it was to keep an eye on her, but Victoria knew there was more to it. He won't last long under my rules, she thought. Years ago, she'd made it clear to her brother and father that their lady-friends and booze-friends were not welcome.

The silence of the house was suddenly immense, making her feel alone and adrift.

*Scared?* That from the malicious voice in her head. "Get over yourself," she said firmly, annoyed at what she considered signs of weakness.

After pushing through her nightly personal hygiene, she jumped into bed, grabbed the remote, and channel-surfed. A mindless reality show would put her to sleep faster than a sleeping pill. "That's what I need, a good night's sleep."

Nando waited until he was sure Victoria would be asleep before returning to the house. He was in no mood for her questions, digs, and accusations. He had pressing problems of his own. He'd had a long day stalking his sister.

At the engineering firm where she was still a partner. Victoria hadn't arrived until after twelve noon. He'd wondered if she'd taken the day off and thought about calling and asking her what time she'd be home, but that would have been entirely out of character.

Nando had decided that if she hadn't arrived by one, he'd try another day, but as he was ready to leave, she pulled into her space.

Once she walked into the building, Nando headed home. She thinks I'm a no-account drunk with no brains, ability, or drive. Maybe she's right—we'll see. First, I need to know what the brilliant, favorite granddaughter is up to in her attic lair.

On his drive back to the house to spy on Victoria, Nando was occupied with how he would find the money to pay off his gambling debts to Billy Slips. He knew he couldn't duck Billy's collector forever, even though he'd moved back into the family home, undetected by Billy's goon, Harold.

Fortunately, the last time he'd tried to return to his apartment, he'd spotted Harold parked and waiting across from the main entrance of his condo. Nando had backed up the street and drove away. After two hours of aimless driving, going nowhere, he stopped for gas, coffee, and burgers, always watching for the familiar black Ford. When he was sure Harold hadn't seen him, he headed for a motel along the highway and checked in for the night.

Safely in the room, he'd bolted the door and shoved a chair under the handle for good measure. When he'd checked his cell phone, there was a text from Billy Slips.

*Hey man, my guy is coming to pick up the package you're holding for me. Let me know by tomorrow, or you could bring it yourself and have a drink with me.* That was code for pay or else. He was on the verge of panic.

Nando had tried to recoup his losses by betting on the horses, but he'd lost even more. His savings account was down to $16,000. Not enough to pay Billy in full.

He thought if he gave Billy Slips ten grand, it would get the mobster off his back for a few days, but he'd be almost broke. He needed to have his allowance fully reinstated. Then he remembered no deposits or withdrawals of ten-grand or more.

What's worse, he asked himself. The IRS or Billy?

# CHAPTER 15

## "DOUBLE, DOUBLE, TOIL AND TROUBLE."
### Shakespeare's Macbeth

Tony was anxious when he entered the stage door earlier than usual. Worried about what he'd find, he held his breath. He disarmed the system and didn't turn on the overhead lights, but he saw the glow from the ghost light. Relief surged through him. He went to his office, dropped his briefcase on the floor, grabbed his cell phone with the pictures he'd taken the night before and walked to the stage.

Nothing had been moved. He walked along the rows of trusses and looked at the sets flying above the curtain line. Climbing the steps to the catwalk, he saw that nothing had loosened overnight.

Maybe my imagination is getting the better of me, he thought. I'd better get focused on the requirements for 'that story.' Although not superstitious, he refused to even think of the title, *Macbeth*. Why take chances?

Returning to his office with new energy, Tony buckled down to work. His crew would arrive soon, and he wanted to meet with them to discuss technical matters.

Taking out the clipboard with his notes from Bernardi-Bono Ballet Company's board meeting the day before, he saw Victoria Asturias's card clipped to the top. He had a visceral reaction to her name. He didn't like or trust her, but he knew that he'd have to work with the company's fairy godmother.

Mrs. B. handed Father Melvyn a cup of coffee. "We have an invitation from my son," she said.

"To what?"

"To a special rehearsal at the theater." Mrs. B. loaded fruits into the colander in the sink. "John is excited. The company had a board meeting yesterday. They've decided to go forward with *Macbeth*, despite the theater's technical issues."

"What sort of technical issues? I hope not safety."

"No. They may have to rent some specialty equipment because the theater hasn't been renovated since the 1980s.

They're a new company, and they can't afford to exceed their budget, but the new board member, Victoria Asturias, has generously offered to cover the additional costs. Anyway, he's invited us to watch."

"I don't understand," Father Melvyn said.

"Being invited to watch a working rehearsal is a big deal," she explained. "I've watched one or two before. It's fascinating. You get to see what happens in rehearsal to make the performance look effortless on stage."

"And he invited me?"

"He was impressed with your reaction to the first ballet you'd ever seen. He thought you might enjoy this perspective."

Father Melvyn smiled. "I think I would. I'll ask Father Declan to be on duty that day.

"By the way," he added, "I heard from Sally Leightman yesterday. She—" The phone interrupted him, and the needs of St. Francis de Sales parish took center stage for the remainder of the day.

With both priests out on calls, when it was time for her to leave, she wrote instructions for heating dinner, set the phone to the answering service, and left.

When she arrived home, Sasha and Ziggy were harmonizing their calls for dinner. One with deep gulps, the other with elongated meows.

"Oh, my," she said, walking in. "It's only six o'clock. Why the fuss? Are you that hungry?" She reached down to pet her darlings. "I know I've been busy, and I haven't spent much time with you. Let's get you some dinner." With that, Sasha stood on his hind legs and pushed on Mrs. B.'s leg to hurry her along.

She moved through her routines, all the while feeling that she'd forgotten something. It was 11:00 p.m. when she was ready for sleep that it came to her.

Father Melvyn had started to tell her something about Sally Leightman but didn't finish. She reached for the Post-Its on her night table and wrote, Ask Father Melvyn about Leightman.

*The music started softly. The Sugar Plum's pink tutu was encrusted with rhinestones and pearls as she danced on the blackened stage. With her every step, the music's volume, and dissonance increased.*

*From behind her, the silver thread became visible, snaking its way forward. Its incandescent glow encircled her. From nowhere, blood dripped onto her tutu, coated the jewels, then puddled on the floor. The Sugar Plum's pointe shoe dipped into it. Her face was almost in view —*

The dream ended. Mrs. B. bolted upright in her bed, disturbing Sasha and Ziggy. She breathed hard; her heart raced in her chest. "Sorry, boys," she said to the cats as they groused, circled, and resettled. It was 2:00 a.m. She slid down in the bed.

While Mrs. B. pulled the blanket up to her chin to hold off the clammy cold essence of trouble emerging from the shadows, a few miles away at the Rue de L'Histoire Theatre, air currents swayed the backdrops flying above the stage. Steps tapped lightly across the floor, and set pieces moved from right to left.

Two ropes unwound, dropping sandbags to the stage floor before the ghost light clicked off.

# CHAPTER 16

## THE PEACE OF ORDINARY DAYS

"Have a good weekend, Mrs. B., and get some rest." Father Melvyn waved, holding LaLa in his arms. Was she coming down with something? She looked a bit peaked.

It was close to dinnertime, and in the dining room, the chafing dishes were set out on the sideboard. "Ummm. The pasta smells delicious. I hope Declan and Joe get here soon," he whispered to LaLa.

Daylight was fading. Father Melvyn set the cat on the floor and closed the window blinds. They'd once had a break-in, and when the culprits were caught, they'd admitted that it was easy because the blinds had been left open after dark.

Shaking his head, Father Melvyn recalled the incident and its connection to the murder of one of his parishioners. Now, he was confronted with the murder of a second parishioner, Adam Leightman.

"It's a terrible way to learn to appreciate the peace of ordinary days," he said aloud.

"What was that, Melvyn?" Joe asked from behind him.

"Ah, you've arrived, and here comes Declan." The clatter of feet in the hall announced Declan's arrival.

"What were you saying when I walked in?" Joe asked.

"I said I'm amazed at how I've learned to appreciate the peace of ordinary days."

*M-E-O-O-W!* LaLa sat in the doorway. The three men studied the green-eyed feline beauty.

"Do you think she agrees?" Joe asked.

"Probably," answered the pastor. "Declan, Mrs. B. left a tray of her wonderful bruschetta in the fridge. Please get it. Joe, you can pour us a pre-dinner drink." Looking down at his regal cat, Father Melvyn said, "And LaLa, a bowl of milk for you." Father Melvyn led the cat back to the kitchen. "And if you don't tell Mrs. B., we won't."

At the end of dinner, over coffee and cookies, Father Joe asked if there'd been any updates on the Leightman case.

"No," Father Melvyn answered. "I spoke to Sally Leightman a few days ago. She's very frustrated. Even though the police let her leave, they keep calling and asking questions. It seems the investigation is going nowhere."

"Has Mrs. B said anything? Can she get anything out of Jake Zayas?" Joe asked. They all knew Mrs. B. and her late husband had graduated from Austin's Citizen Police Academy and had become friends with the detective and his wife.

"Not that I know of."

"Adam was the theater person, right?" Declan asked.

"Correct, and speaking of theater. Mrs. B.'s son invited her — and me, to a working rehearsal. Here's the date," he said, handing Declan a piece of paper. "Can you cover for me?"

Declan took the paper from Melvyn's hand and looked at his phone. "Yes. I can cover," he said.

"Wonderful. That's in two weeks." Melvyn wrote it on a scrap of paper. "I'll tell Mrs. B."

Father Joe watched Declan enter the date in his phone calendar while Melvyn wrote it on a scrap of paper. "Melvyn," he said, "when are you going to learn to use your cell phone calendar?"

The pastor waved his finger in the air. "You keep your technologies and leave me to my dinosaur methods. They work for me..."

The house phone rang. Father Melvyn went to answer. He returned to the dining room. "Emergency at St. David's."

"Go on, we'll clean up," Declan answered.

The doorbell rang promptly at half-past six, and Mrs. B. was ready for her dinner guest, Nancy Jenkins. Even though they hadn't talked for a couple of weeks, as friends do, they quickly settled into the evening.

Mrs. B. handed her a martini and asked, "How'd your week go? Father Melvyn said he thoroughly enjoys his visits to the school, and the kids seem enthusiastic."

"As always, the kids are great, most of the time," Nancy answered. "The parents are a bit more difficult. We had some blowback over the security company that came in to instruct us in active shooter defense. Some of the parents weren't happy."

"Really?" Why would anyone object? It's essential given the world we live in today."

"Ummm. This is good." Nancy sipped her martini. "Some parents felt that it was too scary for the younger kids."

Mrs. B. shook her head in disbelief.

They talked and caught up on the latest events in each other's lives. "Anything new on the Leightman murder?"

Sammi grimaced.

"What is it?"

"Nothing new about the case, but I'm worried about my son and daughter-in-law. They are fully invested in the dance company and the theater." She sipped her decaf coffee. "All this talk of ghosts, theater superstitions, and bad luck, along with the murder—" she paused. "This could be devastating for them." She served Nancy a slice of her lemon pound cake.

"You're going to think I'm crazy," Mrs. B. said. "Maybe I am. I've had this irrational nightmare. It all sounds stupid when put into words." Nancy waited. "It's always the Sugar Plum Fairy from *Nutcracker*, dancing to bizarre music, with blood soaking up her pointe shoe and an iridescent thread looping around her neck, pulling tighter and tighter." She waited a minute, then said, "Crazy, right?"

Nancy leaned forward. "Here's what I think. You are so concerned for John and Lisa that it weighs heavy on your mind."

Changing the subject, Nancy asked, "How about we take a theater trip to New York in the spring."

Mrs. B. perked up. "That's a great idea. Schools will be closed, and the weather in the Northeast will be milder."

Mrs. B. cleaned up after Nancy left, feeling better having talked to her friend, but she wasn't convinced that her dreams were because of emotional overload.

Although it was midnight, Mrs. B. wasn't sleepy. She curled up in bed with "The Valley of Fear," a Sherlock Holmes mystery she'd never read.

On the stroke of midnight, Fr. Melvyn got back to St. Francis. He'd administered last rites to a 90-year-old man at the end of his days. When Fr. Melvyn left the hospital room, the nurses said the old guy wouldn't make the night.

He took out his prayer book and said the final liturgy of the hours, followed by additional prayers for the soul of the gentleman he'd attended. He was ready to sleep when Adam Leightman sprung to mind.

Even though Adam was dead, the seal of confession was sacrosanct. Father Melvyn knew the consequences if he violated it, but he felt incredibly guilty since it was his suggestions that may have put Adam in harm's way.

He chewed on this dilemma. Even though Adam's suspicions didn't fall under the confession itself, it was still a dangerous tactic to repeat anything he'd heard during a confession.

*Until I figure out how to give Jake information about Adam's fears without revealing my source, I must remain silent. I hope the police solve this soon.*

Father Melvyn said a rosary for the repose of Adam's soul. It was 1:00 a.m. when he lay his head down.

Turning his thoughts to the soothing nature of an ordinary day, he drifted off to sleep.

# CHAPTER 17

## "FIRE BURN AND CAULDRON BUBBLE"
### Shakespeare's Macbeth

It was the second Wednesday of October, and the Central Texas rainstorms hadn't let up. Isabel's emotions were magnified by an ominous rumble of thunder in the dark sky as she arrived at the theater for the special rehearsal. In the parking lot, she sat in her car, pressed her fingers to her temples, and fought to clear her head of all thoughts other than the ballet.

Intermittent raindrops splattered the windshield and the ground. Isabel knew she'd better make a run for it before the rain began again in earnest. Looking at the other cars in the lot, she was relieved that the dreaded Mercedes wasn't there, at least not yet.

Another rumble, followed by a hard crack of thunder, made her jump. She ran from the car to the backstage door and grabbed the handle, her dark thoughts temporarily pushed aside by the tingle of excitement coursing through her body. It was the same every time she opened the stage door; she could never have enough. Isabel loved the theater: its atmosphere, its smells, its sounds.

This time, when she stepped inside, she shuddered as if someone had walked over her grave.

Yesterday, the company had been given a half-day off to decompress after weeks of intense work on John Bono's ballet. Instead of resting, Isabel had spent the afternoon with her nose buried in microfiche. She found no supporting documents for her grandfather's claim, but what she learned shocked her.

The Rue de L'Histoire Theatre sat on the section, lot, and block number her grandfather claimed was stolen from his family. This theater was at the center of the mystery. She gave her head a little shake and pushed forward toward the sound of voices coming from the stage. "Focus," she hissed.

Forcing her jumbled emotions aside, Isabel joined the other dancers. At the barre, she stretched, preparing for a short warmup class, but she was riddled with frustration.

John's voice brought her back to the moment. "When the curtain opens," he told the lighting designer, "I want fog and lightning."

The designer nodded. "I saw your notes last week and brought in the fog machine. Will there be sound? Thunder? Music?"

"The kettle drum will create an echo of distant thunder, but no music until the first witch steps down and away from the cauld—." A salvo of thunder drowned his words and shook the walls.

Isabel's muscles twitched.

"Good atmosphere, inside and out," John remarked with a laugh. He did a final review for the lighting designer.

"Each of the witches has a short solo, depicting the opening chant; each of them tells a different part of the prophecy through dance. The scene ends with all of them back on the platform, stirring the cauldron. The stage goes to black, followed by a flash of lightning and more thunder."

"What follows?" the light man asked.

"Macbeth and Banquo enter into the smoky light from stage right."

Isabel shivered. John's instructions to the lighting director and his vision for the mood increased her sense of danger, of forces beyond her control. Tying her pointe shoes, she thought about how all these feelings would serve her role as a prophetic witch.

Standing and shaking out her legs and arms, she looked toward the audience. The house lights were up. Thinking of witches, she was relieved that Asturias wasn't there. Lately, Victoria Asturias seemed to be around all the time, watching. *Her eyes bore into me when she thinks I don't notice.* Isabel winced at the feeling that she was under a microscope. She'd passed a comment to John about it.

John had sounded surprised. "Isabel, you're a dancer. You should be pleased that a board member has taken an interest in you. Victoria told me she enjoys watching you work."

His statement, meant as a compliment, did nothing to soothe her nerves. She realized she couldn't complain about Victoria Asturias at work. The woman had practically been elevated to sainthood for the financial support she was giving the company.

But Isabel knew it wasn't her work that Victoria watched. She believed that Victoria realized who she was at the gala and remembered their collision on the steps of the appraisal office. The ballet company now owned the property her grandfather believed was theirs.

Maybe my mother is right, Isabel thought. Perhaps it is time to give this up… but she had an idea. Was there, perhaps, another owner between Asturias and the ballet company? That's it, she thought, clutching at straws. I'll go back to the Travis County office and trace the property sales. That will be my next move before I give up. Feeling better, she focused like a laser, ready to dance.

John held the stage door open for Father Melvyn and his mother. "Welcome, Father," he said, shaking the priest's hand.

"Thank you for the invite, John. I can't tell you how much I'm looking forward to this."

"We were lucky to get inside before the deluge," Mrs. B. said, shaking out her rain hat.

John smiled and acknowledged his mother with a peck on the cheek. "We're almost ready. Follow me." John led them across the cavernous stage.

Father Melvyn soaked in as much as he could as they made their way across the stage. He found the industrial atmosphere in the bright, overhead light intriguing. Pipes, grids, walkways, lights. All the necessary appurtenances to make magic on the stage. John led them across the stage, past a raised platform where a large black cauldron sat. They walked past the portable barres set up on stage for the warmup, then down the steps on the left side of the apron to the row in the auditorium where several others were already seated. Lisa was there with a clipboard and notepad on her lap.

Several rows behind her, at the center of the auditorium, the priest noticed what looked like a large table. Two men sat behind it. "What is that?" he asked.

"It's a light board. That's where the lighting designer sets the cues," John explained. "Naturally, that won't be there when we perform."

Mrs. B. and Father Melvyn slid into their seats. Lisa scooted across the row to greet them. "Hi, Mom," she said to her mother-in-law. "Father Melvyn, we're glad you could come."

"See you later," John said and returned to the stage. "Okay, everyone," he called out and pressed the button on his boom box.

Lisa waited. Once the music began, she leaned over, pointed to the barre, and whispered to Mrs. B. and the priest. "The ladies getting warmed up are the three witches. The two men are Macbeth and Banquo, who will make their entrance at the end of the prophetic dances. In the performance, there will be other dancers on stage in the background, simulating the battle from which Macbeth and Banquo came."

Father Melvyn paid close attention to Lisa's lecture. "John wants to see how the choreography and the special effects meld." She continued.

"Lighting and fog will create a sense of danger, in the dark with only overhead spots on the dancers. When the witches are done, the cauldron will be raised above the curtain line, and Macbeth and Banquo will enter. The mood will, hopefully, be set for the remainder of the ballet."

Mrs. B. peeked across Lisa. "Who are the other guests?"

"Some of the board members enjoy watching rehearsals."

The audience lights dimmed. "Enjoy," Lisa said and returned to her seat.

"Places," John said.

The stage darkened. A voice at the light board said, "Cue lights," and the stage lit up in sections.

"Amazing," Father Melvyn whispered to Mrs. B. as he watched the atmosphere change with the lighting and the haze winding its way across the stage floor.

An overhead spot beamed down on the three witches stirring the cauldron. Bent over, the three women gripped paddles and moved their arms in small, dramatic circles when a downpour of rain pounded the theater roof drowning out the manufactured sound of far-off thunder.

The first witch stepped down. Music started, and she began her dance. When the witches completed their performances and returned to the platform, the light above the cauldron went black. Macbeth and Banquo entered from stage right in a dim haze.

John stopped the rehearsal. "Lights, please. Good, very good. We had some help from the elements, did we not?" Laughter rippled through the cast. "We'll do it again in five." Turning toward the audience, John called his wife, "Lisa, can you give the ladies notes while I talk to Macbeth and Banquo?"

Mrs. B. and Father Melvyn watched, mesmerized by the process of making a ballet.

"My, that last witch was exceptional. She isn't even in costume and make-up, and she gave me the creeps," Mrs. B. whispered to Father Melvyn.

"I believe that's the intent," he answered.

Lisa walked over to the knot of women standing at the platform. They twittered among themselves.

"Oh, for goodness sake, don't tell me you believe that stuff," said Isabel, the last witch to dance.

"Problem, ladies?" Lisa asked.

Janet whined. "He said 'Macbeth.' You aren't supposed to say his name in the theater."

Isabel mouthed, "You just did."

Lisa looked at Isabel, who rolled her eyes. "I'll remind him, but that is a theater superstition, not necessarily a ballet superstition. We have enough of our own."

In a firm voice, Lisa said, "Now, ladies, here's what I saw." She gave them instructions to improve their performance.

John called out, "Okay, dancers. Let's do it again, even though it will be without the assistance of Mother Nature's rain, wind, and storm."

Turning to Janet, Lisa gave the last note. "Concentrate on tightening your muscles. Make it look like you are encountering more resistance in the cauldron."

A sharp whistle drew their attention up; they stepped back. The cauldron, held by thin wire cables invisible to the audience, was lowered back onto the platform.

Lisa reentered the row to resume her seat. Crossing in front of Father Melvyn and Mrs. B., she asked, "Enjoying this?"

Father Melvyn nodded. "Yes. Quite. The detail that goes into making a ballet is fascinating."

Two hours later, John had run the rehearsal three times. "Okay, everyone. Good work. Thank you all."

Lisa headed up to the stage. "Come with me," she said to Father Melvyn and her mother-in-law. "I have to give the witches a last set of notes."

Mrs. B. and Father Melvyn followed her. When Lisa ran up the front stairs onto the stage, she called out, "Ladies, a minute of your time," before she faded into the dim light.

"I was spellbound," Father Melvyn said to Mrs. B. "I must thank John again for the invitation."

"I can't wait to see it in performance," she answered when a man's voice shouted.

"Watch out!"

Without warning, there was a crash accompanied by a cacophony of metal banging against metal, its echo reverberating before a final enormous clang rattled the stage floor.

# CHAPTER 18

## THE CURSE

Time stopped. Then screams electrified everyone in the theater. Tony reached for the overhead light switch. He swore when he saw the scene from hell, then charged across the stage to the witches' platform, where the cauldron had landed and bounced off. It sat on its side, next to the steel batten that had come down with it. In the harsh light, two women lay on the floor like ragdolls. Volpe kneeled next to the closest, pushing herself up.

"Are you okay?"

Isabel nodded, sat up, and rubbed her knee. "It's Lisa," she whispered and pointed.

Three feet away, Lisa Bono lay unconscious. Blood droplets spattered her face and arm. John reached his wife before anyone else. "Lisa!" he cried out.

Mrs. B. and Father Melvyn ran toward John. When they reached him, Father Melvyn's shoe slid on something. He looked down. Another droplet splashed on his shoe. Looking up, Father Melvyn saw someone kneeling on the catwalk.

The priest yelled, "Up there!" He pointed above his head. "Someone is bleeding up there and needs help." He heard rather than saw boots clatter up the metal steps. Father Melvyn pulled out his cell phone and dialed 911.

"Tony," a voice called from above. "It's Monty. I'm bringing him down. His neck is gashed."

Volpe called out to Charlie, "Open the backstage doors and the loading dock. EMS will need to get in fast."

The few board members present at the rehearsal had run up on stage, trying to help. Everyone was shaken, but all eyes were on Janet, who was on the verge of hysteria.

"I knew it. The curse has been unleashed. No one should ever say the name of this story in the theater. It's a warning!" she cried out, her voice wobbly with fear.

Orlando pulled her away and shushed her. "Stop it now. This is bad enough without you making it worse."

"But," she stuttered.

"No buts. Shut up. Go sit in the auditorium and pull yourself together." He pushed Janet toward the stairs at the front of the stage as sirens announced the arrival of EMS and the police. With one eye on the hysterical dancer, Volpe helped get Monty seated and put pressure on his neck. Blood from the cut in his neck seeped between Monty's fingers into his shirt.

John knelt beside his wife. "Don't try to move her," Tony ordered. Turning to the crew, he shouted orders. "Get the cauldron and the batten out of the way. Put them over there," he pointed to the area away from everyone.

What the hell happened? Tony asked himself. Those wires can hold hundreds of pounds, and the cauldron is a good-looking fake but doesn't weigh enough to hurt anyone. He knew it was the steel batten that had done the damage.

The paramedics rushed past everyone; their jackets glistened with water. "Excuse us," they said. "Everyone, please back away." One medic, with a long blond ponytail, pushed everyone back. Father Melvyn stepped back, taking Mrs. B. with him, but John didn't move.

"What's her name," the medic asked, "and what's your relationship to this woman?" She felt Lisa's wrist for a pulse.

"I'm her husband."

"What's her name?" the medic repeated the question.

"Lisa Bono."

"Has she regained consciousness at all?"

"No."

Father Melvyn heard John's voice catch in his throat. The medic continued to examine Lisa. Noticing the back of her blouse was ripped, and blood had seeped through the tear, she asked John to step away.

"Mike," she called to her partner, "get everyone away. I need to examine her back before we try to move her."

A soft moan escaped Lisa's lips when the medic felt her shoulder blade. "Scapula may be fractured," she said. "Mike, please get the padded board."

Standing with Mrs. B. and John, watching the care EMS was giving Lisa, Father Melvyn saw a shadow fly across the stage. Out of nowhere, Victoria Asturias materialized. The priest wondered where she'd come from. She hadn't been in the audience. He looked for her.

Victoria marched over to the stage manager. Volpe frowned, turned his back, and walked away from her.

Odd, he thought. She isn't at all wet. She didn't even look damp. When she saw Isabel, who had been helped up off the floor by two stagehands, he thought she looked angry. At that point, his attention was drawn back to Lisa.

The medics turned her, holding the affected arm, and slid the heavily padded board beneath her back. Within minutes, they had her on the gurney and were moving toward the door.

John walked alongside, holding Lisa's hand. Mrs. B. was behind her son, and Father Melvyn followed.

Another officer stepped up. "Are you related?"

"Yes, she's my daughter-in-law," Mrs. B. said and tried to sidestep the officer.

The policewoman extended her arm to block Mrs. B. "I need you to stay here and give a statement."

Father Melvyn read the look on his housekeeper's face. There'd be trouble if she were stopped. "Officer, couldn't she give her statements later? I was beside her the entire time, so I can provide as much information as she can."

The officer looked at Mrs. B.'s pale face. "Okay, Ma'am. Give me your name and contact information."

As fast as the chaos began, it was over. The injured were treated and sent to the hospital. Two more police officers arrived. They asked everyone to form two lines, give their names, contact information, and describe what they saw and heard.

Welcoming the opportunity to slip to the back and out of the police officers' sightlines, Father Melvyn passed two stagehands talking alone.

"This wire looks cut. First Adam, now this," one of them said, keeping his voice low. When they saw the priest, they stopped talking.

"Where is the nearest restroom?" Father Melvyn asked. One man pointed, but they both walked away.

The priest went into the empty men's room, pulled out his little notepad, wrote what he'd observed, and then returned to the stage.

He looked at the people waiting to give statements, other than the crew, and realized that as mysteriously as she'd appeared, Victoria had vanished.

# CHAPTER 19

## "WHAT'S DONE CANNOT BE UNDONE."
### Shakespeare's Macbeth

Wearing his clerical garb, which he knew would ensure his access to most areas of the hospital, Father Melvyn walked into the bustling emergency room waiting area where Mrs. B. paced. One look at her ashen face told him that Lisa's injuries weren't minor.

"What's going on?" he asked.

Her voice was thick with emotion. "Apparently, Lisa was pregnant and has miscarried. The trauma of the accident may have caused it, but the doctor said it might have been inevitable." She wiped away a stray tear. "They'll know more after some tests."

The door to the treatment area swung open. John came out and headed straight to his mother and Father Melvyn. "Thank you for coming, Father. Has my mother given you an update?"

"I am sorry about the baby. Did you and Lisa know she was expecting?"

John cleared his throat twice before he was able to speak. "Yes. She was ten weeks along. We were waiting to get past the twelfth week before saying anything."

Father Melvyn knew words were useless; he put a comforting hand on John's shoulder.

John took a deep breath and continued. "Right now, they are preparing her for surgery. She'll need a plate and screws because the impact of the batten not only broke part of the scapula but dislocated the clavicle. Any movement is agonizing."

"Are they going to operate tonight?" Mrs. B. asked.

"Yes, but they're waiting until eight because she ate lunch at noon. They have her arm immobilized, and she's sedated. I'm going to stay with her until she goes to surgery."

"Son, can we get you coffee or something to eat?"

"Nothing. Thanks, Mom." Looking at Father Melvyn, John said, "Please pray for her, Father."

"You know, I will."

Tears wet John's face. "Mom, why don't you go home? I'll call as soon as the doctors come out after the surgery. I'm staying here for the night."

"I can stay with you."

"Thanks, Mom, but it would be better if you could get some things I'll need in the morning and bring them here. Will you do that?"

"Of course, son."

Taking out his keys, John detached the apartment key. "In the dresser, get me a change of underwear — also, a clean, short-sleeved shirt. My toothbrush is in the bathroom – it's the blue one," he said with a sad and lopsided smile. "In the morning, go to the studio and get my computer. I'll text Chelly and tell her you're going to pick it up." With that, John reached out and hugged his mother. He reached for Father Melvyn's hand. "Thank you for coming. I'll keep everyone posted, but I need to get back to Lisa."

Father Melvyn raised his right hand and made the sign of the cross over John before he disappeared through the automatic doors to the treatment area.

"Sammi." Mrs. B. turned. Her friends, Jake and Terri Zayas raced toward her. They all embraced and greeted Father Melvyn.

"I am so, so sorry," Jake said. "How is she? How is John?" Father Melvyn saw that Mrs. B. was overcome with emotion.

He patted her shoulder as if to say, it's okay; then he told them that Lisa needed surgery to repair the damaged scapula.

"Sammi, is there anything we can do to help?" Terri asked.

Mrs. B. pulled herself together and added what Father Melvyn didn't say. "Lisa was pregnant. She lost the baby. Maybe from the blunt force trauma or, the doctor said, she might have lost it anyway, due to some unpredictable chromosomal abnormality." Mrs. B.'s voice became intense.

"They can say what they want. I cannot believe that being slammed to the floor by a heavy piece of metal had nothing to do with it." Her anguish turned to fury. "How could this have happened? Don't they do safety inspections?"

Jake took her hand. "Sammi," he said. "The officers on the scene filed their reports. There is some question about why the cable holding the cauldron broke. They are closing the theater temporarily until the building inspector can assess the situation."

"What are you saying? Are you telling me there are suspicions? Of what? Do you think someone did this deliberately?" Mrs. B. balled her hands into fists and held them on either side of her cheeks. Her voice became louder.

"Ohhh. If this was deliberate, someone has to be held accountable. If I find out, I'll…"

"Sammi," Jake said. "Do not jump to conclusions. If there is something that warrants investigation, please leave it to the police."

She opened her mouth to answer, but Father Melvyn, who'd been watching her building rage, interjected.

"My dear, you are exhausted. You left your car at the theater. Jake. Can you take her to get it? She'll need it in the morning."

"Of course," Jake answered, and turned Mrs. B. toward the door.

"Okay. Yes," she said, pushing her unruly white hair back. "You're right. I will need my car." Behind her back, Jake gave Father Melvyn the thumbs up for derailing the building tirade.

Mrs. B. controlled her emotions until she pulled into her garage and lowered the outer door. When she turned off the car engine, she heard Sasha's and Ziggy's mournful wails from the other side of the kitchen door. She wiped away her tears and went inside. "Yes, my darlings. I know I'm very late." She picked up her cats, went to the nearest chair, and held them on her lap.

Sensing their beloved human's upset, Sasha and Ziggy sat curled up on her lap while she sobbed and stroked their heads. Emotionally spent, she gave herself an order in English, then in Italian, for emphasis: "Enough! Basta!" To her cats, "You must be starving."

The cats jumped down, went to their feeding bowls, sat erect, and waited.

For the next two hours, Mrs. B. moved through her regular routines like a robot. She checked off the list John had given her. She'd stopped at his apartment on her way home for the personal items he wanted. She only had to go to the ballet studio in the morning to get his laptop.

Looking at the clock, she wondered if Lisa's surgery had started on time and how much longer it would take. She was about to dial John's cell number but thought better of it if he was catching a nap. He'll call when it's over, she reminded herself.

Mrs. B. tried to sleep but couldn't. Every time she closed her eyes, the scene in the theater replayed: the bang of metal hitting metal; screams; an injured dancer on the floor; the cauldron on its side next to Lisa, who lay unconscious.

"No sense lying here," she muttered to Sasha and Ziggy, trying to settle down next to her. "It's eleven, so why hasn't John called yet?" She was getting nervous. "This won't do," she said in a firm voice. "I'll have a cup of tea." In the kitchen, Mrs. B. saw the light on her cell phone flash. She grabbed the phone and pressed the button for text messages.

*I didn't want to call in case you were sleeping. Lisa is in recovery. The surgeon said everything went well, and she'll have a full recovery. I'll see you in the morning. Thanks for everything. Love Ya.*

"That's a relief," she said to her cats; they'd followed her to the kitchen. "But I still can't sleep." Taking a cup of tea, Mrs. B. sat at the kitchen table and thought about John, the ballet company, and the Rue de L'Histoire Theatre. She remembered her son telling her that she would enjoy the *Macbeth* superstitions. What the hell, she thought. "Let's see if I can find any stories about ghosts or *Macbeth,* attached directly to this theater," she said aloud. At 1:00 a.m., she was still staring at the computer screen. "Can this be possible?"

A *Macbeth* curse connected to the Rue de L'Histoire Theatre and a ballet?

She saved the page in favorites, turned off the computer, and decided she'd better get some shut-eye. *I'll reread this in the morning. My brain is fuzzy from exhaustion and the day's trauma.*

# CHAPTER 20

## IT WASN'T AN ACCIDENT

On Thursday morning, Isabel pulled herself out of bed at eight. Groggy from a lousy night's sleep, she opened her eyes, wishing the disastrous rehearsal the day before was a bad dream. The hope disappeared when she sat at the edge of her bed.

Her muscles were sore from the fall. Standing up, she tested her leg. Her left knee pinched from the typical feeling of sensitive skin from the scraping it'd received when she fell. Careful not to change the mechanics of her body by limping, she walked to the kitchen and made coffee. Despite the tight, sore muscles, she was relieved that the x-rays taken at the hospital the night before showed no broken or chipped bones and no ligament or tendon damage. It was just bruised.

She drank her coffee and thought about the doomed rehearsal. Standing on the platform; the sound of something rushing overhead; Lisa's hand shoving her hard; hitting the floor face down; banging metal; turning over and looking up. Someone staring down. Isabel shuddered and closed her eyes.

Her grandfather's face swam before her, and she felt the need to touch his photo. Pulling it out of the plastic cover, she hugged it to her chest. The worn, faded picture of him and his father, Rafael, was one of her most precious possessions.

Running her finger over his beloved face, she tried to draw warmth out of the paper and conjure up a live feeling of him. Taking a deep breath, Isabel hoped to summon the aroma of his pipe. She'd always loved the smell of his tobacco.

Nothing.

Her heart ached with memories. "I miss you, Grandfather," she said, staring at the picture that had been taken in front of the Sanchez home in Austin, before it had burned to the ground. Rafael, her great-grandfather, stood with one hand on each of Oratio's shoulders. She peered at the imposing ring on Rafael's finger before she returned the picture to its plastic cover and slid it back in her desk drawer. She needed to stop reminiscing and get to work.

She wondered if there was any word on Lisa's condition. An overwhelming sense of malice gave her a chill. Although sunlight streamed into her bedroom window, she was enveloped in a moment of inner darkness. A feeling of evil crept around her. For a split second, she couldn't move.

"Stop!" she shouted. "Your imagination is running wild. Go to work."

Immersed in worry about Lisa, Mrs. B. didn't enjoy the crisp, clean air and the deep blue sky that had followed yesterday's raging storms. She walked in the door of the ballet studio, where another storm was brewing.

Dancers were gathered in the main lobby clustered around Chelly Bernardi, who made her announcement. "We've canceled *Macbeth*, and the theater is temporarily shut down."

Mrs. B. heard the strain in her voice. "The police, who are already involved because of Adam Leightman, are looking for evidence of foul play." There were shocked murmurs. "And," she continued, "the city inspectors are examining the theater for safety issues." The buzzing voices grew louder.

Chelly had to call for quiet again. "These terrible events are dreadful for those who were hurt and a significant setback for the company, but we will carry on." Taking a breath, she said, Now, about *Nutcracker.*"

Orlando was the first to notice Mrs. B. standing in the doorway. Rushing over to her, he asked, "How is Lisa?" Everyone's attention turned to John's mother, asking questions and expressing sympathy.

Chelly made her way through the cluster of dancers and hugged her. "We are all so sorry about Lisa. I heard from John last night. Is there any word on her condition this morning?"

"Thank you, all," Mrs. B. said. She raised her voice so everyone could hear. "Lisa came through the surgery beautifully. The surgeon put in a plate and pins in the scapula to repair the damage, and they expect her to have a full recovery."

John had asked her to tell the company about the baby, so he wouldn't have to. Looking at the dancers, she said, "Sadly, Lisa was pregnant..." Mrs. B. cleared her throat to keep control over her emotions. "She lost the baby."

"I am sorry," Chelly said again, after an almost imperceptible gasp shot through the group. "We'll do whatever we can to help. Please tell John. And, if you see a need, please let us know."

Overcome with emotion, Mrs. B.'s voice was hardly above a whisper. "Thank you, Chelly." She cleared her throat. "I've come to get John's laptop from his office. Is that okay?"

"Yes, of course," Chelly said. "Do you think my husband and I can visit tonight?"

"I don't know, but I'll tell John to text or call you to let you know." With nothing more to say and relieved the conversation was over, Mrs. B. headed to John's office.

Behind her, she heard Chelly take command of her company. "Studio A, please. Time for class. Isabel?" Chelly called out. "Take the day off. Don't even do the barre. Give the knee extra rest. We need you in good shape ASAP."

Hearing about Lisa's injury and the loss of her baby, Isabel was a bundle of nerves. She followed Mrs. B. into John's office and closed the door. "Mrs. B., can I talk to you?"

John's mother was untangling wires. She looked up in surprise. "You are? Oh, yes, Isabel. How is your knee? I heard Chelly tell you to take the day off."

"The knee is okay, just bruised." Isabel walked over and took the wires from Mrs. B.'s hands. "Let me do that for you."

"Thank you," Mrs. B. said. "I'm afraid to pull on the wrong wire and blow something out. How can I help you?"

Keeping her eyes on the tangled mess passing through her fingers, Isabel's words rushed out. "I have something to tell you, but not here. Can we meet somewhere else? I don't want to be overheard."

"My, that sounds dramatic."

Looking back at the closed door, Isabel's semi-whisper was intense. "What happened yesterday wasn't an accident. That cauldron was coming straight down at my head. Lisa shoved me off the platform. She may have saved my life."

Mrs. B. froze. "What? Why do you think that?"

Isabel was desperate and on the point of tears. "That's what I want to tell you, but not here."

"Do you know where St. Francis de Sales Church is?" Isabel nodded. "Can you meet me at the rectory this afternoon at four?"

"Yes. Please don't tell John until after I get a chance to talk to you."

"I won't tell John, but I will want Father Melvyn Kronkey, the pastor, my boss, and friend, to join us, if that's okay with you."

Isabel thought for a second. "Well, he's a priest, and he will keep my confidence, I'm sure." A knock on the door ended the conversation.

Laurel, the receptionist, walked in. "Can I help you get John's things together?" She looked from Isabel to Mrs. B.

"Thank you, but Isabel came in and did all the work for me. I'm leaving now," Mrs. B. said.

"Isabel, why aren't you in class?" Laurel asked, her tone authoritative.

Isabel bristled. *How dare she question me? She's not the ballet mistress,* but she smiled sweetly and said, "Chelly told me to take the day off to give my knee some extra time. I thought I'd ask John's mother how Lisa was doing. I'm going home now."

Laurel followed Isabel and Mrs. B. from John's office toward the front door. It swung open, and in walked Victoria Asturias.

The hard look in Victoria's eyes made the hairs on Isabel's neck stand up. She blinked and darted out the front door.

"You're John's mother," Victoria said.

"Yes, I came to pick up his computer. I'm taking
it to him at the hospital," Mrs. B. answered.

"I'm so sorry about the accident. I hope Lisa will be back on her feet and fully recovered soon." Without waiting for an answer, Victoria headed to Chelly's office.

Laurel watched the exchange. When Victoria was out of earshot, she touched Mrs. B.'s arm and whispered, "Emergency! The board needs to assess the financial cost of this disaster. I overheard Chelly telling her husband that the board may want to cancel the rest of the season."

Mrs. B. didn't respond to Laurel's inside information, but her heart sank. What would canceling the season mean for John's and Lisa's investment? It couldn't be good.

Nodding at Laurel, Mrs. B. walked out the door, feeling more agitated than ever. And why is this woman talking about company business? Who else does she tell? Mrs. B. wondered. She made a mental note to tell John that his receptionist, while pretty and sweet, talks too much.

# CHAPTER 21

## BATTLE OF THE MACBETHS

Tony Volpe's face was redder than a ripe chili pepper and just as hot. He slammed the phone down, finding it difficult to control his temper. Victoria Asturias had implied that the crew was negligent.

His computer pinged. With no time to recover from Asturias's aggravating call, he read a high-handed email from Inspector Dunne of the building department.

*I will be at your theater this afternoon at 3:30 p.m. Touch nothing before my arrival. I require all crew to be present on stage, and we will conduct a thorough assessment. I expect full cooperation from all techs, stagehands, construction crews, and, of course, you.*

Well, Inspector Dunne, we didn't just sit here on our hands yesterday, Tony thought. After the police and EMS had departed, he and his crew examined everything.

The witches' platform was undamaged because the cauldron and batten had never hit it, but the stage floor had been gouged when the batten landed after hitting Lisa Bono's back. He didn't have a full report from his flyers yet. His stomach was in knots from anxiety. He felt he'd be held responsible for the accident.

Tony looked at his wristwatch. He marched to center stage and gave a sharp whistle. Like magic, the crew appeared. "Listen up, everyone. The building inspector will be here soon. Meanwhile, we are ordered not to touch anything, and we are all required to be on stage and ready to answer questions."

Tony kept his professional face on but smiled internally at his crew's strong words expressing what they thought of the building department's order. He believed if they knew about Asturias's insinuations, they'd really be pissed. "Let's get through this formality," he said, "then we can get back to our assessments of what happened and why."

The crew dispersed and returned to their duties, but Steve and Mel, long-time veterans, hung back.

"Tony," Mel said. "With all the commotion yesterday, we didn't have a chance to tell you, but the wire holding the cauldron looks like it was cut almost all the way through."

"Show me." Tony covered his dismay at the suggestion of a deliberate act.

"I thought we weren't to touch anything?" Steve asked.

Tony matched his sarcasm. "No hands, I promise," he said, "but I want to see for myself before inspector know-it-all gets here."

The three men pulled on work gloves and climbed up on the catwalk where Monty had been working on a light strut when the fly-wire broke, snapped back, and hit him. Mel grabbed the end of the wire and pulled it to them.

Tony took the end and turned it in his fingers. Holding it up, he shone his penlight on it. "Yep. Cut. It's too smooth to have shredded." The strands looked razor-sharp. "No wonder Monty bled so much," Tony said. "Here, look at this, though." He turned the end again and lifted more strands with the end of his pen. "These look like they ruptured from too much weight."

"Someone cut the wire precisely, not going all the way through." Tony sighed. "Whoever it was, wanted it to dangle before it dropped."

"What should we do?" Steve asked.

"Leave it," Tony said, letting go of the wire. If the inspector questions whether or not we found anything, answer truthfully. It's been cut. No sense trying to hide it."

Mel frowned. "This theater is safe, and no one knows it better than we do. It must be sabotage."

Steve was about to chime in.

Hearing the anger in Mel's voice, Tony interrupted. "One thing at a time," he said. "I know you're right, but let's wait for the inspector to give us clearance. Then we can figure out what happened and why before we see the police again."

At precisely half-past three, Tony met Inspector Dunne in the main lobby. The inspector smiled, stuck out his hand, and introduced himself. Tony was pleased that he didn't seem to have an attitude. Together, they walked to the backstage area. Tony answered the inspector's general questions about the theater: how many performances a month, when had the ballet company bought the place, and what changes, if any, were made?

Dunne stopped to speak to several men and women of the crew and took particular interest in the fly system that controlled props and backdrops suspended overhead.

Tony stayed on the floor and watched Dunne climb to the top of the grid. Dunne checked every bolt, pulley, and safety chain. He worked his way down to the floor and then made notes in his book.

"I'm going to check the staircases and areas below the stage, including the orchestra pit."

The crew, Tony included, leaned against walls, set pieces, and trusses waiting for him to come back.

"Let me show you this," Tony said when Dunne returned. He directed the inspector to the gouge on the stage floor.

"Not surprising. I understand someone was injured. How?"

Tony explained that when the cauldron came down, the batten hit a person before landing on the floor. The inspector noted it in his book. After a lengthy and thorough examination, Dunne addressed the crew.

"I think you already know that the fly-wire holding the batten and the cauldron were cut and that I'm obligated to report it to the police. I know they will appreciate it if y'all don't make any repairs or changes."

Dunne looked from face to face. "Other than that, I am clearing this theater. Everything is well-maintained and in good working order, as far as I can see." The inspector slipped his notebook into his jacket pocket. "I will submit my report today. Without a police investigation, it would still take three to five days before the theater could reopen. My superiors will inform the cops, and once their investigation is complete, hopefully within that three-to-five day period, y'all can get back to business."

The crew applauded, satisfied that the inspector recognized the quality of their work. The majority of them had been at the Rue for close to a decade. They knew the theater was old, and they knew it didn't have the most up-to-date technologies, but they also knew that they kept everything in tip-top shape.

Charlie let the inspector out through the stage door and then locked it. He joined the crew on stage.

Tony saw relief and pride in his men's faces. "Okay, I'm sure you all have much to say. Who is first?" he asked.

Charlie raised his hand. He'd been at the Rue longer than anyone else. Like his father before him, he'd started as a stagehand, but after his leg had been fractured in two places in a car accident, his job became more custodial, but when the crew needed extra hands, he filled in.

"Charlie," Tony acknowledged him.

The custodian scratched his head and looked around at the expectant faces. "You young guys don't know everything about the Rue. Now, I'm not superstitious, but—" he stopped.

"Spit it out, Charlie," Mel said.

"You know, there is a story about the last ballet company that performed here," Charlie said.

"C'mon, Charlie. Tell it before the end of the year," Steve said. He thumped Charlie on his back to show he was joking.

The others joined the chorus. "C'mon, Charlie, let's hear it."

Tony noticed the old guy's withered and wrinkled face was unsmiling, but his blue eyes glittered.

"You all know my father was a stagehand here. That's how I got my job, so my stories go back – way back." The crew nodded and smiled. Everyone knew Charlie's deep connection and commitment to the Rue de L'Histoire Theatre.

"This theater was built in 1922. It was a favorite spot for many traveling theater companies from Shakespeare to Vaudeville, to small, European dance companies."

He stopped and mopped his wispy white hair back. "The story goes that a minor British company, the Lovingsworth's Dance Hall Troupe, booked a date in May of '24. At the same time, the Rue's manager was negotiating with the most famous Russian touring ballet company of the time." Charlie stopped to scratch his head. "It would have been a coup if the Rue had gotten them, but the only dates they had available were the same ones the Dance Hall Troupe had already booked."

Tony sighed. "Does this have a point?"

"I'm getting to it," Charlie said, waving his hand. "The Russians offered to do their new production of *Macbeth*. The Rue's manager wanted them, so he asked the Dance Hall Troupe to change. Lovingsworth refused. He said that he was presenting his company's *Macbeth* and that the Russians were 'overrated.'

"The Russians, of course, were furious and said that *Macbeth* shouldn't be performed by just any company. Lovingsworth would be sorry, but the Rue's manager didn't think it right to bump the Dance Hall Troupe since they booked almost every year, so he lost the Russians."

"And?" Mel asked, moving his hands, palms up, in a circular motion.

"Lovingsworth's run turned bad. Ticket sales were poor, and the first incident happened on the second night of the show. A member of the crew lost his footing and fell from the top of the grid." Charlie held up his hands. "I know y'all are getting antsy; hold onto your britches. That guy died a few days later.

"On the last night, Lovingsworth decided he'd perform the role of Macbeth, but he was a drinker, and before the show, he stupidly had one too many and was drunk. His wife, the actress Maureen Welch, tried to cover for him, but he was off-balance. He tripped, fell into her, and his weight pushed her over the apron at the front of the stage. She fell, hit the rim of the kettle drum, and broke her neck; she lay dead as a doornail."

Steve shrugged. "It was an accident brought on by an arrogant fool who drank too much."

"Sorry, Charlie. I don't get the connection," Tony said.

Folding his arms across his chest, Charlie huffed with impatience. "Theaters get reputations. Don't you think it's strange that no other drama or dance troupe ever tried to bring *Macbeth* here?"

Charlie stared at the faces staring at him. "Maybe Maureen Welch is haunting this theater. Maybe she's trying to stop this ballet company from performing that ballet."

"Interesting," Tony said. "But I don't know how a ghost cuts a fly-wire with precision."

"Neither do I," Charlie answered, his tone testy. "But, I've been here longer than any of you, and we've never had a murder or a serious accident. That woman was almost killed yesterday," he said, referring to Lisa Bono. "And what about Adam Leightman?" With the mention of Adam, everyone went silent.

"Any other ideas or questions?" Tony asked. The conversation continued, but no concrete suggestions or alternate scenarios were forthcoming. Tony could see that everyone was actually considering Charlie's story.

"Okay, guys," Tony said. "Let's call it a day. Come in tomorrow morning, and I'll have more information about the season's schedule."

Steve was blunt. "Tony, are we getting laid off?"

Compliments of Victoria Asturias's phone call, Tony knew the company was considering it. "I don't know but, if that happens, you will all be entitled to unemployment. For now, let's not jump the gun."

Glum-faced, the crew made their way off stage. And now, Tony thought, I will call Ms. Asturias, who insisted on hearing Dunne's report immediately.

Tony revealed in his small victory. He could throw her insinuations back in her face. *I'll also email the company's artistic directors with the result of the inspection.* That brought Lisa Bono's injuries to mind.

"What the hell is happening in my theater?" he grumbled, sotto voce.

## CHAPTER 22

## SHE APPEARED AND DISAPPEARED

Isabel pressed the doorbell at St. Francis de Sales, despite her second thoughts about asking Mrs. B. to help.

"Hello, Isabel." Mrs. B. brought her into the front office. "I wasn't sure you'd come," she said.

"Honestly, Mrs. B., I wasn't sure either." A few minutes later, a tall, burly priest with wire-rimmed glasses and a bushy mustache walked in and extended his hand.

"I'm Father Melvyn Kronkey," he said. Isabel looked into the warmest brown eyes and a genuine smile.

As soon as the priest seated himself behind the desk, Isabel blurted out, "I know you're going to think I'm crazy, but..." She bit her lip instead of finishing her sentence.

Sitting beside her, Mrs. B. said, "Why do you think what happened yesterday wasn't an accident?"

Isabel clenched and unclenched her hands in her lap. Taking a breath, she said, "After Lisa shoved me off the platform, I saw someone staring down at me from the catwalk."

Father Melvyn scribbled a note and asked, "Where on the catwalk?"

"Close to the area where the cauldron had been hanging. The backlight made her silhouette clear, but I couldn't see a face."

"Her silhouette?" Mrs. B. repeated. "How do you know it was a woman?"

Isabel squirmed. "I don't know for sure, but," she paused, searching for the right words. "I feel it."

"Ms. Reardon," Father Melvyn sighed. "There must be a reason you feel that."

Isabel's knuckles whitened as she gripped the arms of her chair. "Call me, Isabel, Father. It's a long story."

"I hope you aren't going to tell me it's a curse," the priest said ruefully.

"No." Annoyance nibbled at Isabel. "I don't think it's a curse, but—" She paused. "Please promise this conversation will remain confidential."

"Agreed," Father Melvyn and Mrs. B. echoed.

Taking a breath, she said, "The Asturias family stole my family's land." She watched the expressions on the priest's and the housekeeper's faces become guarded.

Father Melvyn slammed back in his chair, his surprise evident. "Do you have proof of that?" Father Melvyn asked.

"My grandfather has the deed to the property naming Rafael Sanchez, my great-grandfather as the owner." Isabel looked from the priest to Mrs. B. "And I have it now. I also have his diaries. My grandfather wrote about Victor Asturias's bootlegging activities with a gang called Las Cruces Negras, his money, and powerful political connections."

She saw the shock and doubt on their faces. Isabel rushed on. "I went to the appraisal office and the city records, and even the Sanford map collection. There is no documentation of this land belonging to anyone but Victor Asturias, before or after 1920."

"Have you asked your family about this?" Father Melvyn asked. "Most families have stories and memories that pass down through the generations."

"I've tried. My mother refuses to talk about it. Any mention of the Asturias name sends her into a tizzy. 'Those people have caused us enough pain. Don't go stirring up trouble,' is all she says."

Isabel looked at the priest and Mrs. B. Her heart sank. "I should have listened to my mother. She didn't want me to take this job in Austin, and when I insisted, she made me promise that I'd leave all of this buried." A sob escaped her throat. "I broke my promise. Now Lisa and John have been injured. The entire company may be injured because of me."

Mrs. B. handed her a box of tissues. "Sorry," she said, regaining control. She stared down at the damp tissues bunched in her hand.

Father Melvyn spoke. "If your story is true…"

Isabel's head snapped up. "What do you mean, *if?*"

The priest raised his hand in a gesture of defense. "To help you, my dear, we must question everything. So, as I was saying, even if it's all true, you are not responsible for the wrongdoings of others. Just as you have choices in this matter, so does everyone else."

Isabel nodded but felt disappointed by the cautious stance the priest was taking. Coming here had been a mistake. She was about to thank them for their time and leave when Mrs. B. asked, "Will you bring us everything you have, including your photographs?"

"Yes, of course." Isabel was surprised. "I can bring them tomorrow if you like."

"Good," Father Melvyn said. "Check tomorrow's calendar, Mrs. B. Let's see if we can spend at least an hour with Isabel."

"Can we make it late afternoon? I was excused from dancing today because of my knee, but I'm sure tomorrow I'll be working most of the day."

"Half-past five?" Mrs. B. asked.

"Perfect."

"My dear," Father Melvyn said. "Have you spoken to the police?"

"No, and I don't want to."

"Why not?" Mrs. B. asked.

"How can I accuse one of the most prominent families in Austin of stealing land or being criminals-or worse? No one will believe me."

"Do you think you were the target of yesterday's mishap?" Father Melvyn asked.

"Yes," Isabel answered without hesitation.

Father Melvyn became formal. "We promised confidentiality," he said, "and we will keep that promise. But," he poked the air with his right pointer finger, "it may become necessary to involve the police. There are ways to do it without making accusations. That's to be determined."

Isabel was relieved that they hadn't dismissed her story out of hand and accepted Father Melvyn's caveat about involving the police.

When Mrs. B. opened the office door to let her out, LaLa blocked their path.

"What a beautiful cat," Isabel exclaimed.

LaLa emitted a series of meows and chirps. Tilting her head up, she blinked and flirted, looking into Isabel's face. She then rubbed the dancer's leg, giving her a sign of approval before walking toward the back of the rectory.

"Well, she likes you," Father Melvyn said.

*He looks like a proud daddy, instead of the pontificating authority of a few minutes ago.* Isabel smiled at her own thought. "I love cats," she said. "Maybe, one day, after all of this is sorted out, I'll adopt one."

After Isabel left, Father Melvyn and Mrs. B. went to the kitchen. LaLa was already seated on a chair, her head above the table-top, watching them.

The priest switched on the coffee pot. He leaned against the counter, holding his pursed lips between his thumb and forefinger. Deep in thought, he stroked his mustache.

Mrs. B. knew that look. She turned her attention to the vegetables in the sink, waiting to be washed.

Father Melvyn was still leaning against the counter when the pot beeped. The freshly perked coffee was ready. He didn't move.

"Excuse me, Father." Mrs. B. bumped him out of the way and reached for two cups and the coffee pot. She set everything on the table. "Coffee is ready," she said. Still, he didn't move.

"Father." Her tone sharper. "The coffee is ready. Are *you* ready to tell me what you're thinking?"

Father Melvyn came to the table. "That was quite a story," he said. "But what do we know? Only that she thinks the Asturias woman is after her because of their family's history."

"Something doesn't add up," Mrs. B. said, stirring her coffee. "We saw the encounter between them at the gala. But that isn't enough to support Isabel's story. To my son John, and the ballet company, Victoria Asturias borders on sainthood for all she's doing."

"There is something else," Father Melvyn said, his eyebrows arched down over his nose.

Mrs. B.'s eyes opened wide. "Go on."

Father Melvyn took his coffee cup and began to pace.

"Yesterday, after the accident, you left with John and Lisa. There were other people in the auditorium, and they had umbrellas and rain gear. Victoria Asturias wasn't there, and she'd be hard to miss. Did you see her there?"

"Come to think of it - no, I didn't."

"When everyone gathered around the injured on stage, Asturias suddenly appeared, dry as a bone. No hint of having gotten wet. It rained pretty hard yesterday, don't you think? Did you stay dry? I didn't," he said, emphasizing his point. "When she saw Lisa on the floor, she went white as a ghost; when she saw Isabel get up, her eyes glittered with rage."

He sipped his coffee. "Then, after you left with John and Lisa, I looked for a gent's room and heard two crew members whispering something about a wire being cut and Adam Leightman. When they saw me, they went silent." The priest sat down once again. "When the police asked everyone to give their names and contact information, Victoria Asturias was gone. She disappeared."

"Hmmm. So, do you think there might be something to Isabel's story?" she asked.

"I think it deserves a look."

Surprise zinged up Mrs. B.'s spine. "But, Father, I thought we weren't to stick our noses into police matters?"

"We don't have to get involved, but we can help that girl get pertinent information to Jake. After all, Isabel makes a good point. You don't go around accusing people, especially prominent and powerful ones."

"Right." Mrs. B. was relieved by his change of heart. She knew she couldn't and wouldn't stay out of this one. Someone may have deliberately hurt her son and daughter-in-law, and this she wasn't going to tolerate. She took Father Melvyn's reaction as a left-handed blessing.

Mrs. B. left the rectory and drove to the hospital on auto-pilot. Her thoughts filled with the details of Isabel's story. She'd forgotten that she hadn't told Father Melvyn the stories and superstitions she'd found online, including the mysterious death of a stagehand and a dancer at the Rue de L'Histoire Theatre, during a performance of *Macbeth.*

Pulling open the hospital door, she gave herself a strict warning. "Do not breathe a word of this, tonight."

# CHAPTER 23

## THE EPICENTER OF MISFORTUNE

The rectory was unusually quiet after Mrs. B. departed. Father Declan and Father Joe were both out, and the phones were silent. Father Melvyn poured another cup of coffee, his mind brewing the details of Isabel's improbable story. What was going on at the Rue de L'Histoire Theatre? He thought back to Adam Leightman's confession and fears that the theater was haunted. He was still troubled. In his efforts to help Adam, he'd suggested some logical possibilities, and he worried that he'd spurred Adam into action. Whatever Adam did after flying out of the confessional may have been the reason he was murdered.

Was Adam's death somehow connected to yesterday's terrible accident? The theater seemed to be the epicenter of misfortune. Adding to his unease was that it was on the property Isabel's grandfather claimed was stolen from the Sanchez family.

I don't believe in coincidence. The Good Lord has a reason for everything–and so does Lucifer, he thought, then wondered if theater people really believed that ghosts haunted the theaters. He sighed, confident that the ongoing drama was purely human, perhaps informed by evil intent, but not of the spirit world.

He looked forward to examining the documents Isabel would bring the next day.

His musings were interrupted by paws galloping beside him as he walked to the front of the rectory to turn off the office lights and lock up for the evening. LaLa bolted ahead into the office he'd used a short time before with Mrs. B. and Isabel.

The cat made a chattering sound, sniffed, and then peered up at him before continuing her systematic investigation.

"I'm not Mrs. B. I don't speak cat. What are you telling me?"

LaLa continued sniffing.

"I think you like that young woman." Father Melvyn noted the cat's different reaction to Isabel than the one she'd had to poor Sally Leightman.

LaLa blinked her eyes, left the office, and was about to resume her seat on the landing when the back door slammed.

"Hello?" A familiar voice called.

Father Melvyn headed back to the kitchen. "Hi, Joe. I was about to have dinner—Mrs. B.'s leftover meatloaf. There's plenty. Want to join me?"

"Sounds good to me."

LaLa rubbed against Father Joe's leg; he reached down and scratched her head.

The kitchen door banged open in walked Father Declan. "I smell food," he said.

LaLa left Joe and went to greet Declan, then zigzagged between the three priests, looking up at them and blinking her eyes.

Father Melvyn laughed. "Seems our LaLa is happy to have her favorite men around tonight."

Together, they ate a casual dinner in the kitchen and talked about the challenges of living according to Pope Francis's most recent exhortation, "Gaudete et Exsultate," ("Rejoice and Be Glad").

Father Melvyn didn't rush them, but he was anxious to get to his room to make notes and focus on Isabel Sanchez-Reardon's story and the strange happenings at the Rue de L'Histoire Theatre.

Mrs. B. opened the door of the hospital room and walked in. Lisa was propped up on a pillow, her arm trussed like a UPS package, but she was alert and talking to John and Jake Zayas; both men had their backs to the door.

"I'm here unofficially," Jake was saying. "What's most important to Terri and me is how you are feeling." Mrs. B. looked around; Terri wasn't in the room.

"Are you up to telling me what you remember?" Jake asked.

Lisa saw her mother-in-law behind the men. "Hi, Mom."

John and Jake both turned. John echoed his wife's greeting and planted a kiss on his mother's cheek.

"Sammi," Jake said and pecked her other cheek.

Mrs. B. turned to her daughter-in-law. "My darling, Lisa, you sound much stronger than I expected."

"Not too bad," Lisa answered, "but they do have me on painkillers, which I'm going to discontinue tonight," she said, looking John straight in the eye.

Mrs. B. sensed the disagreement between husband and wife regarding the pain pills. She looked from one to the other.

"Lisa is afraid to stay on them too long," John said. "But, I feel that she might need them a bit longer."

"We'll see," Lisa said, dismissing the subject. "Jake, here's what I remember, and it isn't much," she continued.

Jake pulled out his notepad. "I'm ready when you are." He then turned to John. "When she's done, I'd like to hear your recollections."

Lisa explained that she'd gone on stage to talk to the dancers. Then she heard a sound from overhead. "It's hard to describe, maybe like a rushing sound. I looked up. I think I pushed Isabel off the platform, but I don't remember clearly. That's it. My next memory is in the hospital."

Jake made notes. "Do you remember why you pushed Isabel off the platform?"

Lisa looked puzzled. "I thought it was going to land on her."

Jake nodded and continued to write. "John?" he said.

"Were you on stage all night?"

Mrs. B. thought that an odd question.

"I think so," John answered. "I don't remember leaving the stage. At some point, I might have used a restroom. When the accident happened, I was talking to Orlando."

"Who?" Jake asked.

"The dancer portraying Macbeth. All I know is that I heard a loud crash and screams. When I turned, Lisa was on the floor; I ran to her. Someone called for help. I think it was Father Melvyn."

Jake's eyebrows rose. "What was the priest doing there?"

"He and my mother came at my invitation. I thought they might enjoy seeing how a ballet is made. I remember Father Melvyn yelling that blood was coming from overhead, but my focus was on Lisa. I was scared that she was dead."

Jake continued to write and then flipped the cover of his pad down. "Enough for now. If I have more questions, I'll get back to you when you're stronger." Jake tucked his notebook in his pocket and changed the subject." Lisa, when are they sending you home?"

"They're sending me to rehab first," she answered. "Tomorrow, I think. They'll begin physical therapy before I go home. I seem to be okay after the miscarriage." Her voice dropped to a whisper.

John reached over and took Lisa's hand. "The doctor said you are healthy, there's no internal damage, and we can have children whenever we want."

Mrs. B. hugged Lisa. "That is good news."

Jake cleared his throat. "Seems I've lost Terri. I sent her out for coffee, and she hasn't returned. I'm going to find her. We'll come back to say goodbye."

Mrs. B. looked from her son to her daughter-in-law. "I'll come with you, Jake," she said.

They saw Terri walking toward them out in the hall, carrying two cups of coffee in a pulp-fiber disposable carrier.

Mrs. B. waved at her friend and fired her question to Jake.

"Have you found out anything new?"

"No," he answered. When Terri reached them, Jake took the holder so the women could embrace. After they exchanged greetings, he said, "Now Sammi, I do understand how personal this is to you, but leave the investigation to us. You know, curiosity killed the cat, figuratively speaking."

"I know," she answered. Peering at Jake, she thought he looked worried and wondered if he was concerned about the case or that she and Father Melvyn might get involved.
"I just wondered in what direction the investigation was going," she added.

"Unfortunately, what I can tell you isn't great news for the ballet company. The building inspector went in today. He called to say that the theater was safe, but the wire had been cut. The official report will be in our hands tomorrow. We'll need to keep it shut down a few more days to complete our investigation."

Mrs. B. felt the blood drain from her face. "Thanks."

Jake looked from Sammi to his wife. "It's not confidential, but the less conversation, the better."

Terri changed the subject. "Sammi, if there's anything we can do to help, please don't wait. Ask. You know we'd do anything for you and your family."

"Let's say goodnight, Terri," Jake said as he led his wife back into Lisa's room.

Rubbing the chill out of the goosebumps that had risen on her arms, Mrs. B. thought about Jake's words. "That wire was cut."
Isabel's story was becoming more plausible. She'd tell Father Melvyn tomorrow.

# CHAPTER 24

## YOU WILL KNOW WHAT TO DO

Dressed in jeans and an old shirt, Victoria sat at her makeshift desk in the attic of the Asturias mansion. She'd converted the space into a crude office, and she'd installed a new lock on the attic door to protect against her brother's booze-soaked prying eyes.

A cheap carpet on the rough wood floor held down the dust, allowing her to leave blueprints, property acquisitions, deeds, accounting books, and her grandfather's journals spread out. She'd found almost everything, but not Victor's journals. Her grandfather, Oratio, had been adamant that she find and read them.

Since the well-attended and front page double funeral for her father and her grandfather, she'd immersed herself in Asturias Enterprises, determined to uphold her promise she'd made to her grandfather the day he died. She had a duty, but the business troubles were more profound than she'd thought before taking over.

She'd been renegotiating debts and payments, staying one step ahead of the simmering financial crises that threatened ruin. Weight was dropping off her already slender form, and she was having trouble sleeping. The pressure of one wrong move or one creditor refusing to extend the debt further and everything her grandfather did to grow and protect the Asturias name and fortune would come crashing down. Would she be driven out of Austin? Out of Texas? The thought made her ill.

And now the appearance of Isabel Sanchez-Reardon. She stared at the bank statement. It needed reconciling, but her mind was elsewhere. She knew the stories about the Sanchez-Asturias feud, but she thought it was bullshit.

Unfortunately, the day she'd collided with the dancer, she'd been impatient and disregarded the young woman.

It wasn't until the ballet gala that she heard the name and recognized Isabel as the girl she'd collided with. Victoria had tried to smooth it over, but Sanchez-Reardon was hostile. Victoria didn't know why Sanchez-Reardon should suddenly show up in Austin, but whatever the feud, it was over one hundred years earlier.

Victoria had more critical things to consider, but it still nagged her. She didn't need any more controversies concerning the Asturias name.

Her brother's voice broke into her thoughts. She decided she'd better get downstairs fast before he tried to come up. "Be right there," she shouted, running down the steps.

"Hey, Sis, what are you doing in the attic?" Nando shouted, leaning against the wall adjacent to the staircase as she came thundering down.

Handsome as ever, her brother looked somewhat hungover.

"Just cleaning up and going through some things." She wondered what he was doing there. "Judging from the smell of stale booze and sweat, I can guess you haven't been home." Her brother was usually fastidious to the point of vanity.

Nando stood up straight. "Don't start harping. I've called you several times, but you haven't answered."

Victoria knew what was coming. She'd spoken to the accountant on Friday afternoon and decided to ignore her brother's calls.

"You haven't reinstated my allowance. We have to talk about this," he said, his eyes smoldering above the dark circles from lack of sleep.

"Come downstairs," she ordered. "I'll make some coffee." She turned her back and marched down the stairs to the first floor, shocked when he blew past her on the staircase, almost knocking her over.

"I'm not in the mood for you and your high and mighty crap. I came to tell you that I made an appointment with the lawyer—Tuesday at four. This has to be settled," he snarled and flew out the front door, banging it against the wall.

Victoria sat on the steps and held her head. The sound of his expensive sports car squealing out of the driveway was a personal affront to her. She walked to the front door and slammed it shut. "Aahhhh!" she screamed. Tugging at her hair, she said, "I have enough pressure without him."

She went back upstairs and looked at the bank statements again; she couldn't concentrate.

On his deathbed, her grandfather had said there was a fortune. But where? She'd already searched the house for its hidden secrets. She'd found everything, hidden in different parts of the attic, except Victor's journals.

Nando and financial desperation blocked her ability to concentrate on bookkeeping. She decided to search again, starting with the old oak wardrobe she loved, with its ornate carvings.

Gripping the door handles, she opened it. The bottom drawer was warped, and it stuck the first time she'd searched. This time, she grabbed the drawer's brass handles and yanked. The drawer flew out on her foot. She screamed in pain and kicked it away hard, then sat on the floor, sobbing from pain and exasperation.

When the pain subsided, she examined the bluish lump rising on top of her foot and hoped nothing was broken. Limping around to test it, she was relieved it was only bruised.

Victoria reached for the drawer she'd kicked away; it lay upside down, and the wood at the bottom was cracked. She cursed, thinking she'd broken it. When she looked closer, she saw something between the slats. With the claw of a hammer, Victoria pulled apart the splintered drawer.

There, hidden in the false bottom, were black leather-bound books: Victor Reyes-Asturias's journals.

Her grandfather's words resonated. "You are more like him than you know.

"Read everything. You will know what to do."

# CHAPTER 25

## THE PAST NEVER DIES

Midmorning on Friday, Jake's e-mail beeped. The electronic report from the building inspector had arrived.

Re: The Rue de L'Histoire Theatre. My inspection revealed no negligence. The theater's equipment and materials are well maintained. The batten and prop held by the wires of the fly-system did not exceed or approach the maximum weight the wire was capable of holding.

Upon examination, it was clear that it had been cut in such a way that the prop and batten hung suspended until the strain on the last few strands finally ruptured them, and the load dropped. His heart sank. Someone planned this. Why?

Jake knew the stats. Almost half the women murdered in the U.S. are killed by romantic partners or husbands. He had to give that fact weight in this investigation. Could he remain dispassionate? He'd always prided himself on keeping his emotions separate. Still, right now, he was sympathetic to Sammi's son and daughter-in-law, but when he and his wife had visited Lisa Bono at the hospital, the answer he'd gotten to the question he'd asked John wasn't enough to clear him.

The fly-wire holding the cauldron had been cut, but not all the way through, which means whoever cut it didn't want the load to fall immediately.

Jake knew what he had to do. He took off his black-rimmed glasses and massaged the bridge of his nose. "Marv?"

Sitting opposite Jake, at his own desk, Marv raised his eyes from the computer screen. "Yes?"

"I just got the official report from the building inspector. He confirms that the fly-wire holding the prop was cut. You know we have to look at John Bono for this, right?"

Marv nodded.

"Will you handle it?"
"Sure."

Jake filled him in. "John and Lisa Bono danced together in a company in Dallas for years. You will be far more objective with the facts than I might be."

"What exactly does the report say?" Marv asked.

"It says the fly-wire wasn't cut all the way through, meaning someone didn't want the prop and the metal batten to fall immediately. John Bono could have cut the wire and left part of it intact so he could return to the stage before anything happened." Frowning, Jake leaned back in his seat. "Could he have had an accomplice? A girlfriend? A boyfriend? You know the drill."

"Sure," Marv answered. "I'll get on it right away. Give me the name of the company where they danced in Dallas." Changing cases, Marv said, "By the way, have you seen the stuff on the grisly headless corpse found out on Montopolis?"

"Yes. Not looking good."

"When I went out there to ask questions, 'nobody knew nothin.' What else is new? Gang-related, ya, think?"

"Can't see it any other way. We should have the coroner's report in the next day or so, but that's a favorite method of MS-13. Supposedly, that group of monsters hasn't arrived here—not yet, anyway."

"Give me what you've got on Bono and let me get it done, Marv said. "If you're right about the gang, it'd be good if we got the theater case closed before MS-13 buries us. I'll start the background checks on the theater personnel. See if anyone has a rap sheet."

Jake prayed Marv wouldn't find anything suspicious, but he knew he'd made the right decision asking Marv to handle the investigation of John Bono.

His thoughts returned to the facts of the case. There's been a murder and now a possible attempted murder at the theater. Were they connected?

On the Rue de L'Histoire crime board, Lisa's accident was now parallel to the investigation of the Leightman murder. He and Marv had listed all the players in the drama; most were theater employees who had consistent and easy access to the fly-system. He added John Bono.

Jake stared at the board. They never did find the weapon that had killed Leightman. The M.E. believed it was something heavy, like a shovel or sledgehammer, but they found nothing in the theater, and no one admitted to anything being missing. These theater people sure were a close-knit group.

Marv's head popped up. "Jake. Get this. I ran some names through the database. Tony Volpe, the stage manager, has a record. He did time in New York."

"What for?" Jake asked.

"Embezzlement. Over ten years ago."

"See if there's anyone else of interest. I'll research the facts of the case on Volpe," Jake said.

An hour later, Jake's whistle was loud.

Marv smiled. "What did you find?"

"Listen to this. What a scandal. Lots of newspaper reports on it, too.

"Tony Volpe worked as a groundskeeper for a school district on Long Island in New York. Volpe was involved, got caught, and served time in jail as a co-conspirator."

"Another one?" Marv said.

Jake continued. "Yea. Pilfering school monies is on the rise. Volpe and his accomplices stole a few million dollars from this small wealthy school district. Volpe pled guilty and paid back most of his share of the stolen monies. When he got out of jail, he left New York and resettled in Austin."

"We need to have another talk with Mr. Volpe," Marv said.

Jake reached for his phone and dialed. When Tony picked up, Jake put the call on speaker. "Hello, Tony. This is detective Zayas. We have a few more questions for you that we'd like answered today."

There was a pause. "Do you need all of the crew?" Volpe asked.

"No, just you."

"This isn't a good time," Volpe said. "Can we do it tomorrow?"

Jake shook his head while Volpe talked. Trying to beg off is a stupid move, thought the detective. "No. We can come to the theater or have you picked up and brought to the station. It's up to you."

"Come through the stage door," Volpe said and hung up.

Marv heard the conversation. When his partner hung up, he asked, "So, our stage manager doesn't want to meet?"

Jake shrugged. "He knows he doesn't have a choice. I'm not getting too excited, though. His crime in New York was embezzlement, not murder, but who knows, maybe he's graduated." Jake looked at his watch. "Let's go before the afternoon traffic gets bad."

Damn! Tony tapped a pencil on his desk. The inspector said the police would get in touch because the wire had been cut, but he didn't expect the questions to be limited to him.

Stepping out of his office, he called the custodian. When Charlie came over, Tony told him the police were coming to speak to him. "They'll come through the stage door."

Less than an hour later, Charlie brought the detectives to Tony's office.

"What can I do for you, gentlemen?"

Jake didn't waste time. "Let's start with your stay in the New York State Correctional Facility. Tell us about what put you there."

"Listen, fellas," Volpe answered, spreading his hands in supplication. "I did my time, and what does that have to do with this theater?"

Marv cleared his throat. "Just routine. We need to understand all the factors in play here. Answer the question."

Tony proceeded to tell them what they already knew, with a couple of personal notes they weren't aware of. "I was trained in theater production and worked in all aspects of backstage crafts, from building sets to electrical wiring and lighting," Tony said. "When the economy turned bad, in 2002, I was out of work. I found a job in this school district as a groundskeeper. I got involved with some people, took some money, got caught, paid a lot of it back, used more of it for legal bills, and spent a few years in jail. That, gentlemen, is the long and short of it."

"Some money?" Marv echoed. "I think seven million qualifies as more than some money."

Tony felt his face redden, but he didn't answer.

"Why did you come to Austin?" Jake asked.

"I wanted a fresh start. The Rue de L'Histoire advertised for part-time stagehands, I applied, and Leightman gave me a job."

"Did he know about your record?" Tony squirmed. He didn't answer immediately.

"Well?" Jake said.

"No. Adam didn't ask when he hired me part-time, and I didn't offer," Tony said, keeping his voice neutral.

"So," Marv interjected. "Leightman found out and called you out on it?"

"No." Tony felt sweat gathering under his armpits. "Look. Adam was a good guy. Backstage work can be dicey if you don't know what you're doing, so I was on probation like every other new stagehand when he hired me. When the position changed to full-time, I'd earned his respect. He knew I could handle the job." Tony wondered if the past ever died.

"I've learned my lesson," he added. "And, I keep meticulous records of expenditures. I'm whistle clean." Filled with righteous indignation, Tony watched the detectives write their notes and wondered how many times he was going to pay for that mistake.

When they stopped writing, he continued. "I'm good at what I do, and after a while, Adam promoted me to the assistant stage manager."

Jake asked, "Now that you are the stage manager, have you promoted anyone to the assistant position?"

"No. Too many things are happening. We don't know what the ballet company will decide to do, so no sense making staff changes yet."

Jake and Marv closed their notebooks and stood up to leave.

"We will need to meet with the crew again. When would that be convenient?" Marv asked.

"How about right now? The inspector said he's clearing the theater, and it can reopen as soon as you all finish your investigation. We want to get on with it."

"Tomorrow would be better," Jake said. "How about ten in the morning?"

"Fine." More wasted time, Tony thought. "I'll let the crew know."

As soon as they left, Tony whistled for his crew. "The detectives will be here at ten tomorrow to interview everyone. Be ready."

Without further conversation, he returned to his office and closed the door. I don't know what's going on here, but I need to find out fast before this ends up on me. He fought down bitter feelings about how harsh life had been to him.

So, we stole a few bucks from some rich, snotty elitists who thought their shit didn't stink. We got caught, and I paid my debt to society. I don't see how that puts me under suspicion for murder. Tony sat for a long time, thinking about what to do. "I can't run. I'd look guilty as hell, but I can't sit here like a patsy, either."

Throwing his pencil down in disgust, he slapped his hand on the desk. This is my theater now, he thought, even though he was only an employee.

"There'll be hell to pay when I find out who is messing with this place. But how?"

# CHAPTER 26

**RIPPLES**

Mrs. B. watched the clock. Although she and her boss had initial reservations about Isabel's story, after Jake told her the wire holding the prop had been cut, it was looking more plausible.

Danger rippled through everything connected with the Rue de L'Histoire Theatre, including the Bernardi-Bono Ballet Company, John, and Lisa. How could this be?

At 5:30 p.m., the doorbell rang. Mrs. B opened it to a frazzled-looking Isabel, who balanced a box of papers with an armful of albums. When Isabel stepped in, LaLa rubbed against her leg, greeting the dancer with purrs and chirps.

"Hello, Mrs. B.," Isabel said breathlessly, holding the carton. "What's the cat's name again?"

Mrs. B. reached for the albums sliding off the box. "Her name is LaLa, and she has taken quite a liking to you." The two women and the cat walked into the office. "Father Melvyn will be here in a minute."

The heavy tread of the priest's footsteps on the stairs announced his approach. "Let's see what you've got," he said. Not one to waste time, Father Melvyn used both hands to lift documents from the box. He found the deed in question.

Yellowed with age, almost 100 years old, issued by the General Land Office, covered in plastic, the section, lot, and block, dated January 1919, identified Rafael Sanchez as the owner of the property where the Rue de L'Histoire Theatre now stood.

"These do look authentic. And you couldn't find any corresponding records anywhere?"

"No," Isabel answered and reached for another stack. "All other records for that section, lot, and block are registered to Victor Asturias, except for the most recent, which identifies the Bernardi-Bono Ballet Company as the owner."

Isabel repeated her grandfather's story and again declared his certainty that Victor Asturias was responsible for the Sanchez family's misfortunes.

Mrs. B. looked at the clock and sighed. She'd hoped to get to John and Lisa sooner rather than later. "There's a lot here," she said, flipping through the documents. "Would you allow us to make copies, so we can study everything over the weekend?"

Isabel agreed. "I'll help if you like." The phone rang in the hallway. Mrs. B. went to answer. She returned and told Father Melvyn, "You're needed at St. David's, now." She handed him a Post-It with information.

"I must leave you, my dear," Father Melvyn told Isabel. "With your help, I'm sure Mrs. B. can get all of this done. Let's plan to meet again next week. Mrs. B. has my calendar."

After the pastor left, Mrs. B. quickly took charge. "There's a copy machine in the office across the hall. Let's split up the material. You work in there," she gestured toward the other visitor's office, "and I'll work in the staff office. Make two copies of everything."

Mrs. B. copied as fast as the machine allowed, glancing at the clock every few minutes. Knowing that she had to get the priests' Friday night dinner finished before leaving, she was torn between rushing out and asking Isabel to stay for tea. She rationalized that the more she learned about what was going on at the theater and the players involved, the better she could help her son. Lisa was in good hands in rehab and recovering nicely, so she wasn't needed there.

As soon as the papers were copied, she asked Isabel, "How about a cup of tea? This is dry work."

"That would be lovely." LaLa appeared at Isabel's feet and led her into the kitchen.

Mrs. B. didn't steep the tea, as usual. Instead, she used tea bags and heated the cups in the microwave. She wanted information, but she also wanted to leave.

Isabel sat at the kitchen table, and LaLa sat on a chair, opposite with an expectant look in her eyes.

"Does LaLa always do this?" Isabel asked, taking the cup from Mrs. B.'s hand.

"Yes. LaLa suffers from acute cat-curiosity and has a peculiar need to sit in on human conversations. Thank God she can't use words, or everyone's business would be all over Austin."

The cat directed her gaze at Mrs. B., wriggled on the chair, and gave a little chatter as if to say, get on with it.

Isabel blew on the hot liquid. While waiting for her tea to cool, she asked, "How is Lisa doing?"

Mrs. B. appreciated the girl's concern. "She's doing well. As soon as I'm done here," she said, glancing at her watch, "I'm going over to the rehab facility."

"Please tell Lisa and John I've asked for them and tell them how sorry I am about all of this."

"I will." Mrs. B. then said, "Tell me more about your family. You said they left Austin and moved to San Angelo when your great-grandfather Rafael disappeared. How did your mother end up in New York?"

"My parents met in college," Isabel explained. "My father, a native New Yorker, and my mother, a Texan, were students at UT. It was 'love at first sight,' or so they say." Isabel smiled. "My dad is an engineer, and he received a great job offer in New York right after college. My mother graduated with a nursing degree. She could work anywhere, so off they went."

"Your mother's name is Elizabeth, right?"

"Her full name is Salvata Lizabetta Sanchez-Reardon."

It was Mrs. B.'s turn to smile. "Quite a mouthful. How did your mother's family feel about her leaving them and moving to New York?"

Isabel was thoughtful. "I don't know. You see, I was my parents' miracle baby. Mother was almost forty when I was born. My grandparents were older when I was a toddler, and my grandmother was killed in a hit-and-run incident here in Austin. My grandfather became distraught, and my mother and her younger sister, Marie, thought it best if he came to live with us in New York. He and I became very close."

"A hit and run." Mrs. B. shook her head. "I am sorry to hear that. Were you close to your grandmother?"

"Truthfully, I was so young. I don't really remember her, but when I think of her, the memory makes me smile." Mrs. B. was about to say something when Isabel, with a faraway look in her eyes, spoke so softly that Mrs. B. thought she was in a trance. "That hit-and-run was a tragedy that turned into a nightmare."

Mrs. B. was silent. Isabel's eyes refocused on the housekeeper. "Sorry. Got a bit into the weeds, didn't I?"

"We all do it from time to time." Mrs. B. waved the thought away. "Was the driver found and charged?"

Isabel's face became troubled. She sat with her eyes downcast. Mrs. B. wondered what Isabel wasn't saying. She waited for a heartbeat longer.

"Enough for now. You go home and keep that box in a safe place. Give us the weekend to study everything, and we'll talk on Monday. Deal?"

"Deal," Isabel agreed.

They walked to the front door. LaLa, who had resumed her seat in the hall, on the staircase landing, sat with her paws crossed and mewed a dainty farewell as Isabel passed her.

The door barely closed, and Mrs. B. snapped into action, grateful that she'd done the cooking earlier in the day. She just needed to get it all out before the good Fathers arrived.

The back door opened. In walked Fathers Declan and Joe. Mrs. B. greeted the priests and apologized for being behind schedule as LaLa ran to the kitchen, jumped on the counter, and called for her supper with a series of meows that couldn't be mistaken for anything else.

"Let us help you," Father Joe said and walked to the pantry. He took out LaLa's bag of food. The cat jumped down and ran to the priest.

With their help, Mrs. B. had the final stages of dinner ready and set out in no time. Looking around, she said, "I think that's everything."

"How is your daughter-in-law?" Father Joe asked.

"She's doing well. They've transferred her to the rehab facility across from the hospital. That's where I'm going."

"Get on your way then, Mrs. B. We'll be fine," Father Declan said, then asked, "Where is Melvyn? His car isn't outside."

"He was called to St. David's hours ago. I haven't heard from him, so I imagine he'll be back shortly."

"We'll wait for him," Father Joe said. "You have a nice weekend. As always, Mrs. B., thanks for everything."

"You're welcome, Father Joe. I'm going to grab a box of papers from the office and get going."

Pulling onto the street, relieved to be on her way to John and Lisa, Mrs. B. reminded herself not to speed.

After a short visit to the rehab facility, Mrs. B. went home, parked in her garage, closed the outer doors, and sat in the car for a minute.

Lisa looked good, but John didn't. He had puffy bluish circles under his eyes. She didn't want to ask what was wrong in front of Lisa. Maybe he's just exhausted, she thought.

Sasha and Ziggy yowled on the other side of the kitchen door. She grabbed the box with the papers and walked inside. She greeted her cats, fed them and poured her Friday night martini while preparing dinner. "I've earned it," she said aloud to her meowing cats.

Mrs. B. savored her drink and took her time preparing spaghetti with cheese and pepper, one of her favorites.

The box of papers she'd brought into the house sat in the corner of the kitchen. She looked at it, debating whether or not to start reading or wait until morning. She mixed a second drink and was about to eat her pasta when the phone rang.

It was John. Her heart thumped. "What is it, son?"

The news wasn't good, but it had nothing to do with Lisa's recovery. "I think we could be in real financial trouble, Mom," John said. Mrs. B.'s heart ached at the sound of her son's pain.

"Chelly told me there was an emergency meeting at the studio the day after the accident. They've canceled Macbeth and are considering canceling the rest of the season."

She heard the catch in John's voice; she was glad he couldn't see her distress. When he regained his composure, John said, "If that happens, it will mean laying off dancers and crew." His news jogged her memory.

"Yes, I heard there was an emergency meeting when I went to pick up your computer."

"You knew?"

"Seems your receptionist, Laurel, is a chatty sort. Victoria Asturias showed up, and Laurel whispered to me that she was there for an emergency board meeting to consider suspending the season."

"Laurel told you that? Did you say anything to anyone else?" he shouted.

Mrs. B. was surprised at his outburst. "No. Not a word." Thinking fast, she added, "Don't worry about Laurel. I'm sure she thought it was okay because I'm your mother. Has the board made a decision?"

"Not yet, but it's still under consideration. It was to be kept a secret." He huffed, "We didn't want the dancers upset until we had a clear picture of the immediate future, and I don't want to tell Lisa because she'll worry."

"Can you talk this through with Chelly? Canceling the remainder of the season seems drastic." Mrs. B. sipped her drink. "Boards are important, but you, Lisa, and Chelly are the artistic directors and have a better sense of its impact on the company. Board members invest money and time, but they can walk away. You're the ones who will deal with the professional consequences." John didn't speak while his mother continued her pitch.

"What's happened at the theater, and the cancelation of Macbeth is a setback, but not enough reason to make a ballet company disappear, especially since the next ballet on the program is the universal, or at least the American cash cow."

Mrs. B. was relieved to hear John chuckle at her reference to *Nutcracker*.

"You're right. I'm teaching a class tomorrow morning. I'll text Chelly and ask for a meeting. We'll talk about all of it. The Bernardi-Bono Ballet Company is still too new to withstand disappearing for the rest of its first year. It would be a disaster."

"John," she said, hearing the exhaustion in his voice. "You need a good night's sleep. I know you. You're a fighter. Ballet is no business for the faint-hearted. Get a good night's rest. Lisa is recovering well, and I'm sure you will be able to convince the board that continuing is the right path."

It was midnight when they hung up. Mrs. B. was thoroughly agitated and a little woozy from two drinks and no dinner. "My, oh my," she said to Sasha and Ziggy, who watched her pace the kitchen floor. "If this isn't solved soon, John and Lisa will lose everything they've worked so hard for. How could this have happened," she lamented. "It's a ballet company, for goodness sake, not a CIA operation."

Looking at her cold pasta, she scraped it into the trash. I'll just have the salad, she decided. "Now, where is that box?" Her hands were on it before the words were out of her mouth.

Sasha and Ziggy, accustomed to her talking out loud, mostly to herself, sat at attention. They watched and listened.

Lifting the box to the table, Mrs. B. muttered, "I won't sleep after that conversation. I might as well start on these now. Let's see what I can find. You know, my darlings." She looked down at her cats' beautiful faces, "it's good that Father Melvyn doesn't mind me looking into this. He doesn't know it yet, but I think we are going to be very involved. I can't wait for the police to solve the crimes, but they have procedures to follow. I don't, and time is short."

It was past 2:00 a.m. when Mrs. B. went to bed, but her exhaustion did not guarantee a peaceful sleep.

*The dissonance of the music was bizarre. On the blackened stage, the iridescent silver thread squeezed the Sugar Plum Fairy's throat and dragged her forward on her blood-soaked pointe shoes. Her face emerged from the darkness, and her mouth opened. It was Isabel. It was Lisa. A scream!*

She struggled out of the dream, realizing the scream was her own. She climbed out of bed. Her head pounded from the nightmare, no food, two drinks, and little sleep. She swallowed two aspirin and sat at the kitchen table, waiting for the pills to dull her aching head.

Harold looked at the car's digital clock: It was 4:00 a.m. He dialed. "Hey, Billy. I'm covering all the usual places where Asturias hangs out, but this guy has disappeared off the face of the earth, man."

Billy Slips let out a string of curses. "He hasn't been back to his apartment?"

"Nope."

"Okay. You leave Nando a clear message for me, but stay in Austin and keep searching. He's got a sister. Find out where she lives. Maybe he's there."

"Gotcha, boss." He hung up and drove to Nando's apartment. Using a credit card, he slipped the front door lock.

Harold entered and began the systematic work of leaving Nando Asturias a message he'd understand.

# CHAPTER 27

# THE ENEMY YOU CAN'T LIVE WITHOUT

Victoria was at her attic desk, engrossed in one of Victor's journals. "Hey, sis. Where are you?" Victoria's head snapped up.

"What's he doing home on a Saturday night?" she muttered, shoving the journal back in the bottom drawer and running down the steps from her attic office. When she got to the bottom and opened the door, Nando stood leaning against the banister opposite the door, smiling like a Cheshire cat.

"Let's cut to the chase," he said. "I've been up in your little workroom, and I've read all that stuff. Interesting bloodline we have, yes?"

"What do you mean? How?" Her voice wobbled. Her brother had a degree in business administration, and even though he had his own office in Asturias Enterprises, he'd never shown interest or actively participated in the company.

He ignored the question. "You may have taken over the Asturias Enterprises office on Sixth Street, but I have keys and an office there, too." Nando's eyes glittered. "It's a different experience going in there at night when no one is around. I've been going over the books. You're robbing Peter to pay Paul. Good job getting the company in the black again. Dad really wasn't a good businessman."

Victoria forced herself to stay calm. Don't get mad; he's trying to provoke you, she thought, standing like a statue: still and cold. She waited for him to say more. She hated him at that moment.

"Okay, the game's up," Nando said. "Let's go back upstairs and review."

"Yes, the game is up. How did you get upstairs, and what the hell do you think you're doing? I told you to get out of Austin for a few weeks and stay out of trouble." She looked at the flask in his hand. "Need a drink before we talk business? I don't do business with drunks." She spat the words and turned to walk away when Nando grabbed her arm.

"Have a sip." Victoria tried to shrug off his hand, but he tightened his grip. "For tonight, we do things my way."

Nando's voice sent a chill up her spine. She looked into his eyes for the first time. Dark brown and flecked with gold. She'd never seen this level of intensity before. His handsome face was set in hard lines.

"Nerves make the mouth dry. Take a sip," he ordered, pushing the decanter to Victoria's lips, knocking the rim against her front tooth. Victoria allowed a little of the fluid to pass her lips.

"It's water," she spluttered. "That's right, sister-woman. I haven't had a drink in weeks." He released her arm. "Now, shall we have a brother-sister chat?" Nando put his hand in the small of her back and pushed her toward the staircase.

Victoria's armpits were wet with perspiration. So what did he want, besides money?

As if reading her thoughts, he placed his hand over his heart in a melodramatic fashion. "Don't worry," he said. "I don't want to spoil whatever it is you are doing. I want in."

"Victoria," Nando said, all saccharine. "You misunderstand me. I have no problem with how our great-grandfather made his fortune. I rather admire him, but let's not fool ourselves, even if we want to fool others. We are the descendants of a criminal. Deal with it." He poked a finger at her. "Now, tell me what you're up to? I saw the books. A hundred grand to the ballet company? In our financial state. Why? And what's that little diagram I found on your desk?"

She wanted to slap his face, but thought better of it. Instead, she challenged him. "Have you no pride? Don't you care at all about how far our family has come in two generations? How hard grandfather worked to build reputable, thriving, and successful businesses that employ hundreds? How we've risen to one of the most respected families in Austin? The good our foundations do? The charities we support?"

Nando laughed. "Wow. What planet do you live on? They were damned criminals, bootleggers, and worse. They ran illegal alcohol into Texas from Mexico, and I read our illustrious great-grandfather's journals, the ones you left unlocked in the bottom drawer of your desk."

Victoria was stunned by his knowledge and his attitude. Her defenses flared. "So what? You think all the leading families in America started clean? How many of them were opium traders and bootleggers? We are no worse."

She was entirely off her game. She'd taken the diagram from their grandfather's journal and left it on her desk, thinking Nando had no access to the attic. "This is a new you, Nando," she said, trying a different approach. "But how can I trust you? You've never taken an interest in the business. You were always busy with parties, wine, women, and song."

"As you've said, time for me to grow up. Guess you'll have to trust me now, or else."

"Or else what?"

The doorbell chimed repeatedly. "Who is that at 9:00 p.m.?" Looking at the security camera in her phone, Victoria saw Laurel, the receptionist from the ballet company standing at the front door holding a folder, pressing the doorbell again. Shaking her head in exasperation, Victoria ran down the stairs, yelling, "Coming," into her phone connected to the front door. She heard Nando's footsteps behind her. Victoria pulled open the door. "This is a surprise, Laurel. You should have called first."

"Oh, sorry," Laurel said. "I was in the area and thought you might like to see these." She handed Victoria a folder. "They're the notes from the board meeting."

Victoria stepped aside, allowing Laurel to walk into the center hall. She opened the folder but didn't read it; she watched Laurel look around and assess her surroundings.

On the staircase, Nando lounged against the wall in his most debonair pose. "Aren't you going to introduce me?"

Victoria watched Laurel's expression change from nosy to infatuated. Her cheeks turned pink, and she fluffed her long blond hair away from her face. Smitten, Victoria thought. No surprise there. Nando had that effect on women.

"Laurel," she said, "this is my brother Nando." Like an entomologist, Victoria stood back and observed. Nando turned on the charm, and Laurel melted. Victoria almost guffawed. Nando came down the remaining steps, reached out, and shook Laurel's hand, fixing his gorgeous brown eyes on her. Stupid child, Victoria thought, she doesn't stand a chance.

"Thanks for bringing these," Victoria said and nudged Laurel to the front door.

"No problem," Laurel answered.

It was evident to Victoria that the young receptionist was trying to recover her wits and whatever agenda she had for bringing the papers.

"By the way," Laurel said in a stage whisper. "The building inspector cleared the theater and sent his report to the police yesterday. The wire didn't break. It was cut."

Victoria kept her face neutral. She had already spoken to Tony Volpe, but rather than tell Laurel, she asked, "Any word on Lisa Bono?"

"She's in rehab now. They are expecting a full recovery." Laurel took one last look at Nando, standing behind his sister. "Enjoy the weekend," she said.

Victoria closed the front door and stood facing it. She felt Nando step up behind her. "Don't threaten me," she hissed, returning to the conversation before Laurel's arrival.

"Brother or not, if you don't want me as your enemy, tell me what's going on, all of it," Nando growled, his mouth close to her ear.

"It's late. Give me until tomorrow morning? I need to read these board notes and organize my thoughts."

"You mean to organize your lies."

"Don't you have a date or something? Why are you here all the time? Did you lose your apartment?"

Nando smirked. "It's fun living here again. After all, it's my house, too, and it's easier to keep an eye on you. I think I'll turn in, so I'll be rested and ready for our conversation—first thing tomorrow morning." Nando's smile was wicked. "No tricks, sister. If you think I'm your enemy, then know I'm the enemy you cannot live without."

Victoria pushed past her brother. "I'm going to bed," she snarled, ran up the stairs, and slammed her bedroom door. She threw herself down on the club chair wishing she'd taken a glass of wine, her thoughts turning to the tightrope she was walking. Even though she hadn't finished reading all of them, Victor's journals revealed the reasons and methods for his actions.

Yes, Victor Reyes-Asturias was strong, tough, determined, and a bootlegger. He'd commented on how the rich and powerful made the laws then ignored them in his journals. *If it's good enough for them," he'd written, it's good enough for me.*

Victoria agreed. Now that she'd learned what was within her reach, she was determined to keep her standing among the Austin elites once she found it, which meant it was essential she save her home and her pet charities. She was particularly proud of the children's fund she'd started for the underserved and underprivileged of Austin. And, she intended to continue supporting the arts, particularly ballet, which she loved, having studied as a child. Finally, she felt the sky was opening. She'd come this far and wasn't about to allow two unexpected obstacles to stand in her way.

The first was her hard-drinking brother, Fernando, whose cooperation she could never be sure of, but she believed she could manipulate him with money.

The second was more troublesome. "How much does Isabel Sanchez-Reardon know?" Victoria wondered. What was she looking for at the appraisal office? Victoria knew she had to keep a watchful eye on the dancer, and she was relieved not to be forced to spend money on a private investigator. She was on the ballet's board of directors and had an inside track to Ms. Isabel Sanchez-Reardon.

Now that she had Victor's journals, which were a treasure of information, background, and guidance, Victoria felt confident that she was regaining control, but it was tenuous.

Her beloved grandfather always said, 'where and how you start doesn't matter. It's how you finish that counts.' Yes, Grandfather, you were right, she thought. And, I am more like Victor than even you realized.

Nando waited until he was sure Victoria wasn't coming out of her room before going down for a drink. He hated living in the family home again, but he couldn't go back to his apartment. He still owed Billy money, and compound interest piled up fast in Billy's bank.

How could he get his hands on enough cash to keep Billy Slips from having his debt collecting goon, Harold, break his legs or worse.

Nando frowned, thinking about the deceptive Billy Slips. Skinny, short—under six feet tall, he had indistinct features and a delicate, almost feminine voice. He sounded simple-minded and unassuming when he spoke, but underneath, there was a razor-sharp mind and a vicious streak to be avoided. Nando had learned to fear Billy. He didn't know his last name, other than his handle: Slips. He was a master at slipping through police hands.

His thoughts turned to his sister. He laughed. She thought she'd outsmarted him by changing the lock on the attic door. That alone had made him suspicious and determined to get up there.

While she was at work, he'd spent a few hours in her lair examining everything he could lay his hands on, but he didn't understand their meanings. And he didn't understand the half diagram on her desk. What was it, and where did it lead?

He knew something else was going on. Nando suspected if he could get it out of her, it might be his solution to paying off Billy Slips. One way or another.

# CHAPTER 28

## WHAT THE FATES ARE SAYING

Isabel woke up early on Sunday morning with a pang of nagging guilt. On Friday, she hadn't answered Mrs. B.'s question about the driver who'd hit and killed her grandmother. The tragedy that had become an unclear nightmare until her grandfather identified the driver but made her promise she'd never tell anyone that she knew. She still felt her grandfather was afraid of something else.

She got her coffee pot going, then stretched her legs, bending and flexing her injured knee. She knew it was definitely better. The clock said it was time to call her parents. She dreaded the conversation, but they needed to know. *Macbeth* had been canceled. Maybe they could come for *Nutcracker*. No, she thought. I can't say that yet. We don't know if the board will cancel the rest of the season. Isabel pushed aside her worries that the company might fold and focused on what to tell her parents. She crossed herself quickly, raised her eyes to heaven, and prayed. Please, please, Lord, help me. Then she dialed.

"Good morning, darling. How are you?" Lizabetta asked, "And what's the news?"

It was senseless to skirt the issue: Isabel jumped right in. "Unfortunately, Mamá, there's been another accident in the theater." There was no response. "Mamá? Are you there? Did you hear me?"

"Yes. I heard you. What happened?"

Isabel gave her the facts, tried not to lie, but omitted anything that might scare her already nervous mother. "A wire broke, and a heavy prop fell, hitting someone. The theater has been closed for inspection by the building department."

"Who was injured?"

"Lisa Bono, one of the artistic directors."

"And?"

Isabel heard her mother's sigh of exasperation. Still, she didn't answer.

"Don't make me pull the information out of you," her mother said. "What does this all mean?"

"I don't exactly know. Hopefully, we will know more tomorrow but, right now, *Macbeth* is canceled. Do you have your plane tickets yet?"

"I was going to book them today."

Isabel breathed a sigh of relief. "What about Aunt Maria and her family?"

"I'll call my sister after we hang up. I was going to take care of the hotel arrangements, so it's just a matter of a car ride for them." Unexpectedly, Isabel's mother asked, "The curse?"

"Mamá! You shock me. I thought you didn't believe in curses."

She heard her mother harrumph. "Isabel, I don't believe in the kind of curses you superstitious theater people entertain, but I'm beginning to wonder what the fates are saying. Maybe they're telling you to get the hell out of there. Come back to New York."

And she doesn't even know I was hurt, Isabel thought. "Please don't talk that way, Mamá."

"I know you aren't telling me everything. I'm going to talk to your father. Maybe we should come down anyway. See what's really going on."

Sweat beaded on Isabel's brow. Please, not now, Mother, Isabel thought. "Why don't you wait until tomorrow? I promise I'll call you with a full report. I think we are going into rehearsal for *Nutcracker* straight away. You can come for that."

"You are putting me off, Isabel."

"I'm not. If *Nutcracker* is canceled, you can come whenever you want. Deal?"

Her mother sighed. "For now. We'll talk more about it tomorrow. How's the weather? Fall was my favorite time of year when I lived in Texas."

Isabel relaxed. Her mother's peace offering: a harmless subject to chatter on about. Her father got on the line, and they spoke for half an hour more, then the three of them shared their I-love-yous and hung up.

Exhausted by the effort, Isabel exhaled. It was challenging to walk the thin line between truth and lies by omission. She reached for another much-needed cup of coffee. Looking out at the grey skies, she decided that it was a good day to clean and do the piles of laundry when a rush of anger surprised her.

She'd held her mother at bay for now, but the pressure was building. If her mother had been willing to talk about the family's history, Isabel might not have felt compelled to dig up the past.

In his room, Nando channel-surfed the crap on TV. He would have loved to go out, but he knew his finances were low, almost gone. He couldn't sleep. Maybe a cognac would help.

He crept downstairs barefoot, not wanting to alert Victoria that he was moving about the house. Without turning on a light, Nando made his way to the bar in the living room. He poured his snifter and turned toward the front staircase.

A door upstairs closed. Pressing himself against the wall, he waited. In the silent house, the soft creaking on the back staircase to the kitchen was audible. She's probably going down for a snack.

Maybe she's bored, too, he thought, moving fast to get back to his room before Victoria caught him.

# CHAPTER 29

## NOBODY IS GOING TO TAKE THIS AWAY FROM ME

At the Rue de L'Histoire Theatre, two chairs overturned on stage in the pre-dawn hours of Monday morning. One of the rigging ropes unwound and slid across the floor. A slight breeze moved against the fabrics in the wings just before the ghost light clicked off.

Unable to sleep, Tony left his apartment on Convict Hill Road and went to the Rue di L'Histoire Theatre. It felt as much his home as where he rested his head at night. Letting himself in through the stage door, he disengaged the alarm. As soon as Tony stepped in, his heart sank. The ghost light was off.

Turning on an overhead light, he walked out on the stage. The rear curtain was suspended overhead to keep it clean. Two chairs were on their sides. "Shit," he muttered and turned them upright. Then, he walked over to the ghost light and turned it back on before going to his office, wher he flipped the switch on the coffee maker.

Tony was deeply committed to the Rue since he'd been given the job of stage manager. Instead of treading water, this was his chance to build a new life. Because of his conviction, his wife had divorced him. He had one sister who lived in Australia. They weren't close. If not truly happy, he was content, but now something outside of his control threatened his newfound gratification.

Superstitions aside, Tony felt there were forces pushing events in ways that he didn't like. If he didn't do something to snap this streak of weird and dangerous incidents, he feared the management job would be taken from him. With another cup of coffee in hand, he walked out to the backstage area.

He breathed deep, letting the smells that permeated the walls, fabrics, and ceiling fill his nose. He loved the scents of greasepaint, sawdust, fire-retardants, musty costumes, ball-bearing lubricants, and the vague odor of sweat. They were as much a part of the theater as the stage itself.

The auditorium was dark. He looked out at the empty seats. The performers are special under the lights, but back here, out of the audience's sight, it's all in our hands, he thought. The fly-operators, dressers, prop masters, lighting techs, and stagehands. These nameless, black-clad phantoms were the people who made the magic happen.

As he turned, his toe caught on a length of rope on the floor where it shouldn't have been. "What the hell?"

In his office, Tony left the door wide open, sat at his desk, and looked out. Unfortunately, his view of the stage was obstructed by one of the office walls. He needed a better view. Pushing and shoving, he moved his desk back and on an angle, enabling him to see more of the wing area, part of the stage, and the ghost light. He had a plan. It was going to be tricky, but he was sure it would work.

He'd spend as many nights in the theater as It would take to uncover who or what was sabotaging his life.

"Nobody is taking this away from me."

"How'd you make out?" Jake asked Marv as soon as he arrived at the precinct.

"I met with the artistic director of the Dallas Company on Saturday, and she had nothing but praise for John and Lisa. I asked to speak to the dancers, but they were about to break. I was invited to stay and question them on their lunch hour."

Marv turned the page in his notebook.

"Everyone said John and Lisa were missed. They were dedicated to each other and to ballet. You know, one of those couples who finished each other's sentences." Turning another page, Marv continued. "As far as I could find out, there'd never been any rumors of trouble between them, and there were never rumors about love affairs. Neither drank, other than an occasional glass of wine."

"Any questions about their move here?"

"No. Apparently, they were very open with their fellow dancers and the artistic director." Then, Marv read a direct quote: "'John and Lisa told us that it was time for them to retire because they wanted to have a baby,' the artistic director said. When the opportunity came up, in Austin, everyone in Dallas was sorry to lose them but thrilled for their futures. They all asked for contact information so they could send cards and gifts."

Jake heaved a sigh of relief.

It was a busy morning at St. Francis de Sales. Two funeral masses and one luncheon later, Father Melvyn returned to the rectory anxious to discuss Isabel's story with Mrs. B.

"Mrs. B., where are you?" he called out, once back in the kitchen.

She stepped in from the front hall and shushed him. "The Ladies Altar Ministry is in the front office," she whispered, "and they are madder than a swarm of bees."

"I thought Father Declan was working with them?" Father Melvyn said.

Before Mrs. B. had an opportunity to tell him that Father Declan was there with the ladies, a shout reached them.

"No. With her reputation? We can't ask her. Why…"

Father Melvyn sprang into action. "Time for me to help," he said and marched down the hall to the front office.

Hoping the phone wouldn't ring, Mrs. B. stood in the kitchen doorway, listening as Father Melvyn exercised his most charming brogue with the women of the alter ministry.

When everything was resolved, he returned to the kitchen.

"Nice assist," Mrs. B. said when Father Melvyn returned.

"You heard?"

"Of course," Mrs. B. said.

Father Melvyn's eyes twinkled. "Declan could handle it, but those women can be scorpions sometimes. They forget the Lord's command for charity toward others and not judging," he whispered. "Now, is that fresh coffee? Let's talk before the next crisis."

Mrs. B. brought two cups to the table. "I read the papers Isabel left us on Friday," Mrs. B. said.

"I didn't have a chance, but I will tonight." He sipped his steaming brew. "Anything interesting?"

"Very, but there's nothing Isabel can do about the property." Mrs. B. paused and leaned forward. "I need to tell you something."

His eyebrows shot up; his face registered that spit it out, look.

"Father, I know you don't want me getting mixed up in a police investigation again, but I'm afraid for my son's and daughter-in-law's lives. Whatever is going on in that theater has already seriously impacted them. Lisa lost her baby and could have been killed, and as artists and part-owners of the theater, they stand to lose everything."

"I understand your concerns." He put down his cup. "I anticipated your desire to take a hand in sorting this out."

Mrs. B. said, "If I need to take a leave of absence, so the church isn't involved in any way, I'll do that."

"Jumping to conclusions, my dear," Father Melvyn said, wagging his finger at her, but his eyes smiled. Mrs. B. looked puzzled.

"Let's be serious," he said. "I think we should help out. We'll be a bit more circumspect this time. Perhaps we can move the investigation along by helping that lovely young dancer get her information to the police promptly." He picked up his cup. Before he sipped, he whispered, "Well, maybe not so promptly."

Mrs. B. felt the shock of those words register on her face. "And why the change of heart?"

"You understand that there are times I learn things as a priest that I cannot share—ever." Mrs. B. nodded.

"Well, don't ask. Let's just get on with it."

## CHAPTER 30

### I INTEND TO KEEP MY STANDING

Monday morning, Isabel had completed most of her stretches before any other dancers arrived. In twos and threes, they straggled in, talking among themselves. She stood up and hugged Orlando. Together, they went to the barre to continue stretching.

"What do you think is going to happen?" he asked.

"I don't know, but I hope Chelly will give us information before class begins."

Keeping his voice low, Orlando said, "There are some smaller pick-up companies, you know, semi-pros and schools looking for dancers for their *Nutcrackers.* If we aren't doing it here, I have some connections. Interested?"

"Yes."

"Hey, you two, what's all the whispering?" Janet walked over and took the spot at the barre next to Orlando.

"Just shop talk," Orlando answered.

Within minutes, all of the company was in the room preparing for class, chatting, and speculating about the Bernardi-Bono Ballet Company's future.

Chelly and the pianist walked in together. "Okay, company, listen up." The dancers lined up at the barre. "I need everyone's full attention, so when class starts, your minds are on your work and not on anything else because that's how accidents happen," she said, remembering the devastating accident that ended her career because she'd lost focus.

"First, I'm sure you'll all be happy to know that Lisa is doing well. She's in rehab now, and her recovery looks good. John taught his variations class on Saturday, and he'll be back at work this morning." Chelly looked from face to face. "Get-well cards and good thoughts would be appreciated."

Moving to the center of the room, she continued. "I'm sure the rumor mill is working overtime. As you all know, we had an emergency board meeting last week to discuss the problems at the theater and to cancel *Macbeth*."

Isabel held her breath. Like the other dancers, she was worried.

Chelly continued. "While no one thought suspending the rest of the season was a good idea, there was no official vote. On Saturday, John and I talked it through. We made an artistic decision. We will go on with the season as planned. FYI – If anyone asks, tickets sold for *Macbeth* will be transferred and discounted for *Nutcracker*."

There was a quick burst of relieved sighs and applause. Chelly smiled. "So, now you don't have to worry about a layoff or auditioning for pick-up companies because today is your last easy day."

Thank God, thought Isabel.

Chelly clapped her hands to silence the chattering dancers. "The casting is almost complete. For today, we will have technique class, followed by pas-de-deux. John will teach, and I'll observe. We will pair many of you to see how you work with different partners." She waited for that to sink in. "This is not an indication of who might dance which roles. Concentrate. Show me your best selves, and I promise the cast list will be up before you arrive tomorrow morning. Now, let's begin."

With renewed vigor, Isabel placed her hand on the barre and pulled her body erect with her feet in the first position. She was ready to work.

The pianist's fingers on the keyboard played the music for the plie combinations, and the class was underway.

*I can hold off my mother's visit.* Isabel then shut off all thoughts that didn't involve executing the movement as flawlessly as possible.

In her Asturias Enterprises office, Victoria told her assistant she didn't want to be disturbed. The weekend conversations with Nando weighed heavy on her mind. She didn't trust him.

When Nando had confronted her on Saturday, they'd circled each other like two prizefighters looking for an opportunity to land a knock-out punch. He kept hinting that there were things she didn't know. Victoria thought it was a ploy to distract her. Despite her distrust, she was impressed and a little nervous that he'd checked the books and taken the time to learn what she'd done. Well, she had her own surprise. She told him she'd sold off a piece of property in Marble

Falls, and his shocked expression gave her satisfaction. Most of the monies from that sale bankrolled the Bernardi-Bono Ballet Company.

When she rolled out one of the blueprints of the house and the Rue de L'Histoire Theatre, he was puzzled, as she'd been at first, but she had the advantage of the last and most important of Victor's journals—Nando didn't know it existed.

Victoria wasn't sure where any of this was going with her brother. He'd intimated– threatened that perhaps it was time for him to talk with Mr. Smithson, the family attorney, to discuss how she was handling the debt. Maybe it was time for him to consult that board of Asturias Enterprises to discuss her restructure plan, since they'd formally placed her at the organization's head. The thought of this made her stomach knot. She wasn't ready to confront the directors yet.

"That little shit," she growled. "He thinks he can push me around. He'd better think again." She looked at the clock. "I'll deal with my brother later."

She dialed. Volpe picked up. "Good morning, Tony. How is it going there?" Victoria already knew the answers since he'd left a phone message on Friday but understood that he needed the satisfaction of pressing the point. He repeated that the inspector found the theater well maintained by a competent crew.

When she asked about suspects, Tony said there weren't any.

"Can I help with anything technical or mechanical?" She was looking for an in.

"No. By next Monday, I'll be at full crew again. *Macbeth* is canceled, and if the company goes forward with *Nutcracker*, it's pretty routine. We'll be fine."

"Okay, Tony. If there's anything I do, please don't hesitate." They hung up. He hadn't given her anything to work with. Unhappy with that conversation, she dialed the ballet studio.

"Bernardi-Bono Ballet Studios," Laurel answered.

Victoria realized her error. She should have called Chelly's private number. "Good morning, Laurel. Is Chelly available?"

"Good morning, Miss Asturias. No. Chelly is in class with the dancers." Laurel lowered her voice. "She's telling them that *Nutcracker* will go on, and she's filling them in on the police and building inspection. Shall I have her call you back?"

"Yes. Please give her my office number."

"Will do, Miss Asturias. Before Victoria hung up, Laurel added, "You know, it was a pleasure to meet your brother."

"So glad," Victoria answered and slammed the phone down, vexed that she hadn't been consulted by the artistic directors before they made the decision to go on with *Nutcracker*. *If I don't hear from Chelly by noon, I'll call again on her private line.*

She buzzed her assistant, Carl. "Is my brother in yet?" He immediately called Fernando Asturias's extension.

"No, Miss Asturias. Do you want me to leave a message?"

"Yes. Tell him to call me as soon as he gets here." Victoria sat at her desk and tried to focus on the report she was preparing for the upcoming staff meeting. But it was the Rue de L'Histoire Theatre that stayed at the forefront of her thoughts. Her intercom rang. "Yes, Carl?"

"Chelly Bernardi on the line, Miss Asturias."

Victoria picked up. "Good morning, Chelly, or should I say good afternoon," Victoria corrected herself.

"Time flies, doesn't it?" Chelly answered. "Victoria, John, and I met on Saturday and went over everything. As you know, no official vote was taken at the last board meeting, but I didn't feel the board wanted to cancel the remainder of the season."

Already prepared because Laurel had told her, Victoria wasn't taken by surprise. "You're right. No one wants that, but are the dancers up to the task? We know they tend to be a superstitious group...sorry," Victoria said. "I mean, no offense."

"None taken. I spoke to the dancers this morning. Now John and I are calling each board member to explain our decision." Victoria didn't respond. Chelly cleared her throat and hurried on. "Normally," she said, "I wouldn't speak to the dancers until I'd polled the board, but this is a very competitive time in the ballet world. *Nutcracker* looms large. There are pick-up companies that need dancers, and if we were canceling the season, our dancers would need to get themselves out there to audition for other productions. I wanted to ease their minds so they'd concentrate on work."

Still annoyed, Victoria was gracious. "This is good news, and I'll bet the dancers are relieved."

"They actually applauded when I made the announcement." Chelly paused. "Victoria, I hope you know how grateful we are for everything you've done and your contribution enables us to go ahead with *Nutcracker*, which is always a money-maker. It will propel the spring season."

"You know I'm devoted to ballet, and I'm glad to help," Victoria said, but she thought, you're so grateful you didn't include me in the conversation, but added, "One of the perks of being in business for myself is that I can rearrange my schedule most of the time, so if you need me, reach out."

"Thank you again. *Nutcracker* is second nature to dancers at this level. Most companies and ballet schools in America perform some version of it at Christmas, thanks to New York City Ballet and George Balanchine. They've made it an American holiday tradition. Ticket sales from *Nutcracker* often make the difference between a company finishing in the black or the red. But, since you offered," Chelly paused. "There is one thing."

"Yes?" Victoria said.

"You are a formidable woman and a persuasive leader. Maybe you can give the board an extra push to sell out the holiday performances—all of them. We need great ads and a great PR campaign in light of the unfortunate cancellation of *Macbeth.* If we do well enough, financially, maybe we could put it back on the schedule for the spring?"

"My donation was originally earmarked to cover production costs for *Macbeth,* but I think using it now to cover the costs for *Nutcracker* is justified. I'll encourage the board to push hard to make it a great success. After the holidays, we can revisit *Macbeth.*"

Chelly thanked her again. After hanging up, Victoria sat back in her chair. Chelly's words rang in her ears. "*Nutcracker* is second nature to dancers." She understood that she didn't have the same carte blanche to be around the studio. Soon it won't matter, but for now, I need a conduit for theater schedules and information on that Reardon girl. If she starts talking about family histories and suspicions of who did what to whom, it will only complicate matters and cause trouble. *And, if that big-mouthed receptionist, with the need to be important, finds out, the whole town will know about it.*

Victoria recalled her attempt to talk to Isabel the night of the gala. She'd approached Isabel to compliment her on her dancing, but Reardon had rebuffed her. Eyes snapping, she'd stated, "You're the woman I collided with at the appraisal office; I know what your family did." Then she'd walked away. But what exactly did she know? The question troubled Victoria because it could mean the difference between financial survival and ruin.

Victoria knew that Reardon's hostility was futile, but she was looking for trouble.

Why is Reardon searching for records? There's nothing she can do after all these years, Victoria assured herself, but would the Sanchez family try to bring a lawsuit if everything was discovered? That would raise questions about the family's honor and reputation, which brought her brother to mind. If he heard her express such a sentiment, he'd ask, "What honor?"

He can think whatever he wants," Victoria muttered. "We are highly regarded no thanks to Nando's and my father's reputations as society playboys." She worried that while the upper-crust smiled indulgently at their antics, she wasn't at all sure they'd look away if everything came out.

She winced at the thought. We give generously to worthy causes and charities, she thought. That must count for something!

To be accepted into the best country clubs, make the guest lists for the leaders' and shakers' benefits and charity events, and receive party and dinner invitations from the elites meant keeping the family's dirty laundry out of the public eye. "And I intend to keep my standing," she said aloud, but how fast could she find what Victor had hidden and what could she do about it before the Reardon girl choreographed the Asturias's fall from grace?

# CHAPTER 31

## WHEN ONE DOOR CLOSES

Victoria pled a headache and went to bed early. Bullshit, Nando thought. Since the night he'd sneaked downstairs for some cognac, he became aware that Victoria, too, crept around the house when she thought he was sleeping. So far, he hadn't figured out what she was doing, but he followed her lead. "I've had a busy weekend. I'm going to do the same."

Instead of going to sleep, Nando crept down the front stairs that didn't creak and went to the kitchen, where he wedged himself between the refrigerator and the far wall. I hope I'm right, or I'm going to have a long uncomfortable night, he thought.

He heard a light footfall enter the kitchen from the front of the house. The digital clock on the counter said 10:15 p.m. Victoria walked through, opened the cellar door, and flipped the switch. For a split second, she was clearly visible, wearing black clothes with a workman's belt around her waist. He waited until the staircase light went off.

On sneakered feet, he followed. When he reached the basement floor in the dark, he crouched behind an old chair. His eyes needed a few minutes to adjust; he saw nothing in the darkness until weak light penetrated the gloom. It came from the adjacent wall. In a flash, Victoria was there, then gone.

Holding his breath, Nando carefully made His way to the place where Victoria had been visible. It was a wall of shelves. "Where the hell is she?" he muttered, getting frustrated. He pulled at the shelves.

Nothing.

He ran his hands over the sides and front. Nothing.

Wedging his hand between the shelves and the wall, his fingers hit something metal. He pushed up; it didn't move. He pushed it down, heard a click, and the shelves swung away from the wall, almost hitting him. He jumped back.

A dim light came from the opening. Nando eased his body behind the shelves and looked in. The dank, underground smell of packed dirt and no ventilation was intense.

Should I?" he asked himself. "Hell, yes!" He stepped in. How to close the door behind him? He felt the wall to his right and found another lever. What the hell is this? Nando wondered and pushed it down. The wall swung closed.

Facing forward, he noticed crude light fixtures spaced along the side walls. The ground sloped down. He forced one foot in front of the other, his nerves screaming as he wondered where he was going and where his sister had disappeared to.

Tendrils of fear and a sense of claustrophobia tightened his chest. Some parts of the walls were mossy. The deeper in he went, the more pungent the damp smell became. Squeezing his arms close to his body, he avoided touching whatever fungi were growing, but he peered at the walls trying to find other doors or levers. There were none. The only escape was behind him. It felt like he'd been walking forever when the ground leveled out. He came to a turn. The tunnel became narrower. His sense of being closed-in put Nando on the verge of panic. He stopped. It was either turn left or go back.

Sweating from nervousness in the cold, damp underground, Nando forced himself to turn. Once in this new shaft, there were no lights, only dim, watery fragments of light from behind him that grew weaker with every forward step he took.

He stopped again. Fear flipped his stomach. He thought he'd seen a flashlight dangling from Victoria's work belt and wished he'd taken one, too.

Nando refused to allow his mind to imagine what might be on the walls or crawling on the packed dirt floor. It was agony for him to force each foot forward. "Don't think; just move," he ordered. His sister had come this way. She couldn't have disappeared into thin air.

His fear turned to fury; his need for a sense of barriers overcame his distaste for what might be on the walls. Walking forward, he reached his arms out to each side to be sure the walls were still there. He shuffled for fear that if he lifted his foot when he set it down again, there would be nothing there, or worse, something wiggly underfoot.

Perspiration dripped in his eyes. He smelled his own sweat and heard his breath coming in short gasps. He pressed on, one foot in front of the other, hands moving along the walls on both sides.

Bam! His face slammed into something rough and hard. "Uragh!" he screamed, no longer caring if Victoria heard him. He backed up several steps, holding the wall with one hand and his nose with the other. Fighting not to panic, he regained his composure, put his hands out in front and walked forward again. This time his hands hit the stone in front of him. He'd reached a dead-end.

Turning from side to side, he ran his hands over the side walls searching for another way out. "Damn you to hell, Victoria," he snarled. Sweat burned his eyes and the scrape on his nose. His sister was nowhere in the tunnel. Where did she go?

Again, he ran both hands along the wall in front of him, fighting back the urge to turn and run or puke from fear. His fingers hit another piece of metal; he yanked his hand back, as if shocked. On the verge of going to pieces, he reached forward once more and gripped the metal in his trembling fingers. Desperately, he pressed it down.

Without so much as a squeak, the stone wall swung away from him. His heart pounded in his chest. Where was he, and where was Victoria?

Nando inched partway through the opening. It was black as pitch. Afraid to move for fear of falling or banging into something, he stood still and hoped his eyes would adjust. A narrow beam of light provided relief from the unnerving darkness.

Barely visible, a figure held a flashlight in one hand and studied some large folded paper in the other. It was his sister.

"What the hell are you doing?"

She pivoted fast, dropping the blueprint.

Victoria gasped from the force of his grip. "You will tell me everything, not just what you think I need to know," he snarled.

"Okay," she shouted and tried to pull his hand off her face. Nando tightened his grip. Through clenched teeth, she said, "If you do anything to upset my plans, I swear, blood or no blood, I'll kill you."

Nando smiled, and in his silkiest voice, he returned the warning. "Let me assure you, you will not kill me. If you don't come clean, it's the life you love that may die." He released her face and watched as she rubbed her cheeks. "Don't sell me short, Victoria." He glared at her. "The same ruthless blood in your veins is in mine. Tell me here and now. Where are we, and why?"

She'd never seen her brother like this. For the first time, she was afraid. Her heart raced, and she played for time. "We are backstage at the Rue de L'Histoire Theatre. Victor Reyes-Asturias drew this crude blueprint." She waved the folded paper at him.

"Go on."

"I'm looking for a false section of the wall in this room. According to Victor's journal, there's a fortune, probably worth several million dollars in gold, hidden here."

"I've read the journals. There's no mention…"

She changed tactics. "Nando, it's almost eleven. Let's go back. I never know if anyone will come in here at night." She regretted the words as soon as they were out.

"You mean like Adam Leightman?" She remained silent but felt his piercing brown eyes penetrate her soul.

"I think you do have a lot to tell me. Lead the way," he said and swept his arm toward the false door that was still ajar.

When she didn't move, he laughed and said, "You do have the flashlight."

Victoria hugged the blueprint to her. Before moving, she looked around to be sure everything was as she found it when she came in.

Recovering her usual wit and sarcasm, she said, "Speaking of clean, take a shower. You stink."

Back in the tunnel, she ordered, "Use the Metal lever. The wall will close, and the latch will click." When she was sure the hidden door was securely closed, she set a rapid pace returning to the Asturias home. She didn't hear his footsteps, only the sound of his breathing; his presence behind her felt threatening.

Her mind churned with options, and she considered how much to tell him. As little as possible, she decided. He already knew too much.

As the hidden door in the prop room clicked shut, another door opened on the opposite side of the theater.

Tony Volpe disarmed and then reset the alarm. To his relief, the total darkness was broken by the glow from the ghost light on stage.

Leaving his office door wide open, Tony settled into his desk chair in his reconfigured office. When Charlie had seen what he'd done, he was surprised. Tony had explained that he wanted to see more of what was going on when the office door was open. That was true. He hadn't told Charlie why.

Tony set the timer on his watch to 5:00 a.m.,

and silenced the buzzer. His eyes struggled to adjust to the dark as he sipped the coffee he'd brought from home. He couldn't see everything, but he listened for any out-of-the-ordinary sounds.

Unaware of the building's natural creaks and groans during the day, when the theater was a beehive of activity, they spooked him in the absolute silence of the night.

Tony's heart skipped a beat. An almost inaudible noise from above reached him, coming from the backdrops suspended above the stage. He wondered if it was an air current that swayed them or his imagination. He sat in his chair and waited.

Hours later, when the watch vibrated against his wrist, Tony forced his eyes open. Guess I did more than doze, he thought. He didn't move. To his relief, the ghost light was on, its weak beam barely reaching the end of the stage.

Grabbing his jacket, he walked out of the office. After one final look around confirming that nothing had been touch or moved, he reset the alarm and left.

## CHAPTER 32

## GHOSTS OF CRIMINALS PAST

Mrs. B. arrived at the rectory on Tuesday morning to find Father Melvyn waiting for her in a state of excitement. "We need to talk, right now," he said. "Sit down. Don't worry about the door or the phone. Declan is in the staff office. He'll cover."

"My goodness, Father, what is it?"

"I was up until 3:00 a.m. reading Isabel's papers. There is a real situation here." Father Melvyn took two cups from the cupboard when the coffee maker beeped, poured the coffee, and set the cups down on the table.

Mrs. B. looked around. "Where is LaLa?"

"With Declan. She's sprawled out on the desk, assisting him." Father Melvyn chuckled. "He's stamping and signing the confirmation certificates, trying to keep LaLa from paw-printing them."

Mrs. B. sipped the coffee and was pleasantly surprised. He'd managed to make a good cup instead of his usual muddy brew requiring at least one ice cube and milk.

The priest took a quick gulp. "Ummm. Not bad this morning, yes?"

"Yes, Father. Now, what is it that has you in a stew?"

Reaching in his shirt pocket, he pulled out his copy of the photograph Isabel had left. It was her great-grandfather, Rafael standing behind her grandfather, Oratio, as a young boy. Rafael had one hand on each of Oratio's shoulders.

"Look at this," he said, pushing the photo across the table.

Mrs. B. took it. "I saw this. What am I missing?"

"It's black and white and faded, but *look* at the ring."

"Yes. It is quite clear. What are those markings?"

"I almost missed them myself," Father Melvyn said. "I needed a magnifying glass. Is there any way you can enlarge this on the copy machine?"

"I can try, but what is it you think you see?"

"Mrs. B., the ring has the markings of a Piscatorial Ring!" Her shoulders rose, her hands opened, palms up.

"Those rings are worn by popes," Father Melvyn said. "This one looks particularly old."

She stood up. "Let me try to enlarge this." She started toward the staff office and changed her mind. "Let's leave Declan and LaLa there. I'll use the copy machine in the front office."

Mrs. B. returned with the enlarged copy and handed it to him. Despite its slightly fuzzy quality, the ring's markings were distinctive enough for Father Melvyn to make them out.

"Why is this so important?" she asked.

"What do you know about organized crime?"

"As a native New Yorker of Italian descent, I know a lot about the Italian mobs in the

Northeast, but not much here in Texas. According to the History Channel, they've all been decimated."

"Maybe, but that's a different subject." Father Melvyn took a quick gulp of coffee. "You know, it was Prohibition that provided the conduit for dangerous street thugs to become organized crime families. New York gets all the attention, but there were plenty of bootleggers all over the country, including here in Texas."

"Father, you amaze me," she said.

His eyes left the picture. "Why?"

"A nice Irish boy, who prefers coffee to tea and has this interest in organized crime. How is this possible?" she asked, half-joking.

"It's always interested me. And don't be naïve. There are organized crime families all over the world. When I arrived in America, I learned how they changed from running booze to running drugs." He lifted his cup, but before taking a drink, he spoke his tone grave. "They are bigger than ever and don't let anyone tell you otherwise. They've just buried themselves deeper." He held up his hand. "But I digress." He gulped his coffee.

"Here's why I'm concerned. In the years of Prohibition, the Spada Crime family operated in Texas. They were connected to the very powerful New Orleans mob. The Spada used jewelry as a sign of status, and the most important, especially the *made* men, wore rings like this one," he said, poking his finger at the ring in the picture. "It was a sign of position. If a man wore that ring, it meant he was near or at the top and gave orders. The message was, 'My hands don't get dirty any longer.'"

Father Melvyn continued the crash course on mob history. "Only the kingpin, the Don of the Spada family, and a few very important underbosses wore these rings. Perhaps they considered themselves the popes of organized crime." He shook his head in disgust. "Looks like they were designed like the old poison rings worn in the heyday of Papal power and corruption." He tapped the picture.

She stared at her boss. "Are you saying Isabel's great-grandfather was a criminal?"

"He might have been. If he was, Isabel might be opening a can of worms she's not prepared to confront." Father Melvyn was thoughtful. "I think we need to speak to her. Can you arrange to get her in here this afternoon?"

Mrs. B. went to the phone. As soon as Laurel picked up, she realized her mistake but couldn't hang up—they had Caller ID. After Laurel's greeting, Mrs. B. said. "Good morning, Laurel. I need to leave a message for Isabel. Please tell her to call me at this number."

"Of course. How's Lisa?"

"Improving every day. Thank you for asking."

"May I tell Isabel what this is about?"

Nosy. Mind your own business, Mrs. B. thought, but said, "No. Just ask her to call. Have a good day." She hung up, leaving Laurel no time for another question. Turning to Father Melvyn, she said, "That receptionist is too nosy by half. I should have called Isabel's cell number."

M-e-e-e-o-o-o-w. The plaintive cry from the doorway interrupted their conversation. "And good morning to you," Mrs. B. said.

Father Declan followed LaLa into the kitchen. "Good morning, Mrs. B. I hope you and Father Melvyn had enough time," he said.

The pastor looked at his watch. "We did, and thank you, Declan. I'm going over to the church to say the funeral mass for Mr. Ortiz this morning."

Father Declan told them, "I'm meeting with the Ladies of the Altar Ministry. We're going over to Martha's house to ask her to join."

"Great. Is everyone on board? No more objections?" Mrs. B. asked.

"Our lone dissenter decided to leave the ministry," he answered.

With that, the phones rang, and a busy day at St. Francis de Sales began.

The ballet company broke for lunch. Laurel walked back to the break room, sought out Isabel, and said, "Isabel, John's mother wants you to call her. Getting cozy with the artistic director's family, are we?" Laurel asked, sweet as pie.

One day I'm going to smack that bitch, Isabel thought. She looked up to see questioning looks from some of the other dancers. She knew there was no point trying to explain; it would only make things worse. Instead, she told Orlando, "See you back in rehearsal."

Isabel walked outside and called St. Francis.

Mrs. B. answered and immediately apologized. "I'm sorry, Isabel. I shouldn't have left a message with Laurel. She is nosy."

"Yes. That she is."

"Isabel, will you be able to stop by this afternoon after work? Father Melvyn has found some information he wants to discuss with you."

Promptly at 5:30, Isabel arrived at St. Francis. For the first time, LaLa failed to greet her. Instead, she remained on the staircase landing, paws crossed through the spindles, mouth slightly open, panting.

"Hi, LaLa," Isabel said, walking toward the cat. LaLa hissed, jumped up, and ran up the stairs. Surprised, Isabel stepped back. "Did I do something to upset her?"

The housekeeper's brows furrowed over her nose. "No. Sometimes she gets that way." Isabel felt a strange vibe from both the housekeeper and the cat.

"Glad you could come in," Father Melvyn said, dashing into the office, carrying books and papers. He dropped the load on the desk.

He opened the first book to the page where he'd stashed a copy of Isabel's photo. He placed that alongside the picture that Mrs. B. had enlarged. "Isabel, look at these. What do you see?"

She saw it immediately. "It looks like the same ring Rafael is wearing." She looked up. She didn't like the look in the priest's eyes. "Why is this important?" she asked.

Father Melvyn explained the design of the piscatorial rings worn by popes and the history of the poison rings from Medieval and Renaissance times. He told her how mobsters, godless men though they were, often used religious symbols.

Tired from a long day of rehearsal, Isabel showed her impatience. "This is all very interesting, Father, but—

Father Melvyn opened a second book. He showed her pictures of the rings worn by the Spada crime family. "Look at Rafael's ring and look at these pictures."

"So?"

"Your great-grandfather disappeared in the height of Prohibition," Father Melvyn said. "The ring he wore is exactly like the ones worn by the Spada." Father Melvyn sighed. "You must face the possibility that Rafael was a high-ranking member of that Italian crime family. And that may be the reason he disappeared."

"Stop." Isabel jumped up. "My great-grandfather was not a criminal. It's the Asturias family. They were and probably still are criminals." "And," she blurted, "It was Fernando Asturias, the second, who ran down and killed my grandmother. Why aren't you investigating them?"

Father Melvyn stood up. "Please calm down, my dear. I'm trying to explain..."

"No." She flew to the front door and yanked it open hard enough for it to hit the adjacent wall. "You are a liar. I came to you for help. I thought you were on my side!" she shouted and ran out of the rectory.

## CHAPTER 33

## ADELINA CABRERO-SANCHEZ

Nando half-listened to his sister's plan. He had questions. Things didn't fit. Where was she getting her information?

"Nando, pay attention, Victoria snapped. "If you screw this up, I'll--"

"I won't screw it up, but what makes you think there's gold hidden in the theater?"

"Victor's journals."

"Are you delusional? Where are you getting all of this? I've read Victor's journals. They don't say anything about Rafael Sanchez, gold, or the Italian mob."

Victoria didn't answer.

"You'd better tell me. Where are you getting these stories? I swear, Victoria. I'll blow this whole scheme wide open."

Victoria stared at him.

"I mean it."

"There's one more journal you haven't seen."

Nando grabbed her wrist. "Bitch! Still holding out on me. Where is it? Get it—now."

Victoria pulled her arm away. "Fine."

Nando heard her run up the stairs to her bedroom. When she returned, she dropped the last journal on the table.

Nando flipped through the pages. "Some of the ink is faded, hard to read, but I will, and I'll come to my own conclusions."

"There's no time." Victoria's words were clipped. "We caught a break when the theater closed, but it will reopen next week." Then, almost to herself, she added, "I know where the hidden room is, and I think I've figured out the best place to breakthrough."

"Is that what you were looking for the night you killed Adam Leightman?"

Victoria's stare was hard as granite.

Nando looked away. "And what's your problem with the dancer, that Reardon girl? What does she have to do with all of this."

"She's nosing around. I think she's trying to find proof that the land under the Rue de L'Histoire Theatre belonged to her great-grandfather. But, of course, she can't prove it."

She pointed at the journal in Nando's hand. "Victor hated Rafael Sanchez because Sanchez ran booze for the Italian mob, and he was good, too good. He was cutting into Victor's profits." Victoria paced while she talked.

"Victor was the head of Las Cruces Negras, the most powerful Mexican mob at the time. He drove the Italians out and took control of all the liquor coming into Texas. His journal says that he 'took care' of Sanchez, but he didn't want a turf war with the Italians, so he started a rumor that Rafael had betrayed the Spadas and disappeared with a fortune in gold, leaving his family behind.

"According to Victor, Rafael's house was set on fire by the Spadas. Victor moved fast. He took over Rafael's booze customers and drove the remaining Italians out of Austin, then used his political connections and bribery, paid off someone in the Land Office, and got Sanchez's properties deeded to him."

Nando flipped through the journal. "Can't make this shit up. Nice family. We could sell it to Hollywood," he quipped.

"Cut the crap," she snarled. "It's called survival of the fittest."

"How do you know the dancer is searching?"

"Because I collided with her on the steps of the appraisal office a few weeks ago. At the ballet gala, I tried to speak to her nicely, but she was hostile."

"Did she say anything?"

"She said, 'I know what your family did.'" Victoria shrugged. "I don't understand what she thinks she can do, but if she runs her mouth, it could dust up trouble. And if she has any inkling about the gold — "

"But she wasn't specific?"

"No," Victoria said.

"And you're *sure* there's no other reason for her hostility?" Nando asked, then paused for dramatic effect, grinning like a Cheshire cat, enjoying his sister's discomfort.

Victoria's eyes glittered. "If you know something, spit it out. We don't have time to play twenty questions."

"Don't like it when I hold out on you?"

"You're wasting time," Victoria retorted.

"Twenty-five years ago, Dad was at a party in Dripping Springs. He drove home drunk. It was early morning and foggy. He managed to get back to Austin without being picked up by the police, but he fell asleep at the wheel, hit a woman on her way to early mass, and then fled the scene. The woman died a few days later. Grandfather called in some favors. It was recorded as an accident. The story was he thought he'd hit a deer."

"I know all that. What has it to do with the Reardon girl, and how did you find out? It was supposed to be a big secret."

Nando laughed. "The advantages of having your father for a drinking buddy. He blabbed the whole story. Did you ever wonder why he always had a driver?"

"Extravagance. Why else? Honestly, until he drove the business into the ground, I never gave it much thought."

"No, sister-woman. After grandfather fixed the inquest, he imposed the condition that Dad could never drive again."

Victoria slammed her bottle of water on the counter. "And how does that relate to Reardon?"

"The woman he killed was Adelina Cabrero-Sanchez."

"So?" Victoria almost shouted the word twirling her hand, indicating he should get on with it.

"Adelina Cabrero-Sanchez was Reardon's grandmother!"

Nando let that sink in. "Adelina's husband was distraught and swore he'd kill Dad. After the hearing, Oratio Sanchez was picked up a couple of times for stalking him." Nando went to the refrigerator for a bottle of water. "I overheard Grandfather telling Dad that he'd hired a P.I. to track the old man. Sanchez was shipped off to New York to live with one of his daughters." Nando folded his arms across his chest and grinned. "So, now, you know."

"Stop gloating." Victoria paced. "That might explain Reardon's hostility, but does she know about Rafael's gold? She could try to make a claim, and that I can't have."

Nando watched Victoria and thought he could see the wheels turning in her head. "Guess I'd better read this journal, fast," he said, waving it at Victoria.

"Guess you'd better," she snapped. "I'll deal with her later." Victoria pointed her finger at her brother. "Read all you want, but you'd better stay focused because we need to act fast and act now."

# CHAPTER 34

## SNOW QUEEN

On Wednesday morning, Isabel took her spot at the barre. Her arms and neck muscles felt tight. It was a miracle that her whole body wasn't one big knot of tension after she'd met with Father Melvyn and Mrs. B. She was offended that the priest would even suggest that her great-grandfather was a mobster.

The music began. The opening exercises didn't require much instruction from John. He walked along the line of dancers, moving an arm here or a leg there.

Isabel tried to focus. She paid particular attention to the knee that was still sore from the fall and the scrape.

"Don't force it," John whispered as he passed her. Isabel nodded. The shape of the bandage under her tights was visible. She'd thought of taking it off before class, but the scrape still oozed a bit. It wouldn't do to have any bloody fluid seeping through.

John adjusted her free arm. "Shoulders down, Isabel. Too much tension in your hand," he said, tapping her thumb with his forefinger.

Isabel took a deep breath, and without changing the position of her fingers, she used her mental power to relax the muscles. She'd always taken pride in the fact that everyone said she moved her hands beautifully. She saw John's questioning look. "Breathe," she ordered through clenched teeth.

By the end of class, when they did the most difficult jumps, Isabel felt her knee functioning without any stiffness, and she'd successfully refocused on her technique.

The dancers gathered in the corner and prepared for the Grande Jetés sequence. The pianist chose "Mack the Knife' by Kurt Weill and upped the tempo to drive the dancers into the air and across the floor.

"Lift. Split. Front and back legs at the same level. No drooping. I want to see the full split at the top of the jump," John ordered. He called out different corrections as each dancer flew across the stage.

Isabel took her start position in the corner. In two steps, she propelled herself from the corner and lifted high. She felt free and powerful like she could jump to the moon. When she finished, Orlando smiled. He and some of the dancers moved their hands in a silent clap. Others looked away. She understood the different body languages in the class.

When every dancer had completed the jumps, John didn't wait. "Reverence," he said, and the sweaty company assembled in the center of the studio for the last set of exercises.

"Take a fifteen-minute break, and then report to your rehearsals. After the break, Isabel and Orlando, you'll begin work on the Snow Pas," John said and left the room.

Dancers chatted and whispered, but Isabel sat alone on the floor in the back corner of the studio and adjusted her pointe shoe. This was a sensitive time.

Whenever cast lists were posted, there were always disappointments. Some dancers hoped for specific roles and didn't get them; others were annoyed at who was chosen for principal purposes.

Isabel had been cast as the Snow Queen. She knew whatever jealousies they felt would be over by the end of the week. They needed some space. Isabel smiled internally; she'd experienced her own disappointments and jealousies from time to time.

"How's the knee?" Orlando asked, dropping down next to her.

"It's fine," she answered.

"Good. You looked a little tired at the beginning of class today. Everything okay?"

"Just a bad night's sleep." She changed the subject. "Have you seen the video of the duet we'll be learning?" she asked.

"Yes. Have you?"

"I did. It's beautiful. Very athletic. Lots of jumps and turns."

"That's why I was happy to see your Grande Jetés fly across the toom," Orlando whispered and nudged her with his elbow.

Isabel smiled at the compliment. "And that shoulder sit from a running start!" she exclaimed. "It's exciting. Dramatic."

While they waited for John, she let her guard down, and her mind wandered back to the confrontation with Father Melvyn the day before.

Forget it! She gave a mental order, reminding herself not to let anything spoil this. Finally, she and Orlando stood up and shook out their legs.

John walked in. "Ready?" he asked.

# CHAPTER 35

## TAIL ON FIRE

Mrs. B. placed two cups of coffee on the table. Father Melvyn couldn't hide his bewilderment.

"So, Mrs. B, what did you make of Isabel's reactions yesterday?" Father Melvyn asked.

"I wasn't surprised. She was shocked. You know she adored her grandfather and never heard even a whisper that her great-grandfather was a criminal. People don't exactly brag or advertise those connections." Mrs. B. stirred her coffee. "She doesn't understand what it has to do with the situation at the theater, and honestly, Father, neither do I."

"Perhaps nothing," he answered. "But I didn't have a chance to explain; she flew out of here like her tail was on fire. Of course, yesterday was the first time Isabel mentioned that it was an Asturias who ran down her grandmother and got away with it." Father Melvyn shook his head. "This feud goes deep. That alone might explain the hostility, but I don't know." He grimaced. "Nothing makes sense."

"You're right. It doesn't." The girl can't hurt Victoria or her family. The theft of property was too long ago, and the hit and run? Well, it's more recent, but again, there's nothing to be done." They sipped their coffee.

Lala sat on the chair at the far end of the table, watching them. Almost to herself, Mrs. B. said, "LaLa knew something was going to happen." She told Father Melvyn about the cat's reaction as soon as Isabel arrived, but the priest wasn't paying attention.

Father Melvyn was far off. He stroked his mustache. "First, if Isabel knows there's nothing she can do about either the property or the hit and run, so does Asturias." He held his finger up, stressing the point. "So, why is Victoria hostile? What is she afraid of?"

Father Melvyn reached for one of Mrs. B.'s cinnamon rolls. "I looked up the family on the internet," he said between bites. "They've had plenty of negative publicity because of her father, now deceased, and her brother, both flagrant drinkers and playboys."

"I did too, and I found something else. Asturias Enterprises filed for Chapter 11. That means they are restructuring. Doesn't that usually mean financial troubles?" She nibbled one of the rolls. "Why, then," she wondered aloud, "has Asturias become the financial savior of the ballet company, and why is she hanging around there so much?"

"Pieces are missing from this picture," the priest added.

"Perhaps it's time to call Jake?" she suggested.

Without warning, Lala jumped off the chair with such vigor that it flew backward. She began to growl and galloped into the hall before the bell rang.

When Mrs. B. arrived at the front door, there stood Jake Zayas. Mrs. B. smiled. Speak of the wolf, and the wolf appears. She kept that thought to herself.

"A few minutes of your time, please, Sammi?" Jake leaned over and pecked her cheek.

"Sure. Come in. Coffee? I just made a fresh pot."

He nodded. "How is Lisa doing?" he asked.

"She's doing well. I think she'll be home in a few days. The doctors are pleased with her progress. She's mending quickly."

In the kitchen, Father Melvyn greeted Jake and handed him a cup of coffee.

"Cinnamon roll?" Mrs. B. offered.

A series of meows made them look down. LaLa sat at Jake's feet. "Is she preparing to bite, scratch, or pee on my leg?" he asked.

Father Melvyn laughed. "None of the above. I think she's just greeting you."

"Sammi, there's something you should know, and I wanted you to hear it from me."

Mrs. B.'s eyebrows lifted. "And that is?"

"You know enough about police procedure to understand that we investigate everyone connected to a crime or its victims." He paused. "Has John mentioned that he's heard from friends in Dallas?"

"No. Why would he?"

Jake sighed. "I sent Marv Clingman there to speak to his former company about him and Lisa." Jake paused. "You know spouses are always first in line as suspects, but we don't see any evidence, at this time, that John had anything to do with it."

Mrs. B. sputtered in frustration.

Father Melvyn saw a pink sunrise creep up her neck.

"Now, Mrs. B.," the priest said in his most soothing tone. "Jake didn't have to tell you at all. They have a job to do."

Mrs. B. sucked in a breath. "I do understand, but if you have reservations about my son's relationship with his wife," she said, pointing at the detective, "you are wasting valuable investigative time."

"I agree, Sammi," Jake answered and changed direction. "Do you know the stage manager, Tony Volpe?"

"I know of him."

"Do you know what his relationship is with the ballet company? Has John mentioned any arguments or disagreements with him?"

"Not that I know. John's never said anything about any problems. Why are you asking me?"

Jake stared at her. "I'll be asking John, too. I thought if there was a problem, he might have mentioned it to you."

"Are you looking at the stage manager?"

"We are looking at everybody who works in the theater."

"I haven't gotten any hints or complaints from my son about the theater crew."

"Thanks, Sammi." Jake headed to the front door then turned back. "Give my love to John and Lisa." He paused. "And if you do hear anything, you will call me, right?" Mrs. B. nodded after a heartbeat's hesitation.

After Jake left, Father Melvyn asked, "Think he suspects we have information?"

"Right now, I'm annoyed, and I don't care what he suspects. Looking at my son for attempted murder!" Mrs. B. waved the subject off. "I don't like it even if he's only doing his job." She looked at her boss. "Before he arrived, I had suggested telling him, but it's not time. He has to go through the process of investigating everyone. I'm not sure he's ready to hear this story."

Father Melvyn agreed. "Anyway, after her abrupt and emotional departure yesterday, we aren't sure if we are ever going to hear from Isabel again."

The priest felt that he'd failed the young woman.

## CHAPTER 36

## MAYBE IT IS A GHOST

After spending the night in the theater, Tony went home to catch a few hours of shut-eye. He returned to the theater at his usual time, worried that his plan wasn't going to work. Sitting at his desk, he mulled over the situation when there came a triple knock on his door. "What's up, Charlie?"

"Maybe you better come out and see this." Tony followed Charlie across the stage. In the wings, a sandbag sat in a puddle of dust. Its rope was unwound from the pulley and hung loose. "How can this be?" he muttered. Charlie was about to tie the rope. "Leave it," Tony said. "When the crew gets here, I want them to see." Tony caught Charlie's knowing look.

"Was everything okay when you left?" Charlie asked.

"What do you mean?" Tony's heart thudded.

"You left at six last night, right? Was everything secure?"

Keep your wits about you, Tony warned himself. "Yes."

The stage door opened; the crew had arrived. Tony gave a loud whistle, then shouted, "Over here, please." They assembled. "Anybody know why this rope should have come loose?" There were curses and murmurings, but no one could account for it.

"Check the condition of the rope," Tony ordered. "See if it's frayed. Check the pulley too. Maybe it's loose, and the rope slipped off."

"I check those ropes every day, and I make sure the pulley handles are set and locked. This handle is in the release position," Mel said.

"Maybe it is a ghost," Charlie said and laughed. "Can I clean this up now?" he asked before anyone could chide him for the ghost joke.

Tony was cross but overlooked Charlie's remark. He returned to his office. Tonight, I will come in earlier, he decided.

Even though Sammi had gotten mad as hell, Jake was relieved that he'd told her that they'd looked at her son as a suspect. He picked up Marv at the precinct, and they headed back to the Rue de L'Histoire Theatre, this time without giving Volpe the benefit of notice.

"He has a good motive for Leightman, but I don't understand cutting the wire and causing the accident," Marv said.

"Maybe a smoke-screen. An attempt to take attention off him. Let's see how he reacts to our unannounced visit," Jake answered.

When they arrived at the theater, the stage door was locked. Jake put his finger on the buzzer. A few minutes later, the custodian opened it. Not depending on Charlie's memory, Jake and Marv flashed their badges.

"Is Mr. Volpe in?" Marv asked.

"He's backstage. You're barking up the wrong tree," Charlie said with a grin.

"And why is that?" Jake asked.

Charlie waved at them to follow and led them into a side hall. "I've been here longer than anyone else. I'm telling you, forces are pushing against this ballet company."

"What kind of forces are you talking about?" Marv asked.

"You're talking about the curse," Jake said, keeping his voice neutral.

Charlie looked from one to the other. "Laugh, all you want. Not everything is of this world."

Jake drew a breath. "Even if there are otherworld-forces, they are operating through humans, and we intend to find them and punish them."

"Do you have any ideas about who might be in league with the dark side?" Marv asked.

Charlie looked at them. "Tony is over there," he said, pointing toward the other side of the stage, then turned and walked away.

Without comment, Jake and Marv headed across the stage and flashed their badges. The men stopped talking. Tony stepped forward. "We have more questions for you, Tony. We can talk here or at the precinct. Your choice," Jake said.

Tony gave a few instructions, checked something on his clipboard, and handed it to Mel. "Finish this for me, and make sure these floors are swept clean before someone slips and falls."

Jake felt the unfriendly stares thrust at them and heard unhappy murmurs from the crew. He said, "We'll be back to talk to all of you."

Two hours later, the detectives left Tony's office, giving him a final warning. "Don't leave town."

After the door closed behind them, Tony saw his crew hanging about across from the stage door; they scowled at the detectives. Charlie stood with them, his arms folded across his chest.

Tony turned to his men. "Mel, did you finish the checklist?"

"Yep. All done. Everything is in order. That sandbag coming down must have been a fluke. There's no reason for it to have happened."

Charlie harrumphed, shook his head, and walked away.

Tony wasn't in the mood for ghost talk. "Okay. Let's knock off for today. We'll resume tomorrow."

"Join us for a beer, Tony," Steve said.

"Thanks, fellas, but the cops blew my schedule. Too much to catch up on. I'll take a raincheck."

Tony sat in his office pushing papers around, looking busy but accomplishing nothing. He was worried. He needed to find answers fast, or he'd end up back in jail.

With his headlights out, Tony circled the Rue de L'Histoire parking lot at 9:30 p.m. As expected, there were no cars. He left the theater and drove to another street, parked, and walked back, keeping to the shadows.

He let himself in quickly, moved to the alarm pad, disarmed it, then rearmed the system to ensure no one could enter unannounced.

His nerves were on edge because something had happened in the theater after he'd left the night before. He decided he'd stay all night, and when Charlie arrived in the morning, he'd say he fell asleep at his desk.

He passed his office door and was relieved to see the glow from the ghost light. Tony headed up the dark fly loft. Using his flashlight, he looked down on the stage and checked the equipment within his reach. Everything was secure. He looked at the levers: all locked. He looked up at the flies, nodded, and returned to ground level.

The masking curtain, hiding equipment, nuts, bolts, and pulleys from the audience, was down. Though it was pitch black behind it, Tony walked from one side of the stage to the other, sweeping his flashlight back and forth. A pile of wood was stacked precariously outside the prop room. He'd have the crew move it first thing the next day. He twisted the knobs on the storage closet and prop rooms—all locked.

Content, he went back to his office, sat in the dark and sipped his coffee, fighting the desire to close his eyes until something jerked him like a bolt of electricity, but the sensation was almost imperceptible.

He wasn't alone. The atmosphere changed, and suddenly all sleepiness left him. Hairs rose on his arms; his heart beat faster. Straining his ears and eyes, he saw and heard nothing. Beads of sweat formed at his hairline.

Careful not to make a sound, he moved off his chair. In the doorway, he thought he saw something move at the edge of the ghost light. Was it coming toward him? Tony froze and held his breath.

It stopped.

Not sure if he wanted to hide under his desk or run out of the theater, Tony stood still and waited until his breathing evened out. He listened intently. No unusual noises. The ghost light shone steady.

Gathering his courage, forcing one foot in front of the other, he left his office and circled behind the masking curtain again. This time without the benefit of his flashlight, his steps were slow and deliberate; he was glad he'd walked through when he first came in.

The old trusses and rigging ropes gave him cover until he reached the pile of lumber on the other side of the stage.

The prop room door was ajar, and a faint light seeped out. Something scraped. Crouched below the trusses, he didn't dare go any closer. He angled his head to hear better.

Tap, tap; tap,tap,tap.

Did he hear the sound of metal teeth cutting through wood?

His heart raced, but he remained motionless. A strange pungent odor assailed his nostrils, making his nose wrinkle. Ugh. The stink overpowered the usual smells of greasepaint and wood dust. Did someone gag, or did he?

He heard ghostly murmurs, shuffling, faint sounds, but nothing came out of the prop room. More scraping, and then the door to the prop room squeaked closed, cutting off all light.

He turned and crawled back the way he'd come, looking over his shoulder as often as he could, expecting something to hit him from behind any second. Controlling his urge to run, Tony reached the office side of the stage before he stood up.

Terrified and breathing hard, he crept into his office and sat on the floor behind his desk, where he remained until his pulse and breathing evened out. Okay. Let's try again, he thought, pocketing his cell phone.

Inching his way back to his position behind the stacked lumber outside the prop room, he was accompanied by the faint scurrying of invisible night creatures. All remained dark. The next time he risked a look at his watch, it was 3:00 a.m. The feeling in the theater had changed. Whoever or whatever it was had left the building. But how?

He stood up and went to the prop room; the door was unlocked. Ignoring his thumping heart, he used his cell phone for light and stepped in.

Moving the cell phone light methodically around the room, he saw that everything was in its place. The shelves were neatly stacked, as always. Nothing had been touched. Small props were on the shelves, and the sign-out sheets were on the desk, but a heavy film of dust covered them.

"What's this?" He aimed the light on his cell phone. A faint crunch under his shoe. Tony squatted down and ran his finger through it more dust. It was gritty. He didn't move, just allowed his light to follow the trail. It was heaviest in front of the only cabinet in the room.

He walked over to it and opened the doors. The weighted canvas sheets were neatly stacked, as always. He closed the doors and looked around the room—heavy dust on the left side.

Sliding his hand behind and along the edges of the cabinet, he felt nothing unusual. When he pulled his hand out, the back of his finger hit a rough edge in the wall. That's Odd.

Turning his palm to the wall, Tony reached as far back as he could. The wall was broken. "What the hell is going on?"

He nudged the cabinet away from the wall and saw the shape of a rough opening. Pushing harder, he made a space between the wall and the cabinet that he could squeeze through.

Ignoring the dank, moldy, and odd smells that made his nostrils curl, Tony raised his cell phone for light; his jaw dropped.

The rough-hewn stone of this hidden,

unfinished room astonished him, but not more than the stack of gold bars and what looked like canvas sacks. He walked over and lifted the top bar. It was heavy.

Moving toward the bags, he noticed something crawl behind them. Looks like coins, he thought and backed away, using his cell phone to scan and illuminate small areas.

He turned the light to the opposite side of the room; shock jerked his arm. The phone fell and hit the floor in front of his foot.

With trembling fingers, Tony reached for it and again pointed its light at the horrifying vision that had knocked the phone from his hand.

Lying flat, with its skull at an unnatural angle, was a skeleton.

Fighting the urge to run but regaining his wits, he snapped pictures of the bones with their tattered clothes, then turned and snapped photos of the gold and the sacks. He backed out of the room, slid out from behind the cabinet, and gulped for air as if he'd run a ten-minute mile.

As fast as he could, Tony made sure everything was as he found it, then he crept across the stage and back to his office.

He needed to think—and he needed a drink.

# CHAPTER 37

## PHANTOMS

Hey, Tony!" Steve yelled. "The Nutcracker truck is here."

Right on time, Tony thought. He left his office
and headed to the loading dock. He'd spoken with the artistic directors the week before. Since there were no other performances scheduled at the theater, they'd agreed to have the sets delivered earlier than usual to give the crew more time for adjustments and repairs, but he struggled to keep his mind on business.

Thoughts of last night's discovery possessed him, making everything seem surreal.

The driver and his assistant dropped the ramp to help the stage crew take everything off the truck. When it was time for the grandfather clock, it took three men to move it.

"Doesn't it have rollers under it?" Tony asked.

Steve looked at the manifest. "Supposed to," he said. "Looks like they're broken. This thing needs some work." Steve raised the masking curtain to keep it from getting too dusty from the incoming sets, making all of the cavernous backstage area visible.

"Leave it there," Tony said, pointing to the back wall opposite the prop room. When the clock was in place, Tony walked over to check its stability. Flat on the floor, it was solid. His hand accidentally hit the front panel just below the clock's face. It swung open. On closer inspection, Tony saw that the spring door had a dark screen set in it. He looked inside the clock. There was a little shelf seat. He realized that was for a dancer to hide. He'd ask the artistic directors.

Tony and Steve checked off the items as they were unloaded to ensure everything on the list made it into the theater. "Thanks, fellas," he said when the delivery was complete.

Charlie locked the loading dock door, and the crew began the work of storing the incoming sets and backdrops. They knew their jobs. Tony didn't interfere. "If you have any questions, I'll be in my office."

The company had ordered a ramp for the end of the first act. In the fake falling snow, the corps, followed by the Snow Queen and her Cavalier, would exit up the ramp into the wings as the curtain descended. Dramatic, Tony thought. His crew would build it along with a staircase for the dancers to descend beyond the audience's view. He decided to look over everything else after the men had the pieces situated, but he walked out of his office and gave a loud whistle to get everyone's attention.

"Tomorrow, the artistic directors will be here. We'll put some of the set pieces on stage, so let's keep the house set from Act 1 easily accessible." The crew nodded. Looking back at the grandfather clock, an idea came to him.

At quitting time, Tony called his crew. "How about that rain check?" he asked.

Charlie chose to stay longer to clean up some of the grime that came in with the sets.

"When you're done here, join us," Tony told him.

At the bar, Tony laughed and joked with his men. Charlie joined them late, but they welcomed him. It took all of his self-control not to look at his wristwatch. At 9:00 p.m., he yawned.

"Okay, fellas, this is it for me. Gotta get home and get ready for tomorrow. I've got lots of notes to review."

A half-hour later, Tony sneaked back into the theater and went straight to the grandfather clock. He opened the false door under the clock face, stepped inside, and pulled it shut. After peering through the screen, he stepped out again and unlocked the prop room, praying that his not-so-dead ghosts wouldn't come back yet. Returning to the grandfather clock, he rocked the heavy piece into position to see into the room. When he was satisfied that he had the maximum vision, he locked the prop room, climbed back into the secret compartment, and waited.

He wasn't very comfortable in the narrow space and hoped that something would happen soon. To take his mind off the feeling of claustrophobia, he thought about last night's discovery and wondered who these phantoms were, where they came from, and how they got in without setting off the alarm. He shuddered and rejected the thought that they materialized out of thin air.

Tony worried that nothing would happen when the prop room door opened and light filtered into the blackness. A figure stepped out. From inside the room, an unseen voice said, "Make sure no one is here."

The shadowy figure headed to center stage and into the weak circle of light from the ghost lamp, but that was out of Tony's field of vision unless he opened the clock's false door. He didn't. A few minutes later, the shadow's voice came closer. "There's no one here." It was a man's voice. "Looks like a lot more stuff back here tonight," he said.

"Sets were delivered today. Come in here, and let's get this done." The voice sounded like a woman. How did they know the theater's schedule?

The dark shape walked toward the grandfather clock. Tony's heart skipped a beat. Afraid the whites of his eyes might be visible, Tony squeezed his eyes shut and held the door handle so it couldn't pop open accidentally. He felt rather than saw the black mass standing in front of the clock. Hands ran up and down the clock, making a soft swishing sound. Tony barely breathed.

Louder this time, the feminine voice said, "What are you doing out there?" The shadow moved away. Tony relaxed but controlled his breathing; a loud sigh wouldn't be wise.

"Come on." Tony was sure it was a woman. "We have at least two hours of work here. I want this finished tonight. There will be too much activity in this place starting tomorrow."

Definitely not ghosts. The dim light from the prop room allowed him to see two figures intermittently: one tall, one short. He heard the scraping sound and knew they were moving the cabinet away from the wall to get into the hidden room. Who the hell are they? he wondered.

Twitching with impatience, Tony wished he could get out of the clock and watch. He couldn't, but he strained his ears to hear. The higher voice said, "Here's the wheelbarrow, but the wheels are wobbly. I think more than six will be too heavy. We'll have to make more than two trips. When we're done, I'll repair the wall."

"Can't wait to finish this. It's creepy, and it stinks," the man said.

"Don't be such a ninny. The smell was worse last night," said the other.

"My God. You are cold-blooded," the man answered. Tony heard sounds like wheels scrunching on the floor from the heavy load. Then the light went out, and the room was silent. How were they getting in and out, and where did they go? The question drove him crazy.

Letting himself out of the grandfather clock, Tony crept to the open prop room door that they'd forgotten to close. He looked in. No one.

New sections of wallboard were on the floor waiting to be used. He stepped into the secret room, pulled out his cell phone, and took another series of pictures. The coin sacks were gone along with some of the gold bars, but the skeleton hadn't been moved. He wondered if they intended to take it out.

He checked the rough, far walls of the secret room, searching for a door. Nothing. Backing out of the room, he used his foot to blend his footsteps into the dust. He was about to return to the clock when a long edge of light appeared on the far wall, and a panel of shelves swung open.

I'll be damned! he thought as he ducked out of the room, finding cover behind the open door. Peeking through the space between the door and the jamb, he saw two black-clad figures walk through the poorly lit opening.

When they stepped around the cabinet and into the hidden room, Tony returned to the safety of the grandfather clock.

Hours passed. The phantoms moved in and out of his field of vision. Once more, they disappeared, and the prop room went black for a while. They returned and were silent, only grunting occasionally from the effort of reconstructing the wall. Hope they know what they're doing, Tony quipped to himself.

Wood scraped on the concrete floor. Tony surmised that they must be pushing the cabinet back in place.

The higher voice said, "Wait." The smaller figure came out of the prop room and headed to center stage, and the faint illumination from the ghost light went out.

"Why did you do that?"

"I'm a ghost." The answer was followed by a high-pitched laugh.

"We're done. Let's go." Definitely a man's voice. The taller shadow stood in the doorway of the prop room.

"Make sure you lock this door. You forgot last night."

That voice. Then it hit him.

It's her!

Tony almost fell out of the clock. Now it all made sense. His legs felt weak from shock. He sat on the seat inside the clock's compartment for what seemed like an eternity.

Looking at the time on his cell phone, he realized he'd been in the grandfather clock for two hours since they'd left; they weren't coming back. Tony left the clock, unlocked the prop room, and went inside.

There was very little dust; they'd cleaned up after themselves. He angled the cabinet away to see the wall. The opening had been covered over with the new wallboard. First, he snapped two pictures, then pushed the cabinet back into place. He looked at the wall where he'd seen a sliver of light but was afraid to search for a way to open it; his mind was reeling.

It was 4:00 a.m. when Tony left the theater. He contemplated calling the police on his way home, but how could he tell them such a fantastic tale? Now he knew the identity of the ghost haunting the theater. Did she kill Adams? Did she cause Lisa's accident?

When he got home, Tony was still wired. He printed out the pictures he'd taken on his cell phone. He could be a righteous citizen and report what he'd seen, but the police would never believe him. He wondered if Adam had surprised her, and she'd killed him, but accusing her would be folly. "No. I'm not suicidal," Tony muttered and looked at the pictures again. These asked more questions than they answered. He made notes.

- How did she know about the hidden room?
- Where does that secret door lead?
- What will she do with the gold?
- She and her accomplice resealed the room. Did they remove the skeleton? He'd taken multiple pictures of everything, both nights. The hole in the wall behind the cabinet, the secret room, the gold, and the skeleton hidden in it.

Tony labeled a folder INSURANCE and placed all of the photographs, notes, and questions in it. He was about to put it away, but something wasn't right. He took the pictures out again and lined them up. The removal of the gold bars and canvas bags from one night to the next was evident. He looked at the pictures of the skeleton.

There was a distance shot and a close-up taken the first night. He'd taken two more close-ups just a few hours ago. Placing them side by side, he compared the pictures. There was something on a finger, maybe a ring in the earlier pictures, but it was gone in the photographs he'd taken earlier, and so was the finger. "Ugh."

His stomach flipped. That's ghoulish, he thought.

# CHAPTER 38

## HOME FREE – ALMOST

The canvas sacks leaned against old furniture in the basement, and the gold bars were on the floor in disarray.

"Don't damage the bars. Stack them so I can see how big a hole I need to make in the foundation," Victoria said. She looked around. There were sections of heavy wood beams. "I'll saw these to shore up the opening. Don't want to weaken the foundation."

"Aye-aye, mon Capitan," Nando saluted. Victoria waved him over to the gold.

"Get to work," she said.

While Nando bent over the gold, Victoria pulled out the sledgehammer that had crushed Adam Leightman's skull. She'd hidden it behind a box. Bigs of dried blood and hair were stuck to it, but there was no time to worry about that. Then, taking a deep breath, she looked away and swung it as hard as she could.

"Ahhh!"

Nando screamed as the sledgehammer exploded against the concrete wall. "You scared the hell out of me!"

Victoria chuckled. I could just as easily have smashed it against your fool head. "Here, you do it," she said, handing it to him. "You're stronger, and it will go faster."

When he took his turn swinging the sledgehammer, any remnants of Leightman's skull were gone or covered with cement dust.

The sun was shining through the dirty basement windows when they shoved the old breakfront back in place. Thanks to Victoria's engineering skills, their basement hiding place was secure.

Stuffed in the roughhewn cavity were the gold bars, coins, and bills left in the secret room of the theater all those years ago by their great-grandfather, Victor Reyes-Asturias.

"Tomorrow, I'll make a concrete form the size of the opening for a door," she said, writing measurements on a scrap of paper.

Sweaty, grimy, and tired, Victoria pushed wisps of hair off her face and looked at her brother. She began to laugh.

"What's so funny?" Nando asked. "You don't exactly look like a beauty queen."

"Six months ago, if anyone told me you would be my accomplice, I'd have laughed at them. You actually look pretty good. You've lost weight."

Nando ignored the compliment. "So, we have the money. We've sealed the wall in the theater. Now what?"

"First, we have to convert those bars into cash. The coins and bills in the canvas bags will be a different problem. We'll need a good coin dealer, several, probably. And the bills are probably out of circulation. We'll concentrate on the gold because we need an immediate infusion of cash. The creditors are pounding at the gates again, and Smithson is getting antsy. He wants us to sell the house. We were supposed to have it on the market already."

"I still think we should sell it. You can get a beautiful apartment downtown, and we'll have a great cover for the cash we'll get from the gold."
Victoria smiled at her brother and mimed applause.
"Bravo, brother. Well thought out, but I'm not ready to give up this house. Anyway, it'll take months before we've converted everything to cash. We can't do it too fast. It will draw attention. And, we need to seal off the tunnel on both ends and make the place real-estate pretty for potential buyers."

Victoria headed up the cellar steps. In the kitchen, she took out two bottles of water, handed one to Nando, and drank deeply from her own.

"Once you convert the bars, how are you going to get the money past Smithson?"

"I have a piece of property west of Houston. Smithson doesn't know about it. I'll cover some of it that way." She looked at Nando. She didn't tell him everything.

"Over the weekend," she continued. " I'll do some research. Don't want to sell the gold here in Austin. Too much chatter." She took another swig of water. "Any ideas?"

" Maybe." Nando stretched, yawned, and moved toward the stairs. "Get some sleep, Victoria."

Exhausted from the mental and physical strain, Victoria went to her bedroom, but even after a hot shower, sleep wouldn't come. She took the pad and pencil she kept on her bedside table and made notes:

- Find Gold Dealers

- Nando – will he keep his mouth shut? Stay away from booze, women, and gambling?

- Reardon – Any new information?

Victoria had sent her brother to romance Laurel, the Bernardi-Bono Ballet Company's receptionist. Laurel was a talker. From the first time she'd laid eyes on him, Laurel had become smitten with Nando.

Victoria felt she was almost home free and rid of the past if only she could get rid of that damned dancer. She returned to her list.

Sell the Houston property – private sale by owner, principals only. Satisfied with her plan, Victoria dozed.

Nando stripped and prepared to shower. His muscles ached from unaccustomed physical work. He felt like he'd aged twenty years in two nights. He could still smell the must and decay that had rushed out after Victoria opened the wall in the theater.

Desperate to get in a hot shower, he pulled off his sweaty, dirty clothes. Something hard fell and hit the floor with a dull thud. He picked up the tissue-wrapped lump. It was the ring he'd taken from the skeleton.

Last night, Victoria wouldn't let him near it for fear of bacteria. Tonight, he'd waited. When she was busy placing the gold bars in the wheelbarrow, he'd swallowed hard, reached for the skeleton's hand, and pulled off the lump of metal, dislodging a digit, which almost made him vomit.

Now, with a queasy stomach, he unwrapped the ring. With another tissue, he pulled the remnant of bone away and flushed it. Bile rose in his throat. Shuddering, he filled the sink with hot, soapy water and dropped the ring into it, then he stepped into the hot shower. Before he went to bed, he emptied the dirty water, and refilled the bowl with hot, soapy water and left the ring to soak. He looked forward to seeing it all cleaned up.

In bed, on the verge of sleep, the idea came to him. His eyes flew open. "Brilliant!" he almost shouted the word. He had a solution for Billy Slips.

## CHAPTER 39

## UNDERCURRENTS

Friday morning, sitting in rush-hour traffic, Mrs. B. thought about the pieces of the Rue de L'Histoire Theatre puzzle, and Isabel. They hadn't heard from her since she'd flown out of the rectory, furious at Father Melvyn for suggesting that her great-grandfather was a mobster. Mrs. B. sighed. Things didn't add up.

When John, Chelly, and Lisa had decided to go ahead with the rest of the season, Victoria went to bat for them with the board. She'd convinced the others to support and actively promote *Nutcracker.* If Asturias Enterprises was in such financial difficulty, why was Victoria spending time and treasure on the company?

Then there was Jake's investigation into John's and Lisa's backgrounds. She was still annoyed, but John hadn't mentioned it.

Still troubled, Mrs. B. arrived at the rectory to find Father Joe marking papers and drinking coffee at the kitchen table.

"Time does fly," she said when he told her he was preparing exams for the end of the first semester.

"I can't believe it either. Tempus Fugit." LaLa, who had installed herself on his lap, looked up and meowed. "I know LaLa. Time flies for kitty-cats, too."

Heavy footsteps approached from the hall. "Good morning," Father Melvyn said in his usual cheer. "Beautiful day, once again. Ahh, I love November."

M-e-e-o-o-w. As soon as the pastor entered the kitchen, LaLa jumped off Father Joe's lap and headed straight for the boss. In one leap, she was in Father Melvyn's arms, rubbing her head under his chin.

"Now, that's what I call a greeting," he said and sat down. Mrs. B. set his coffee down in front of him.

Father Joe excused himself. "It's off to class for me. See you later." He gulped the remains of his cup and headed out the kitchen door.

"Where is Father Declan this morning?" Mrs. B. asked.

"Early hospital call; he's not back yet. While it's quiet, let's talk about Thanksgiving. It's a few days away, can you believe it?" he asked.

"Who'will be on call?"

"I will." Father Melvyn scratched LaLa's head. "Joe was invited to spend it with friends from the university, and Declan was invited to join them. I didn't see any reason to spoil the day for them, so I said I'd take the morning mass and be on call. What are you doing?"

"John and Lisa are coming for dinner, and you are welcome to join us. If you're needed, the service will call your cell phone." She sat at the table and twisted her cup in her hand. "I called Isabel last night."

"How is she?" Father Melvyn asked, his tone guarded.

"A little cool. We only talked about the holidays. Her parents won't be here until the last *Nutcracker* performance, and they'll stay through Christmas. Her aunt and cousins from San Angelo will be here too." She paused. "I invited her for Thanksgiving."

"Did she accept?"

"Not at first, but I told her that John and Lisa were coming, so I guess she felt safe that we wouldn't speak of anything painful, or she doesn't want to offend her boss's mother. Either way, I wanted to break the ice."

"Do John and Lisa know?"

"Yes. They know I've taken a liking to Isabel. I told him that she'd called often to ask about Lisa because she didn't want to bother him at the studio."

"How is Lisa doing?" Father Melvyn asked.

"She's back at work. The Pilates instructor at the company is certified in physical therapy and has taken over Lisa's sessions." Father Melvyn waited for more. "John told me a couple of interesting things. First, he said ticket sales are through the roof. It seems that Adam's murder, coupled with the prop that plunged and injured Lisa, and the ghost rumors have been picked up by the papers."

Mrs. B. sipped her coffee. "People are buying tickets like crazy. The company is thinking about adding a performance, as suggested by Victoria. Go figure."

"That is interesting. So, Asturias is still very active with the company. Is she still hanging around, making Isabel nervous?"

"I don't think so, but someone else is. Her brother is now a frequent visitor, which relates to the second thing John said."

"Which is?"

"He, Lisa, and Chelly feel a strange, edgy undercurrent in the company, and they can't get a handle on it. The dancers are antsy and high-strung, and there was a peculiar tension between Tony Volpe and Victoria at the last production meeting."

"Did Isabel hint at anything?"

"I asked her if the dancers were excited about their first *Nutcracker* at the Rue. She said they were, but Victoria's brother was annoying everyone."

Mrs. B. reached for the coffee pot. "Isabel said that Nando is dating Laurel, who is strutting around like a peacock, sticking her nose into everyone's business, especially Isabel's." Mrs. B. refilled their coffee cups. "When Nando picks Laurel up at the studio, he takes the liberty of looking in on rehearsals, and he's always asking the dancers questions."

Distracted, Mrs. B. stirred her coffee. "Isabel said there's something about this guy they don't like, and Laurel brags that because of her, they may have another Asturias on the board, so no one dares complain."

"Maybe Victoria sent him to spy," Father Melvyn remarked.

"That's a thought," Mrs. B. answered, taking his dismissive response seriously.

"Any word from Jake?" he asked.

"No. I had dinner with him and Terri a couple of nights ago. He didn't discuss the case, only said there's nothing new.

"Right now, he and his partner are immersed in the gruesome beheadings. There've been two more. It's all over the papers."

With a series of chirps and twitters, LaLa jumped off Father Melvyn's lap and ran to the staircase landing, a heartbeat before the doorbell rang for the first time that day.

# CHAPTER 40

## GIVING THANKS AND MELTING ICE

Bright sunshine did nothing to alleviate the cold, blustery weather on Thanksgiving Day. Inside, Mrs. B. lit a fire in the fireplace and scrutinized the dinner table. Everything looked warm and festive, but she had second thoughts about the wisdom of having invited Isabel. The doorbell rang. Too late now, she thought and opened the door to three smiling, windblown, shivering faces.

"Happy Thanksgiving," they chorused.

Isabel smiled, but the reserve in her eyes was unmistakable. "Thank you for inviting me," she said and handed Mrs. B. a box of cookies.

M-e-o-o-w came the cry from the floor. Sasha and Ziggy waddled out from under the coffee table to greet the guests.

"You have cats, too. What are their names?" Isabel asked.

"Sasha and Ziggy. Feel free to introduce yourself before I lock them away. Otherwise, they'll invite themselves to the dinner table — with or without us."

Mrs. B. hung their coats and told them to sit in the living room and enjoy the fire. "John, pour us some wine," she said to her son.

John took over the bar duties and asked, "Is Father Melvyn joining us?"

Mrs. B. noticed Isabel's expression cloud. "No," she answered casually. "He's on hospital call today." Once she said that, Isabel visibly relaxed. Looks like Father Melvyn was right. Isabel is more comfortable without him here. Instead of going to the kitchen to finish preparing dinner, Mrs. B. stayed in the living room to goose the conversation.

"Bruschetta!" Lisa reached for one of her favorite appetizers.

"Better take one quick," John told Isabel. "My wife will eat them all."

Isabel took a bruschetta and held it. She was quiet.

"John," Mrs. B. said. "Do you remember that Thanksgiving Day when Kalya called a special rehearsal?"

John burst out laughing. "I haven't thought of that in years." He went on to tell the tales of his early ballet training with a Russian master. She'd call rehearsals at the last minute and at inconvenient times, and no one dared not show up.

Once Mrs. B. got her son talking about growing up in ballet, sharing memories and antics, Isabel visibly relaxed, and they roared with laughter at John's stories.

"I'd better get into the kitchen, or we may never eat," Mrs. B. said, excusing herself, but she continued to follow the conversation.

"Isabel, how old were you when you started to dance?" Lisa asked. At that point, Mrs. B. poked her head into the living room.

"Time for dinner," she called out, interrupting the conversation.

At the table, they joined hands. John said a Thanksgiving prayer. Then Mrs. B. served the turkey soup and regaled them with tales of life in her Italian-American community, where everyone watched out for each other–or spied, depending on your point of view.

"How did you celebrate Thanksgiving?" Isabel asked.

"To my parents," Mrs. B. explained, "Thanksgiving was a sacrosanct, American holiday, and my mother and grandmother wouldn't hear of anything Italian served that day."

After the soup, Mrs. B. carried the bird to the table and set it down in front of John. "Turkey time," she said and handed him the carving knife.

John stood up and ceremoniously carved with great care. "By the way, Mother, have you spoken to Corinne?"

"Not yet."

"Get ready. Corinne said she and her crew will arrive on Christmas morning. It will be like an invasion."

Mrs. B. laughed. "Your sister and her family can invade anytime!"

"My family will be here in time for the last Nutcracker performance," Isabel said.

"Wonderful. We look forward to meeting them. Are they staying through Christmas?" asked Lisa.

"Yes. They'll go back on the 30th, before the New Year's rush."

Mrs. B. thought Isabel's eyes were bright with excitement or was it the wine? Either way, Mrs. B. was happy she was enjoying the day.

It was 8:00 p.m. when John, Lisa, and Isabel took their care packages of food for the weekend.

"Mom. Fabulous dinner. Thanks," John said, pecking her cheek.

Lisa, kissed her mother-in-law. Turning to Isabel, she said, "We're so glad you joined us."

"Thank you for having me," Isabel said. She smiled at Mrs. B. and gave her a warm hug.

Waving goodbye, Mrs. B. closed the door and leaned on it, satisfied with how the day had gone. She was grateful that her son was a natural-born raconteur.

She felt that Isabel's icy distrust had definitely been broken down, and she hoped Isabel might begin to trust her again.

# CHAPTER 41

## FADE TO BLACK

Black Friday was just that. Black. Not only had the warmth of Thanksgiving Day faded, but the overcast skies also made the day grey and broiling–as if the atmosphere suffered its own holiday hangover.

Mrs. B. woke up exhausted. Thanksgiving had been a lovely day, but the nightmare had disturbed her sleep again. This time the Sugar Plum's face shifted from Lisa to Isabel and back to Lisa. She felt violated, vulnerable, and afraid, as if something evil was sneaking into her head at night while she was defenseless.

Taking a cup of coffee, she turned on the TV. The news carried reports and videos of mobs crushing each other to be first in the stores for the Black Friday sales. Good day to stay home, she thought over her morning coffee. Sasha and Ziggy ate contentedly. Mrs. B. scanned the kitchen. Clean. Pots and pans sat on the drainboard next to the sink, but she was restless, unsettled. She called Father Melvyn to tell him she was dropping leftovers at the rectory.

"Are you sure he's reliable?" Victoria asked. Her tone was quiet. She and Nando seemed to have arrived at an uneasy truce. She hoped his cooperation meant that he now understood their survival depended on them getting along.

Nando nodded and listened to Victoria go over the timetable again.

"On Monday," she said, "you take four of the gold bars to the dealer you found in San Antonio. They are worth at least $250,000.00. He knows you want cash, right?" Again Nando nodded. She continued. "I have a buyer for my property outside of Houston. They've agreed to $300,000."

"You listed it for $475,000. Why so low?"

"Cash deal. I will record the sale at half a million, which covers the cash you'll bring back. Most of that will go to creditors, two of whom will be paid off. That will make old Mr. Smithson happy. After Christmas, let's make the next sale in Dallas."

"Okay." Nando was quiet.

Victoria continued to punch numbers on the calculator. "By the way," she said, "the ballet company opens with their *Nutcracker* next Saturday. Be sure you are here for it. I want you at the gala." With a sly smile, she added, "I hear Laurel loves her new sense of importance, but have you learned anything about the Reardon girl?"

"She's dancing two major roles. One in the first act and the other in the second. It seems there are lots of jealousies in the company."

"I know that. Anything about her personal life?"

"The artistic director's mother called asking for Isabel. Laurel thinks Isabel is cozying up to John's mother to advance in the company."

Victoria made a dismissive face. "Nothing else?" she kept punching keys on her calculator and making notes.

"Isabel's mother called and left a message. Looks like Isabel's family will be here for Christmas."

Victoria's head popped up. "Hmmm. Stay on that. The mother is a Sanchez, right?"

Nando nodded and continued. "Nosy Laurel asked when they were coming. Mrs. Reardon told her the dates."

Victoria stopped punching keys on the calculator and sighed. They should have stayed the hell out of Austin, she thought, with disgust.

"I can't wait to be free of those meddlesome people," she snapped.

# CHAPTER 42

## DOUBLE CROSS

To his left, the red prelude of a sunny day streaked the dawn sky as Nando sped south on the wide-open highway not yet congested with rush-hour traffic. Thanksgiving was over, and the Christmas rush was about to begin. He hoped this year he might be able to enjoy it.

He anticipated his sister's reaction to what he was about to do but pushed his worries aside. Once he got past this crisis, he'd smooth it over with her. His fear of Billy Slips was greater than his fear of Victoria. Besides, he thought, blood is thicker than water. She'll forgive me.

Nando had contacted Billy the day before Thanksgiving. Nando was servile in his apology, knowing the deceptively sweet voice in this ordinary-looking man camouflaged a quick wit and a diabolical and vicious character.

"Hey, my man," Slips had said. "Where've you been? My guys have been looking for you."

"I know, Billy. I'm so sorry, really I am," he said, "but I've got what I owe you with interest.

Having control of all of the gambling, horse racing, and other betting venues, Billy asked, "Where'd you get the dough? Robbed a bank?" His voice was silky-sweet.

Nando answered that he had inherited gold from his late grandfather and wanted to exchange it for cash.

"I'm not a bank," Billy stated.

"No. But I'll take a lower exchange rate since I owe you money." He was taking a calculated risk. Nando knew that using gold was the new big thing in Europe and was taking hold in the States because the crackdown on drugs made it more challenging to launder cash.

Billy laughed. Cat and mouse time, Nando thought. "What kind of gold?" Billy asked.

"Bars."

"Won't your sister have something to say?"

"No. This is mine," Nando lied. Better the gold is missing than her brother, he thought.

"Okay. My place in San Antonio. Monday." Billy's tone changed. "My guy will look at. If the gold is worth the price, we have a deal." He paused, lowering his voice. "You're sure about this gold? Because if my guy says it ain't for real, well, you know how that will end."

The memory of Billy's stern warning sent chills up Nando's spine, but he was sure this was his best chance to get out from under Billy Slips. He knew he'd probably get screwed over with the cash exchange, but this was his best chance.

"It's real. You'll see," he'd assured the gangster. He knew Billy would take an additional fifty to cover the interest on his gambling debts, so he'd be bringing $200,000 back. Sorry, sis. He made a mental apology. If I don't pay this off, it won't just be my kneecaps that go missing.

Billy and his gold expert were waiting for him. After the connoisseur gave the thumbs up and departed, Billy counted out the monies. "Nice stuff," he said. "Any more where this came from?"

Nando kept his face neutral and his eyes on the bills as Billy counted. "No. You know how these old-timers were. They hoarded, so you never knew what you'd find, but this is it."

A funny look came over Billy's face. "Old-timers, huh? You mean like the old-timers in the Las Cruces Negras?"

Nando's heart skipped a beat. He shrugged.

Billy laughed. "You guys. You get respectable, then you get amnesia. You're related to Victor Asturias, right?" Nando nodded. "He was one of the greats. In the '20s, he ran Las Cruces Negras. They switched products when Prohibition ended. Didn't you know about him?" Billy didn't wait for an answer. "He screwed over the Eye-talians who came down from Dallas. They wanted to get their hands on Victor, but they never did. It was Victor who got his hands on a few of them."

Nando remained silent. It never occurred to him that mobsters kept track of their histories. Victoria wouldn't be pleased, but who were they going to tell? No one in her circles.

Slips pointed to the cash on the desk. "You owed $35,000 plus $25,000 interest. You get $190,000."

Billy nodded, indicating that Nando could pick up the money. "You're sure there's no more?" Billy asked, adjusting his voice to its usual sweet sound.

"Nice doing business with you, Billy, but I don't have anything else to offer."

"We have a big game on Friday night. The usual place. Want in?"

"I'll pass," Nando said. Looking into Billy's snakelike, glittering eyes made his skin crawl; he couldn't get away fast enough. In his car, he wondered if he'd even be alive on Friday when his sister saw how much he brought back.

Billy watched Nando drive away. "Harold," he called out.

"Yeah, boss?"

"Did you leave Nando a message, like I said?"

"Yeah, boss, but from his reaction today, I'd say he ain't been there yet."

"He'll go home now that he's paid up. Get going. Watch him. See if he tries to sell any more gold. I got a feeling about this." Billy ran one finger over the smooth surface of a gold bar.

When she walked into the house at 6:00 p.m., Victoria hoped that Nando would be home waiting for her with the money. He wasn't. Had she done the right thing trusting him? She thought about his insistence that he'd found a dealer, off the books, in San Antonio ready and willing to deal, and she wanted a quick and untraceable cash infusion for the business.

Kicking off her shoes, she sorted through the mail with the speed of a professional card dealer. Mostly junk. She tore another hand-written envelope that looked like junk. No return address, the word personal stamped in red. That's a new twist, she thought and dumped it in the discard pile. Sorting complete, she was about to throw it all away when part of a picture slid out. It was a gold bar.

"What's this?" she muttered. She searched through the torn paper. The rest of the picture was in the envelope with the word personal stamped on it. Victoria pulled the paper scraps out and matched them.

I KNOW WHAT YOU DID, was pieced together with cut letters on one sheet. The second matched the half in her hand. There were two pictures. One was of the gold bars stacked on the hidden room floor, and the other was of the skeleton.

She dropped down into a kitchen chair, covered her mouth, and stared. She didn't move until she heard the garage door go up. Her brother was home.

"Hey, sis. I picked up some burgers and fries." Nando placed the bag of food on the kitchen table. The smell of the fast food and the pictures in her hand turned her stomach.

"How much?" she asked.

"Two hundred," he lied. She didn't move.

"What's wrong, Victoria?"

She held up the two sheets of paper.

Nando looked at them. "I don't believe it. Demands?"

"Not yet. This is just an introduction."

"How did this happen?" he asked, handing the papers back to her.

"I don't know, but someone was in the theater—or do you believe in ghosts with cameras?" She slapped her hand on the table. "You weren't thorough when you checked the theater, were you?"

"I damned well was," he insisted.

"Bullshit!" she shouted, shaking her head. "Now, explain why you only brought back 200 instead of 250. What happened?"

"The guy drove a hard bargain and misrepresented the exchange rate he'd pay. We won't use him again, that's all."

Victoria shook her head. "I'll find the next dealer in Dallas," she said. "Maybe I'll bring the gold myself."

"Whatever. Nothing I do is ever good enough for you." He grabbed food from the bag and headed toward the stairs. He wasn't waiting for her to count the money.

Victoria watched him go. "Remember!" she yelled. "Saturday night is the opening of the company's *Nutcracker,* and I want you at the gala."

He answered by slamming his bedroom door. She gave her brother a mental drop dead, took a burger from the bag, and heated it in the microwave.

Chewing without tasting, she focused on this unexpected twist. Speed was now critical because someone out there knew.

She wondered at her brother's carelessness. Would he ever learn? That's why she hadn't shared other steps she'd taken.

Nando didn't know about the account in Belize, where the monies would be deposited before transferring them to the business accounts in the U.S., and she hadn't told him about Chapter 11, either.

There would now be a court-appointed trustee to assist the reorganization and prevent creditors from putting undue pressure on her even though she intended to pay them in full. She didn't want Asturias Enterprises in the news for being a deadbeat company.

Frustrated by the new turn of events, Victoria threw away the fast food remains, took the duffel bag, went to her bedroom, and slammed her door. At that moment, she felt she could kill Nando. How could someone have been in the theater without them knowing?

Could it have been Isabel? But how would she have gotten in? She might have hidden in a dressing room or a locker room and waited until the crew left? But then she'd need to get out. Does she know the alarm code? That scenario didn't make any sense, she thought, but Nando needs to work harder and get more information on the dancer.

She looked at the duffel bag. I'll count it tomorrow, she decided and flung it into her closet.

# CHAPTER 43

## GLITZ, GLAMOUR, AND A GALA

At 5:00 a.m. on the first Saturday of December, LaLa was curled up at the foot of Father Melvyn's bed, but he wasn't in it. The priest sat at his desk with his old cardigan buttoned up to his chin in the chilly morning air. Deep in thought, he stroked his mustache and tapped the pen in his left hand on the papers. There were three books opened and articles scattered across everything.

LaLa opened one eye and meowed as if to say, "Knock it off and turn out the light." She huffed and went back to sleep. "Disturbing you, am I?" Father Melvyn asked, eyeing his cat. "I'm disturbed too." He stared down at the picture of the ring.

Despite Isabel's violent reaction to his suspicion that Rafael might have been a high-ranking mobster, he'd felt compelled to continue his research. Using a magnifying glass, he saw the markings on the ring were distinct.

Rafael's ring was like those worn by the notorious bootlegging Spada crime family leaders in Texas during Prohibition. Father Melvyn reread the article and marveled at the human need for status, even within criminal societies. Rafael, although not Italian, was influential in the organization.

Then, the old, powerful Mexican crime family, Las Cruces Negras, also ran booze from Mexico to Texas. There was no indication that they sported any vanity jewelry.

He thought it all fascinating and troubling. Realizing the time, he closed the books. It was time to face the day. Then he remembered what day it was.

Tonight he would be John Bono's guest at the gala after the opening of the *Nutcracker*. Father Melvyn smiled. I've never seen that ballet. Not even one of the renditions on TV. This should be fun, he thought, but first Matins.

Reaching for his prayer book, he forced everything else from his mind and devoted his thoughts to the Lord.

Victoria had been mad as hell, as Nando knew she'd be. He'd lied again and played the fool, telling her that he must have miscounted. Instead of 200 grand, he'd brought back 190, but what could she do? She'll get over it, he thought. Relieved to have Billy Slips off his back, he enjoyed his newfound freedom.

He was happy to return to his apartment, which he found trashed. He knew who'd done it, and he knew better than to complain. Billy's thug had also knifed his bed and sofa for good measure. "Bastard," he muttered. "I'll call a private carting company to pick it up."

Nando knew he'd have to lay low and use his allowance to refurbish his apartment. No gambling and no nightlife — not for a while, but it didn't feel too bad since he was busy with the ballet company. The new experience in the world of theater was entertaining — for now.

Pursuing Laurel was Victoria's idea as a way to get information about Isabel Sanchez-Reardon and he'd agreed to do it. Victoria had taken him to the ballet studios under a false pretext and introduced him around. He'd played his part, making a point of chatting with Laurel, the pretty receptionist, while Victoria took care of business. Before they left, Nando asked Laurel if he could call her. She, of course, agreed, and now here he was, getting ready for a ballet gala. Courting her hadn't been a hardship at first.

He returned to the present. Black tux, black shirt, and black bowtie. Very debonair, he thought. I'm sure Laurel will approve, too. *Not that her opinion matters.*

Nando sighed. Laurel was fun in bed and fun to be with, most of the time, but she was getting too possessive. He hadn't intended to accept her invitation to the opening night gala, but Victoria insisted.

"Do I have to watch the ballet?" he'd asked his sister. "Couldn't I just show up for the party?"

"No. I want you there in the lobby, listening to peoples' conversations. No one knows you, so they won't be as careful about what they say."

"What am I listening for?" Nando had asked.

"Anything about the dancers, especially Isabel Reardon."

He'd rolled his eyes. "I hope I don't fall asleep. Ballet is boring."

"I'll be sitting next to you. I'll poke you if you snore," she'd teased.

Nando arrived at the theater alone. Laurel was working the VIP room, and she'd be busy between acts, too, which left him free to roam and listen.

He bought a drink and spotted Victoria as she worked the lobby. She's good, he thought. He made his way to one of the benches and waited for the auditorium doors to open. People around him chatted about the mundane. Carpools, teachers, soccer, softball, hair salons.

The elders, dressed in their finery, one-upsmanshipped each other with which parties they'd been invited to.

Bored and wondering what he was doing there, he twisted the ring on his pinky. It had cleaned up well, and he liked wearing it. It was too nice to be left behind with a skeleton, and Victoria hadn't noticed.

Flipping through the program, Nando read one one bio. Over the past few weeks, when at the studio, he'd watch Isabel's rehearsals. Although sweaty from the strenuous dancing and not wearing makeup, he'd still thought her pretty.

The auditorium doors opened, and he found his seat, one off the aisle. Victoria came in and sat next to him just before the lights dimmed.

"No snoring," she whispered.

The first act unfolded. Nando yawned. The Christmas tree on stage grew to new heights; toys became giant-sized, soldiers and mice filled the stage and fought. A life-sized Nutcracker soldier marched forward to battle the three-headed rat-king who almost killed him. Clara threw her slipper at the rat, and the Nutcracker won the battle.

I'm never going to stay awake through this, Nando thought as the music changed.

Wearing matching beaded white costumes, Isabel Sanchez-Reardon, and her partner, Orlando, in the roles of Snow Queen and Cavalier, stepped out from the wings. Nando thought they looked regal as his eyelids drooped.

The Snow Queen waved goodbye to Clara and the Nutcracker, who'd magically turned into a prince. Nando kept blinking, trying not to fall asleep. Then everything changed.

The Snow Queen began to dance, and his boredom evaporated, replaced by fascination.
He was awake and utterly riveted.

Isabel was spellbinding. The music swelled; she took a running leap from the front corner of the stage, turned in the air, and landed on her partner's shoulder with her hands over her head. Thunderous applause erupted, his included.

"Wow," he whispered to Victoria.

The end of the Snow scene marked the end of the first act. The Snow Queen and Cavalier stepped out from behind the closed curtain for their solo bows. Nando's applause was enthusiastic. He felt his sister's eyes glowering while she gave an unflattering golf clap.

"Remember who you are romancing and remember what I need to know," Victoria hissed.

At the end of the ballet, the house lights came up, and Victoria slipped away.

Laurel appeared at his elbow. "Come with me," she said, grasping his hand and strutting through the lobby to the stage door.

"You look lovely," he whispered, admiring her figure in a sexy black cocktail dress, her identification badge hanging around her neck. Nando walked beside her, aware that she was showing off and showing him off.

"Excuse us," Laurel said and pulled him past the people gathered at the stage door. She showed her badge, and the guard let them through. Laurel made a point of introducing him to anyone she could rope as the caterers converted backstage into a holiday party space.

Well aware of his reputation as a local celebrity playboy, when the professional photographer aimed her camera at him, he warmed to his role. Laurel pulled his arm around her waist and hugged him; they smiled brightly at the picture.

Nando saw his sister and waved her over, but when Laurel tried to pull her into their little circle, Victoria slipped away to speak to the artistic directors.

Smattering applause drew Nando's attention. The dancers, now in their party clothes, joined the festivities. Laurel took Nando over and introduced him to the principals. "Have you met Fernando Asturias, Victoria's brother?"

Nando forced a smile, shook hands, and congratulated them on their performances, not that he knew one part from another.

The remarks about what a striking couple he and Laurel made annoyed him, though he smiled and said thank you. Nando looked around, trying to figure out how to escape when Isabel walked in.

"Isn't that the girl who danced the snow thing?" Nando didn't wait for an answer. "Introduce me," he said, dragging Laurel toward Isabel. He felt Laurel's displeasure.

"This is Fernando Asturias, Victoria's brother." Laurel's tone was cold.

Nando stepped up. Isabel smiled when he took her hand in his. "I was mesmerized," he said, raising her hand to his lips and then covering it with his left. "You're beautiful."

Her smile froze; her hand became rigid in his. Isabel gave a slight cough. "Excuse me, please, I- uh, forgot something in the dressing room."

"Hmm. How rude," Laurel said.

Nando ignored Laurel and watched Isabel walk away, wondering what had caused her sudden coldness.

# CHAPTER 44

## GET YOUR GAME FACE ON, GIRL!

Isabel ran into the dressing room and leaned on the long makeup table in front of the mirrors, trying to calm down. She knew her abrupt departure was discourteous, but she couldn't help herself.

At first, she was happy for the praise and didn't mind smiling at an Asturias, despite Laurel's steely-eyed glare, but when he raised her hand to his lips and covered it with his left, she saw the ring on his pinky. It was exactly like her great-grandfather's. "How could that be?"

"Get your game face on, girl," she said, giving herself a mental shake. Then, regaining her composure, she returned to the gala.

Within minutes she felt eyes boring holes through her back. Glancing over her shoulder, she saw Laurel staring at her. God, she thought. If looks could kill, Victoria would have nothing to worry about.

Ignoring Laurel, Isabel scanned the crowd. Then, smiling and nodding, she moved from group to group, exchanging pleasantries and thanking people for the praise they offered.

*There!* Mrs. B. and Father Melvyn were standing to the side, sipping wine. She hesitated, worried that the priest might refuse to talk to her after her outburst at the rectory, the day she'd called him a liar. It took all her self-control to walk straight at them, smiling, with her hand extended. She thought they looked surprised and apprehensive.

"Thank you for coming," she said and kissed Mrs. B. She shook the priest's hand. When she was sure her conversation was perceived by those within earshot as the usual backstage chatter, she whispered through clenched teeth. "See that handsome man Laurel is hanging on to?" She tilted her head in Laurel's direction, where Nando and Laurel were posing for another press photographer. "He's Victoria Asturias's brother. Look at the ring," she whispered.

Once their eyes landed on Nando and Laurel, she spoke in a normal voice. "I'm happy you enjoyed the show. Happy holidays to you both," she said and moved on to the next group of patrons.

"Follow my lead," Mrs. B. said and walked over to the couple. "So lovely to see you again, Laurel." She introduced Father Melvyn and identified Laurel as a valued employee of the company. God, Mrs. B. thought. If Laurel were a peacock, her tail feathers would be fanned out.

Laurel reached back possessively for Nando's hand. "Meet my boyfriend, Nando Asturias, Victoria's brother." They all shook hands. Father Melvyn was last.

Mrs. B. noticed the angry glint in the young man's eyes. She surmised that he didn't like being referred to as Laurel's boyfriend.

Nando raised the glass in his left hand to his lips. Father Melvyn jumped on the opportunity. "What an unusual ring," the priest said, pointing to Nando's finger. "Quite extraordinary. Is it an antique?"

Nando looked at the ring and smiled like a Cheshire cat. "I think so," he answered. "It belonged to my grandfather."

"Would you think me rude if I asked to see it more closely?" Sheepishly, Father Melvyn peered at the ring.

"Not at all." Nando slid the ring off his finger and handed it to the priest, who turned and tilted it in his fingers, admiring it. He returned it to Nando.

"Beautiful. Wear it in good health."

Mission accomplished, Mrs. B. thought. "Enjoy the evening, and we wish you a blessed and happy Christmas." With that, the little group broke up.

When they were away from Laurel and Nando, Father Melvyn whispered, "That young man is lying."

John approached. "Did you enjoy the evening, Father?" he asked.

"Absolutely." Father Melvyn shook John's hand and thanked him for the invitation.

"Son, it was wonderful. We enjoyed all of it. The company was terrific," Mrs. B. added. "We'll be on our way, and I'll talk to you tomorrow." Mrs. B. looked around. Lisa was involved in a conversation with another group. "Tell Lisa goodnight for us."

Mrs. B. led Father Melvyn toward the backstage door. At the exit, a wizened old fellow sat on a stool, keeping watch. His name tag said Charlie Lyman.

"Good evening," Mrs. B. said. They all wished each other happy holidays before Charlie pushed the door open to let them out.

"I remember him from the rehearsal when Lisa was injured," Father Melvyn whispered.

They drove in silence. At the first red light, Mrs. B. asked, "Why do you think Nando Asturias is lying?"

"That ring wasn't his grandfather's."

"How do you know?"

Father Melvyn yanked the seatbelt away from his neck and slid it under his arm.

"You know that's not legal."

Ignoring her warning about the seatbelt, he answered her question. "The carving inside the band."

Shortly after Father Melvyn's and Mrs. B.'s departure, the party began to thin out. Nando stepped away from Laurel's discussion with another staff member about the nuts and bolts of the cleanup.

Bored, he looked around and spotted Isabel standing alone. Her unexpected reaction when they were introduced still rankled; he felt challenged. Finally, turning to Laurel, he said, "Get your things while I use the restroom."

Laurel walked toward the lockers to get her purse and overnight bag, but not before she looked back and saw Nando make his move.

"I'm sorry to be pushy," Nando said when he reached Isabel, unaware that Laurel was watching. "But it's hard to have a real conversation at these things. May I take you out to dinner sometime?"

"Aren't you with Laurel?"

"We date, but we aren't exclusive. Can I call you?"

Isabel smiled. "Give me your number. I'll call you."

Nando took out a pen and wrote his number on the napkin she was holding. "Promise?" he asked, giving her his most charming smile. Laser-focused on Isabel, he was startled by the voice behind him.

"Nando, darling. I'm ready to go."

Isabel peeked around him. "Hi, Laurel. I hope you didn't work too hard tonight." Smiling with exaggerated sweetness, Isabel added, "have fun."

Laurel's glare was murderous.

Isabel picked up her handbag and headed to the exit. "Hey, Charlie," she said to the ever-present stagehand turned custodian. "Have a good night, whatever is left of it," she joked.

"You too, Miss Reardon," Charlie said and waved.

Isabel walked to the parking lot with a spiteful grin on her face. She had no romantic interest in Nando. He was, after all, an Asturias, but his compliments in front of Laurel were a fun payback for all the times Laurel implied that Isabel was cozying up to John's mother to advance herself in the company.

Enjoying a moment of perverse glee, she wished she could be a fly on the wall of their bedroom.

## CHAPTER 45

## BLOOD FEUDS DON'T DIE

As soon as Mrs. B. walked into the rectory Monday morning, Father Melvyn pounced. "I've been working on this Sanchez-Asturias thing all weekend. Look what I've found." He pointed to papers strewn across the table.

And good morning to you, too. Mrs. B. thought, looking at his disheveled appearance. She followed his finger. "Old newspaper articles?" she asked, puzzled.

"Look at this one," he said.

BLOODY GUN BATTLE LEAVES
12 DEAD ON DALLAS STREETS.

The bold headline was in good shape, but the faded print with the date was difficult to see. Only the year was clear: 1920.

Flipping through the articles and screwing up her nose, she said, "They wrote graphic descriptions of the bodies." While she read on, Father Melvyn paced and stroked his red mustache with his thumb. LaLa walked back and forth beside him, looking anxious.

"Has LaLa been fed?" Mrs. B. asked, trying to redirect his attention.

"Yes."

She pushed the paper aside when she saw the freshly brewed coffee on the counter, filled two cups, and set them on the table. "Now, talk before the phones and doorbell start ringing. What has you so agitated?"

The priest sat down. "The Spadas were Italians and the major crime family in Dallas," he began. "Their network reached Austin soon after Prohibition became the law of the land." He gathered and stacked articles about the Spadas into one pile.

"Their main competitor was Las Cruces Negras, the major Mexican mob." He made another stack. "Look at the top one." He pointed to a grainy picture of a man with his hands cuffed behind his back. In small print, the caption read: Victor Asturias brought in for questioning.

"Asturias was the alleged boss of the Mexican crime family, but I've never found another article referring to him." He lifted the cup, then put it down. "How powerful was he that no one ever wrote anything about him again?" Father Melvyn paused to drink his coffee. He continued.

"Bootlegging was a multi-million-dollar racket, and it laid the groundwork for the smartest and most ruthless of the street thugs to organize into crime families. When Prohibition was repealed, the mobsters already had their networks in place and switched to drugs."

Mrs. B. sat back and crossed her arms. "You really surprise me. You're a priest! This interest in organized crime didn't start with Isabel's story, did it?"

"Read Sun Tzu." He looked at Mrs. B.'s questioning face. "He was a brilliant Chinese military strategist who lived 500 years before Christ. In his philosophy of war, he advises knowing your enemy." Father Melvyn gulped his coffee. "Organized crime is an evil endeavor pushing every degrading vice and addictive drug. It is the enemy of law, order, and civil society. It shreds ethics, moral values, family life, and a healthy, productive environment. I could go on and on." He drained his coffee cup. "But that's for another day," he said, holding the cup out for a refill. "Today, we concentrate on how this informs the Sanchez-Asturias feud."

Mrs. B. refilled his cup. "Any mention of Rafael Sanchez?" she asked.

"No. Nothing, other than the missing person notification, on a back page of this edition. Isabel isn't going to like this," the priest continued, "but we must get her in here. If this feud goes deeper than a personal battle between two great-grandfathers, she may be in dangerous waters. The mob doesn't like coming under scrutiny, even for its past. "And," he added, his tone dark, "neither do families that had their start in nefarious businesses. Oftentimes, blood feuds don't die."

"It might also explain the Sanchez family's reluctance to talk about Rafael," Mrs. B. said and headed for the phone. "It's Monday. The company is off. I'll call her."

As soon as she opened the door, LaLa ran forward, meowed, and rubbed against Isabel's leg. Mrs. B. hoped that was a good sign, because the last time Isabel was there, the cat hadn't greeted her.

"Isabel, you were beautiful in the *Nutcracker*. We enjoyed it very much."

"Thank you," Isabel answered.

Father Melvyn bounded down the stairs and into the office. He greeted Isabel and sat down in his chair behind the desk.

LaLa surprised them. She jumped on his lap, made one circle, and settled down, with her head above the desk, her eyes focused on the dancer.

Mrs. B. wondered if she was there for moral support. But for whom?

Father Melvyn began. "I have found more information about the Asturias family back in the 1920s." He outlined Victor Asturias's connection to Las Cruces Negras.

"I know about them," Isabel answered.

Mrs. B.'s eyebrows shot up. "And you didn't think to tell us?"

Before Isabel answered, Father Melvyn steered the conversation. "But you didn't know about your great-grandfather, did you?"

Isabel shook her head. "I was shocked, and I'm still not sure how I feel about it."

"At the gala, that ring jolted you," he continued.

"Yes," said Isabel. "But is it the same one? Does it have anything to do with my great-grandfather?"

Father Melvyn pulled out the picture of her great-grandfather wearing the ring and photos of the rings worn by the Spada Crime bosses. He placed them side by side. "The night of the gala, I coaxed Nando to let me have a look at it."

"And?" Isabel asked.

Father Melvyn took a breath. "Consider this, Isabel. Nando's ring looks exactly like your great-grandfather's on the outside. But it's what's inside the band that's telling." He stopped, watching Isabel's eyes. Was she getting it?

"RS/Spada, was carved inside the band of the ring Nando wore. Combine that with the other similarities, and the connection cannot be ignored."

Father Melvyn pointed to the markings on the pictures. "If the ring belonged to your great-grandfather, it couldn't have been handed down by Victor Asturias because Victor, as we now know, was the head of the Mexican crime family. So, the question is, how did Nando get that ring?"

Isabel paled.

"Are you okay, dear?" Mrs. B. asked.

"I don't know," she answered truthfully.

Mrs. B. asked, "When did you find out about the Mexican crime family?"

"I searched back newspapers looking for anything about Rafael Sanchez's disappearance. I found nothing other than a missing person's notice. I did find one article mentioning Victor Asturias. He'd been picked up and questioned by the police."

"This one?" Mrs. B. asked, reaching for the picture Father Melvyn had on the desk.

"Yes."

"Was there anything on that site before the theatre?" Father Melvyn asked.

"My grandfather told me that it was farmland, and there was a barn, but I'm not sure where exactly it was located. I could go back…"

"No, dear. I don't think so." Mrs. B. was firm. "We have the section, lot, and block numbers." She turned to Father Melvyn. "Before I come in tomorrow, I'll try to find the city's record of property sales. Maybe I can find out if anything was on the site where the theater stands."

"There's something else," Isabel said. The priest and the housekeeper waited. "The day after Thanksgiving, Black Friday, I sent copies of that article to the society columnists for three newspapers. This morning I saw this online." Isabel pulled a printed page out of her purse and handed it to Mrs. B., who read the short article questioning the Asturias pedigree, based on the 1920 picture and news report; she passed it to Father Melvyn, who pursed his lips and stroked his mustache.

"Why?" he asked.

Tears welled up in Isabel's eyes.

"No time for tears now, Isabel. That was not wise. What if it's traced back to you?"

"It won't be. I mailed it from Fredericksburg, with no return address." Isabel firmed her chin. "The Asturias family needs to be shaken up." She then blurted out, "And, the night of the gala, Nando Asturias asked me out."

The tension in the room was palpable. LaLa stood up and arched her back. "You are not going to see him," Father Melvyn said, his voice a whispered command.

"I didn't give him my number. I took his. Maybe I'll meet him for coffee. Maybe I can get information from him."

LaLa wailed, pinned her ears flat, jumped off the priest's lap, and ran from the room.

Father Melvyn's eyes flashed. He exhaled hard, fighting to control his exasperation.

"Here's what I think you—we should do," the housekeeper said, heading off the pastor's ire. "Don't call Nando yet. Give us a couple of days. Then, I'll look at the records again, and Father Melvyn will continue his research of the criminal 'enterprises,'" she said for lack of a better word. "Promise me you won't call Nando before talking to us again."

"Okay, but my family gets here in couple of weeks. I need answers."

## CHAPTER 46

## THE CLOCK IS TICKING

Victoria leaned against the kitchen table and massaged her forehead; she was tired and worried. So close, she thought. She could hear the clock ticking in her mind. Staring at the picture taken at the Ballet Gala, with the short blurb under it, made it feel as if the walls were closing in on her.

"Well-known Austin society bad-boy, playboy Fernando Asturias, III, smiles with his date at the Bernardi-Bono Ballet Gala.

According to an anonymous source, there are questions about this family's road to riches. The Roaring Twenties and booze were windfall years for many who now occupy the upper stratosphere of American society. Was the Asturias family among them?"

She flung the paper on the table. "These newspapers are all tabloids now." She knew contacting them would only fuel the reporter's quest for more dirt.

She took her frustrations out on the mail, tearing open envelopes and ripping up garbage.

The pictures increased her fury.

MORE WHERE THESE CAME FROM. YOU HAVE ONE WEEK TO GET ONE MILLION DOLLARS IN CASH. I'LL SEND FURTHER INSTRUCTIONS FOR THE DROP. NO TRICKS. IF ANYTHING HAPPENS TO ME, THE POLICE WILL FIND AN ENVELOPE WITH ALL YOUR SECRETS.

Victoria dialed Nando's cell phone. "Damn you!" she shouted at the answering message. "I don't know where you are, with whom or what you're doing. Get Home!"

She needed to calm down. Making decisions while in an emotional state would be folly. Victoria turned to the only thing that relieved her stress.

Not even changing into exercise clothes, she stripped down to her underwear, set the treadmill's pace to 4.6 miles per hour, and didn't bother with a slow warmup.

An hour later, she stepped off, breathing hard but feeling better. By the time she took a quick shower and dressed, she heard her brother's voice call from downstairs.

Without greeting him, she ran down the stairs. "The clock is ticking," she said and handed him the blackmail letter.

Nando read it. "A million?"

"If I start liquidating that fast, it will raise red flags all over the place, and I'm not about to hand over that much money without a fight. Here's what we'll do. We'll bring a portion of it; then negotiate."

"What if the blackmailer refuses?"

"Assuming it's a man, what's he going to do? Go to the police and say, 'Hey, I tried to shake down these people, and they didn't cooperate; Boo-hoo?' I don't think so. Besides, think about this. What does this person have on us?"

"The pictures, for one thing. And murder?

"What murder?" Victoria asked.

"Let's think," Nando spoke as if to a child. "There's a skeleton walled up in the theater. Why? And there's Adam Leightman. Remember him?" Nando snapped. "And let's not forget the accident on stage a few weeks ago. Bet the police would love to tie them all into a neat little package."

"No proof," Victoria said, not feeling as confident as she sounded. She thought about the sledgehammer she'd removed from the theater. She'd hidden it in her basement and used it to knock a hole in the foundation when she created a hiding place for the gold. It was still there—in her basement.

Could a forensic lab still find DNA traces that would match Adam Leightman? She'd have to get rid of it somehow, but not now. "Look, I'm not playing chicken," she said. "I just know that we can't get a million in cash fast without unleashing other problems. We pay part of it and say we need time to get the rest, which isn't a lie. And maybe we learn the blackmailer's identity."

"We don't know where or when to make the drop," Nando said.

"Right. We have no choice but to wait. Then we can adjust our plans."

Going on offense, Victoria challenged her brother. "Have you found out anything else about Isabel? I suspect she might have something to do with this," she said, pushing the society page in front of her brother.

Nando's eyebrows shot up when he saw the hit piece in the newspaper. "What the hell? I didn't think this stuff was public knowledge, but—" He stopped.

Victoria eyed him. "But what?" she asked, wondering what he wasn't telling her.

"Look, Sis. Our family wouldn't be the first to have a murky start. Even this crappy little piece alludes to that," he said, backhanding the paper.

"But how many have their skeletons on display–literally?" Victoria asked. "You've read the last journal. You know what Victor did. The Italians were powerful, and Victor wanted everything they had. He considered Sanchez a traitor for working with them, and Sanchez was good, but Victor stopped him. That's Rafael Sanchez's body behind that wall, and wouldn't Isabel love to get hold of that information?"

Nando looked at Victoria. "And?"

She looked at him. "What else?"

"The drunk driving incident? Does Reardon know that it was Dad who struck and killed her grandmother? Will she try to dredge it up?" He stared at his sister. "Maybe Isabel Sanchez-Reardon's quest isn't to prove the land steal. Maybe it's revenge."

Victoria blew out a breath and held her head. "We'll be dragged through the mud for years if this comes out."

"No, we won't! Even if it comes out, people will forget by the next scandal."

"Average people. The circles we run in won't. They barely accepted Grandfather when he parlayed his father's money into billions. Wouldn't they just love to ostracize us now?" Victoria stared at the newspaper. "I don't think it's the land or the hit-and-run," she said, her voice soft, pensive. "I'll bet Rafael left some kind of record or letter, and she's gotten wind of the fortune in gold that he was hiding when he was killed."

Nando folded his arms across his chest. "Okay, Victoria. What do you want to do?"

# CHAPTER 47

## AN OUT OF CONTROL FREIGHT TRAIN

Father Melvyn sat at the kitchen table while Mrs. B. made her call. "I didn't wake you, did I?" she asked as soon as Isabel answered the phone. It was Friday, and Mrs. B. knew the company had performed the night before.

"I'm awake and getting organized for tonight."

Mrs. B. didn't waste time. "I couldn't find anything more about what buildings might have been on the property."

"Disappointing, but not unexpected," Isabel said. "Thank you for trying."

"Before we give up, Father Melvyn is checking the newspaper archives. Building a theater was no small matter—it still isn't. He's researching history on the Rue de L'Histoire Theatre, so all is not lost."

"I didn't think of that!" Isabel sighed. "I know I had a bad reaction when Father Melvyn first told me about the ring, and I owe you both apologies. I'm very grateful for all you've done."

"Apology accepted, but do I hear a 'but?'" She kept her tone light, covering her concern. She was afraid Isabel was going to do something foolish, like meet Nando Asturias.

Isabel giggled. "I know you're worried, but I think it might be useful to have coffee with the love of Laurel's life."

"I don't think it's a good idea," Mrs. B. said. "Nando may not be the only danger."

"What do you mean?" Isabel asked.

"I'm not sure about Laurel's stability." Mrs. B. bit her tongue; that was a word too far.

"I don't understand," Isabel said.

Mrs. B. couldn't tell her that John, Lisa, and Chelly had developed concerns about Laurel. They thought she'd been acting strange since taking up with Fernando Asturias, who was at the studios regularly. No one wanted to complain and risk offending his sister. Victoria's generosity and commitment were a blessing to the company.

"Just a feeling." Mrs. B. pressed on. "Can we agree to give Father Melvyn the weekend to complete his research?"

"That works for me. I've been scheduled for double the performances this weekend because my alternate is sick, so I wouldn't have time for anything social. And tonight, instead of getting out fast after the show, all the dancers are on notice to show up at the new donors' party."

Mrs. B. chuckled. "A necessary part of the job, sometimes. You just take care of yourself, and congratulations. I've seen the wonderful reviews you've received, both in the paper and on the dance blogs."

"Thank you. I try to remember my mother's advice not to take the good ones too much to heart, because sooner or later you'll get a bad one that will hurt. You can't let yourself be governed by them."

Mrs. B. laughed. "That's what I told John when he was a young dancer."

"I knew you were a wise woman. Just like my mother."

"Merde, tonight," Mrs. B. used the accepted French term to wish good luck. Then, hanging up, she turned to Father Melvyn. "I'm afraid time is short for Isabel and the company. Now, we have another complication."

Mrs. B. explained that in addition to Nando hanging around, Laurel was snooping around the dancers' lockers and dressing rooms at the theater. John caught her and asked what she was doing. She said that knowing how hard they worked, she was checking to see if anyone needed anything.

"And why is that suspicious?" Father Melvyn asked.

"Because dancers have their own precise and individualized prep routines. It's not likely they'd let someone, especially a non-dancer, get them anything."

"Did John say anything to the dancers about Laurel?"

"Not yet. He doesn't want them to be distracted or worried, but he, Lisa, and Chelly are watching her."

Nando was getting restless. He wanted to go out but had no money. Grumbling, he was making a sandwich in the kitchen when Victoria, dressed to the nines, in a flattering, well-cut black cocktail dress came downstairs. She wore their mother's expensive pearls and diamond stud earrings that peeked out and shone from under her sweptback black hair.

He looked at his sister and whistled. "Wow. You look fabulous. What's going on?"

"Our PR efforts have paid off, Victoria said. "A lot of new firms have moved to Austin, and we've generated more corporate interest in funding the company." She wrapped her velvet shawl around her shoulders. "Tonight, after the performance, we have a special party planned for them. All of the company staff will be there. The dancers have been told to show up and be at their best." Victoria looked at her brother. "And what are you doing tonight?"

"Nothing. Shall I chauffeur you?" He knew that in better times, she'd have hired a limo.

"Not necessary. I'll drive." She grabbed her purse, then turned back. Then, with a not-so-sweet smile, she said, "Swing by. Your charms may be useful." Victoria swept through the kitchen and into the garage. "Ciao," she waved airily.

She never stops, he thought. When she wants something, she'll use anything and anyone to get it. His own smile was sardonic. Why not? He thought.

Nando arrived at the theater in time for the final curtain. When the crowd let out, he strode through the lobby to the stage door. Although the party was private, the guard recognized him and let him pass. Aware that male and female heads turned to look him over, he smiled, knowing that he looked devilishly handsome in his tux and bowtie.

Amid the hubbub of activity, he found his sister talking with John and Lisa Bono. He congratulated them on another excellent performance. "Packed house, again, tonight," he said, even though he hadn't been in the house.

On the other side of the room, he noticed Laurel tied up with guests; he felt her eyes on him and was relieved that she couldn't break away.

The dancers arrived in small groups.

Holding a glass of wine, Nando watched the potential donors, many of whom were newcomers to the world of ballet, ooh and ahh, as they recognized individual dancers; he was waiting for his opportunity.

When she was alone, Nando approached. "Isabel. Congratulations. You've been getting great reviews," he said, holding out his hand to shake hers.

"Thank you."

Nando held on to her hand a moment longer than necessary. "You promised to call me. I've been waiting."

Smiling, Isabel answered, "I know, but I've been crazy busy with extra shows and getting ready for my family to arrive. I have a few days off early next week. I'll call you then."

Isabel's eyes abruptly widened. Her face grew pale; she stepped away.

What the hell, now? he wondered until, from the corner of his eye, he saw Laurel. Like an out-of-control freight train, she steamed toward them with blazing eyes and a flushed face.

Glancing over his shoulder, Nando saw John, Lisa, and Victoria, talking with guests, but they were watching, their eyes filled with apprehension. For a nanosecond, he considered letting Laurel make a scene. But instead, he stepped forward, caught her in his arms, and kissed her. "Hey, I wanted to surprise you. I came to take you out for a late dinner," he lied.

"And you needed to make a pit stop with the Snow Queen?" Laurel hissed.

Nando laughed. "Don't be silly. I just congratulated her on the great reviews she's receiving. After all, she is becoming one of the most promising dancers in the company."

He hugged Laurel's rigid frame to him. "You know," he whispered, "after the fiasco with Macbeth, Victoria worked hard to get support for the rest of the season." He maintained his grip on her shoulders. "My sister has staked her reputation on this company and this theater. It's in everyone's best interests to make sure she's not embarrassed."

Laurel frowned, but he felt her body relax. He steered her away, thinking that his sister owed him big time.

# CHAPTER 48

## SHREDDED

Isabel left the theater after midnight, relieved that she'd held Nando off, almost grateful to Laurel for her ferocious charge. It had left Nando no choice but to waylay her.

Happy to be on her way, she walked out of the stage door and stopped. It was snowing; Isabel turned her face up to the falling flakes. There was already a light coating on the ground. The snow made everything, even the service yard where the dancers parked, look clean and peaceful, unlike real life.

Exhausted, she sat in her car and waited for the engine to warm up. Her alternate was sick, so she'd danced both the Snow Queen and the second act Arabian for both the afternoon and evening shows. John had told her that she'd have to double up again Saturday and Sunday, but he promised Monday and Tuesday off, completely off. That would be a relief.

Her mind turned to the Asturias mess. How could she tell her mother about Rafael's possible criminal past? Or did she know? Was that the reason her mother never wanted to talk about family history? And now, another Asturias has another Sanchez in their sights: Me.

She turned on the headlights. The tire light illuminated. "Damn! What's going on?" Then she remembered that cold could lower the tire pressure, and she'd hit the curb parking in front of the post office earlier in the day. "I'll take care of it tomorrow," she mumbled and shifted into drive. Her only desire was to get home and crawl into bed. Her car slid on the frosty streets. When she got on the highway, she tapped the brakes to further slow down on the glazed road.

*Pop!* The sound was outside, but she knew as the sterring wheel pulled left as the left front fender tilted down. Blow-out!

Although the car shimmied, Isabel remained calm, fighting her instinct to brake hard while it rode unequally; icy patches made it worse. Grateful that there were no other cars on the road, Isabel held the vibrating steering wheel tight and angled the car toward the shoulder.

She tapped the brake pedal and edged the car into a soft hill at the side of the road. The front wheels scrunched when they rode over frost and dirt, followed by an unexpected shriek of metal hitting metal.

"What the hell?" She shifted into reverse. The wheels spun, but the car didn't move. "I'm so damned tired. I don't need this!" In her purse, she found the AAA membership card. Mentally, she thanked her father for insisting she join, dialed— then waited.

Within minutes, the tow truck pulled up. After the driver examined her car, he told her that the tire had blown, and she'd dented the passenger door when she hit a guardrail. "Let me tow it to the service station. They'll take a look at the door and change the tire."

"Where?" Isabel asked.

"The Big-Boy Garage on Lamar. Do you know it?"

Isabel shook her head. "I'll find it in the morning. Can you give me a ride home?"

"Sorry. Company policy. I can take you to the garage, and you can call a cab."

Sighing from exasperation and exhaustion, Isabel grabbed her dance bag and climbed into the truck's cab. At least it was warm in there.

At the garage, the driver lowered the ramp and brought the car down to the ground. He filled out a form then pushed it, with the ignition key, through the slot in the door while Isabel called a cab.

"It's cold out here. Wait in the truck," the driver said. A few minutes later, she saw him wave to the approaching yellow cab.

Isabel thanked him and tried to tip him. "You've been very kind."

"Thanks, Ma'am, but no tip necessary."

It was after two when Isabel finally unlocked her apartment door. She went straight to her bedroom, threw her bag on the floor, and unzipped the top to let everything get air before she stripped off her clothes, pulled on a sleep shirt, wiped the makeup off her face, and fell into bed. She was asleep within minutes and slept until daylight bled through her blinds.

The digital clock said 9:15 a.m. Snuggled deep in her pillows, Isabel drifted peacefully, ready to go back to sleep until the unwelcome memory of her car intruded. "Oh shit. I'd better get up and find out what's going on."

Dragging herself to the kitchen, she put up a pot of coffee and looked out the window. There was snow on the street in front of her apartment, but she knew it would melt before noon. She found the card for the Big-Boy Garage.

When the mechanic came on the line, he said, "I found a nail in your tire, ma'am."

"Oh. I must have driven over one," Isabel said, unconcerned. "Were you able to patch it?"

"No. I had to replace your tire. The nail was in the sidewall."

"What does that mean?"

"Ma'am. You don't drive on the sidewall of a tire."

"How long could it have been there?" she asked.

"Probably not long, but that's why the tire blew. Didn't your tire light come on?"

"Not until last night."

The mechanic changed the subject. "Your passenger door is dented. I can recommend a body shop so they can bang it out and paint it, but the door opens and closes, so it's not an emergency. When you pick up the car, I'll give you the information."

"Thank you." Isabel hung up. Murphy's Law, she thought. I guess it could be worse. She thought about whom to call and ask for a ride to the gas station but decided not to bother anyone. She'd call a cab instead, and the door repair could wait until the *Nutcracker* run was over.

After two cups of coffee, feeling more energetic, Isabel went to her bedroom to empty her dance bag and repack it for the day's performances. Reaching in, she pulled out her soiled dance clothes and threw them in the hamper.

She reached for her pointe shoes. Pulling them out one by one, she examined each. I'll need new ones today, she thought, happy that she'd already sewn ribbons and elastics on two new pairs. She grabbed the fourth pointe shoe, gasped, and dropped it as if it had burned her hand.

"NO!" She looked at the shoe in horror.

Someone had slashed it over and over. Turning the shoe in her hand, she saw where something sharp had gone all the way through the leather-board shaft, and the vamp and wings, the most visible satin parts of the shoe, were slashed to ribbons.

Isabel burst into tears. "No!" she cried again and hugged the shoe to her chest. Outraged, Isabel placed the murdered shoe on her bed. She felt as if someone had dragged that blade through her heart.

Sobbing uncontrollably, Isabel went to her closet and took out the two new pairs ready for use. Tears flooded her eyes. She put them on by feel rather than by sight. She stood up and went through her routine of breaking the shoes down just enough so they wouldn't be clunky on stage but still firm enough to give her the support she needed; she never stopped crying.

"Who would do this?" she asked, her clogged throat making her voice hoarse. Feeling vulnerable and frightened, Isabel locked her bedroom and bathroom doors before stepping into a hot shower. She allowed the water to run down her head and her body. Closing her eyes, her muscles began to relax until the mechanic's words echoed: "You don't drive on the sidewall of a tire." Her eyes flew open. She shivered despite the hot water.

The mechanic at the Big-Boy Service station showed Isabel where the nail had penetrated the sidewall.

"Lady, this ain't no accident. Someone had to do it deliberately. Be careful where you leave your car."

Driving to the theater, two thoughts went round and round in her head: Someone hates me enough to shred my dance shoe, hates me enough to try and cause an accident that might kill or maim me. Laurel's malicious face came to mind. She'd been in the theater as much as the dancers, working the VIP room. Between acts, when the VIPs returned to their seats, the staff was free to do as they wished.

Then there's Victoria, she thought. She, too, was in the theater last night, because of the party.

Isabel shouted, "Stop! Focus, or you'll never be able to dance."

In the parking lot, Isabel saw the artistic directors' cars. She parked alongside them, somehow feeling safer, even though logic told her that she wasn't.

As soon as she walked into the dressing room, Janet looked at her and asked, "Are you okay? You look pale. I hope you're not getting sick."

"I'm fine. A bad night's sleep is all," Isabel answered, tearing the wrapper off one of the energy bars she'd packed. As she applied her makeup, a sudden longing gripped her.

Granddad, I wish you were here, she thought, fighting off fear and uncertainty.

# CHAPTER 49

## TOUGH SHOW

Isabel woke up Sunday morning feeling better. Saturday's shows had gone well. Neither Laurel nor Victoria had been in the theater, and none of her belongings had been touched. She hoped today would be the same.

She wished she could skip the routine Sunday call to her mother, but that wouldn't be wise. She dialed. After a few minutes of pleasant chit-chat, Isabel hurried off the phone. "Everything here is good, Mamá, but my alternate is sick. I must get to the theater to dance both roles in the matinee, as well as tonight."

When she arrived at the theater, the stage was a beehive of activity. Dancers stood at the barres on stage stretching and getting ready for the warm-up class. Offstage, the prop-master looked over the prop table, making sure everything was where it belonged and clearly marked.

To her great relief, there didn't seem to be any Bernardi-Bono Ballet Company staffers or board members around.

In the dressing room, she took what she needed from her dance bag, including one pair of pointe shoes, and then, rather than leaving it under the makeup table, where it would be easily reachable, she secured the bag in her locker as she'd done the night before.

Forcing everything but the music from her mind, Isabel danced her roles with passion, and the matinee was a great success. Between shows, Isabel and Orlando went out for a snack before returning for the evening performance.

At 7:00 p.m., the lights in the dressing room flashed. The perky, Allegro Giusto strains of the overture began. Isabel took a deep breath and focused her mind on the Snow Scene she'd be dancing shortly.

Taking her time, she made her way to the wings for her entrance; Orlando was there waiting for her in his matching white, beaded costume. For their preparation, they held hands, stared into each other's eyes, and breathed in sync, waiting for their entrance.

"Ready?" a voice whispered in her ear. Isabel spun around. Laurel's face was almost touching hers. The wicked gleam in Laurel's eyes shattered Isabel's focus.

"What are you doing here?" Orlando hissed. "Get out of the way." He elbowed Laurel back and away from Isabel.

Laurel stepped back into the shadows, but once Isabel and Orlando were on stage, she walked forward and stood at the edge of the wing.

Isabel's muscles tightened.

"Loosen up," Orlando whispered, not moving his lips. But she couldn't. Only the power of muscle memory pulled her through. Her mind flew off helter-skelter, considering different possibilities. *Did Laurel do it? Was she a psycho, or was it Victoria?*

Orlando held his hand up over Isabel's head for her to use his finger as a balance aide in her pirouettes. "You're gripping my finger too hard. It's twisting," Orlando hissed. She loosened her grip and felt herself shudder and wobble in her turn. Their Snow Pas-de-deux, which always received enthusiastic applause from the audience, received a tepid reaction at best.

In the second act, Laurel appeared again at the edge of the wings. Isabel's concentration shattered like glass under Laurel's hateful stare.

At the end of a mentally agonizing performance, Isabel apologized to Orlando. "I'm sorry. I was really off."

"You're tired," he said. "You'll have off all day tomorrow and Tuesday, get some rest." He kissed her cheek and reassured her.

Laurel breezed past them. "Tough show, tonight," she said with a Cheshire cat smile. "Ta-Ta."

# CHAPTER 50

## IT'S TIME

After a sleepless night, Isabel dialed the rectory early Monday morning. "Mrs. B., I need help," she sobbed. "Can I come in and speak to you and Father Melvyn?"

"Of course, dear."

Drying her eyes, Isabel put the shredded pointe shoe in her purse and drove to St. Francis. The sun was bright, and she noticed that all of the snow from Friday night was gone.

At the rectory, LaLa rubbed against Isabel's leg and sat beside her chair. Father Melvyn pushed a box of tissues across the desk. "What happened?" he asked.

"Someone drove a nail into the sidewall of my tire, and on Friday night, I had a blowout. And—" She reached into her purse. Tears splashed down her cheeks. With trembling hands, she held out her shredded pointe shoe. "Oh, no!" Mrs. B. gasped.

Recovering her voice, Isabel said, "Maybe it's time to talk to the police. Will you help me contact the detective in charge of the investigation? Can I talk to him here?"

"I'll contact Jake right now." Mrs. B. set the shredded pointe shoe on the desk and went to make the call. When she returned, she told Isabel and Father Melvyn that she'd left a message on Jake's cell.

Pointing to the tattered dance shoe, Mrs. B. said, "This was a loathsome and vicious act."

Isabel nodded, relieved that she didn't have to explain.

"About the tire," Father Melvyn said. "What did the mechanic say?"

"He said the nail couldn't have gotten there by accident." Her thoughts tumbled out. "It could have been Laurel or Victoria. They were both in the theater Friday night, and things were tense at the New Donors Party." She explained how Laurel had almost created an ugly scene, but Nando stopped her.

"Then yesterday, Laurel stood in the wings glaring at me while I danced. I could feel the malice radiating from her. It really put me off my game."

While she listened to Isabel's story, Mrs. B. repeatedly checked her cell phone. Jake hadn't called back. An hour later, they still hadn't heard from him.

"He must be in the middle of something important," Mrs. B. said.

"Go home, Isabel, and lay low for today," Father Melvyn said. "As soon as we hear from Jake, we'll call you."

At the front door, Father Melvyn squeezed Isabel's shoulders as they walked out into bright sunshine. "Hang on, dear," he said, "and be careful. Make sure you're never alone in the theater."

"Do you want me to tell John?" Mrs. B. asked.

"No. Please don't. He has enough to think about," Isabel said.

A ray of sunshine flashed off a sequin on Isabel's shoe. Mrs. B. looked down. "Adorable sneakers," she said. "I love the sparkly flower patterns."

Isabel held up one foot and smiled for the first time that day. "They're new, and they cheer me up. But more important, they're incredibly comfy." Isabel headed down the steps and turned back. "Thank you both for everything."

Isabel exchanged her sneakers for thick socks at home and climbed into her most comfortable sweats and a tee shirt. Bone weary and in need of comfort, she took out her favorite picture of her grandfather. Her mind buzzed with senseless, random thoughts. More tears. If I don't stop crying, I'll dehydrate, she thought and reached for a napkin on the coffee table. Picking it up, she noticed writing. *What's this?* She smoothed it out. There was Nando Asturias's phone number.

She heard the echoes of Father Melvyn's and Mrs. B.'s warnings against trying to get information from him. Consequences be damned, she thought and dialed.

Jake didn't return her phone call until seven at night. He'd spent the day gathering evidence in the wild growth behind a run-down strip mall, where another headless corpse had turned up.

"Hi, Sammi," he said, sipping the scotch his wife handed him. "Sorry I didn't call you back earlier. It's been a helluva day."

"Everything okay?" Mrs. B. asked.

"Yes, all work-related. What's up? You have something new on the theater case?"

"It's one of the dancers in the company. She came to see Father Melvyn and me right after the incident that injured Lisa. She believes she was the intended target. Things are happening that make it look that way." Jake didn't speak. Mrs. B. continued. "It's a long story. She wants to meet with you, but she's asked if she could do that at St. Francis."

"What's her name?" Mrs. B. didn't answer. "You want me to help, but you won't tell me her name?" Jake snapped.

"Isabel Sanchez-Reardon."

"What makes her think she's a target?"

Mrs. B. sighed. "As I said, it's her story to tell, but this isn't her imagination. On Friday night, on her way home, she had a blowout. The mechanic found a nail had been driven into the sidewall of her tire. She also found one of her dance shoes slashed to ribbons, and to a ballet dancer, that's a personal attack."

Jake held his temper. "I know you wouldn't have called me if you weren't sure this was real, but you've done exactly what I told you *not* to do. Instead of leaving it to the police, you've become involved!"

Mrs. B. didn't answer.

Jake swigged his scotch. He didn't want to argue with her. If there was any possibility that this young woman was in danger, it was his job to meet with her. He had to go with it. "Okay," he said. "Tell her I'll meet with her at St. Francis tomorrow morning at ten, and you and Father Melvyn can be present."

"That won't work. Father Melvyn has a funeral mass at ten."

Annoyed, he exhaled hard. "How's five in the afternoon?"

"Fine for us. I'll tell Isabel. Thank you, Jake." After he hung up, Jake felt something was about to break big. He went to the kitchen and took a second scotch.

*The stage was brightly lit. A long shadow moved forward and, like black liquid, poured over the front of the apron into the orchestra pit. The Sugar Plum Fairy danced to a slow, discordant dirge. Her pointe shoes were blood red and shredded; the ribbons holding them in place were wrapped around bloodied and slashed ankles.*

*At the front of the stage, her arms, slashed and bloodied, flew out at her sides in supplication. The iridescent thread tightened around her neck, snapping her head up. Her eyes were dead, like fisheyes. Her mouth opened. There was no sound to her scream; it was Isabel.*

Mrs. B. woke from the horrid nightmare and bolted upright in her bed - the clock said 4:00 a.m. Trouble was here. She felt it creeping like an all-consuming fog.

LaLa howled, waking Father Melvyn. He looked at his watch: 4:00 a.m. The cat jumped straight up from her sleep and stood on all fours, back arched, tail bushy from fear, ears pinned back flat. She continued to yowl.

"What is it, old girl?" Father Melvyn reached over to soothe her, but LaLa jumped down and squeezed under the bed.

The priest crossed himself against the icy tendrils crawling up his spine. A sense of wickedness enveloped him.

# CHAPTER 51

## BOOZE, BROADS, GAMBLING AND DEATH

Wendell's Diner was busy at 7:00 a.m. Holding his coffee, Jake slid into the booth across from his partner, Marv, who was eating breakfast.

Jake was brisk. "We're going to meet one of the dancers at St. Francis this afternoon, 5:00 p.m. She wants to meet there, and don't ask why because I don't know." Marv nodded and kept eating. "I spoke to Sammi last night. Supposedly, this dancer has a story and information connected to the theater crimes."

Pushing his empty plate back, Marv said, "I've got some news, too. It's not just MS 13 that has arrived in Austin. It seems Billy Slips has been spotted."

"That's never good," Jake answered. "Is his goon Harold with him?"

"My snitch says he is. Wonder who they're after this time. Well, if we find another body, I have the feeling its head will be attached, but its kneecaps might be missing."

Jake downed his coffee. "Gambling isn't our purview unless it involves a body. Make sure Vice knows."

"Done, but you'll need to move the dancer to another time. The commissioner has scheduled a meeting of Homicide, the Gang Unit, and Drugs this afternoon at four."

Jake nodded. "I'll call Sammi. I just hope this isn't a missed opportunity in the theater. case."

In the rectory office that afternoon, Father Melvyn faced Isabel, who'd stopped by on her way to her appointment. He stroked his mustache; his eyes glittered with concern. "This is a bad idea!"

"I know you're worried," Isabel said, "but it's just coffee, and we are meeting at Café Russ, on Lamar. It's a bustling place. Always lots of people. When I agreed to meet him, I didn't know we had an appointment with the detective, but he's canceled, so I'm going to keep my coffee date with Nando."

"Isabel, you are playing with fire!" Father Melvyn stated.

Isabel shrugged. "Maybe it will force Victoria's hand."

I wouldn't be forcing Victoria Asturias's hand about anything," Mrs. B. chimed in, poking her finger in the air. "Let's not forget about the tire and the pointe shoe."

"I'm not forgetting," Isabel said. She checked her watch. "But this must come to an end. Gotta go," she said. "I'll call you when I leave the café; I promise."

Mrs. B. and Father Melvyn stood at the door and watched Isabel drive away.

"What are we going to do?" Father Melvyn asked.

"Follow her, of course."

"Great minds do think alike, Mrs. B. You drive."

Nando drove out of the garage. He was wrapped up in his sister's plans and overlooked the black Prius following him. He marveled at his sister's toughness. Her risk had paid off.

They'd followed instructions for the ransom demand and made the drop, but instead of one million dollars, they'd left $300,000 and a note telling the blackmailer they needed a few more days to raise the balance without raising suspicions.

The following day, Nando was in the kitchen when the phone rang. "Payphone!" Victoria said, looking at the Caller ID. She held the phone up so Nando could hear.

The disguised voice said, "Last chance. Tuesday night. Inside the theater. Come in through your tunnel and come alone. Eight o'clock."

She hung up. "He knows about the tunnel, so it's someone from the theater. Probably Volpe!" she exclaimed. "If he were smart, he'd have taken the $300,000 and run."

Nando didn't answer. His sister didn't seem as confident after she saw the Sunday newspaper's blockbuster announcement.

## BOOZE, BROADS, GAMBLING, AND DEATH.

A new three-part series on Prohibition in Texas, beginning January 1st.

That was followed by a short piece directly involving the Asturias name.

Asturias Enterprises has filed Chapter 11. Was the recent, shocking sale of one of its stellar assets, the 100-year-old Rue de L'Histoire Theatre, because of financial troubles? Stay tuned.

Outraged, Victoria tore the paper to pieces, shouting, "Isabel is behind this. I know it. I feel it. She's angling to get that gold."

Coming back to the present, Nando found himself at his destination, unaware of the drive getting there. He wasn't happy about this part of Victoria's plan, but she'd been right about everything else so far. He turned into the Café Russ parking lot.

Billy and Harold sat outside of Nando's apartment and waited until he left. "Let's go," Billy said.

Deftly, Billy used his tools to unlock Nando's front door. "No mess this time," Billy instructed. "I don't want him to know we were here."

It took less than an hour for them to do a clean sweep. "Nothing."

Back in Billy's car, Harold said, "I followed him to his sister's house. If there's more gold, maybe it's there."

"There is more gold, I'm sure of it. Nando doesn't have a poker face. That's why he loses so much when he gambles." Billy laughed. "You followed him to a gold dealer in Dallas. He hasn't used any in Austin. Why?"

"Why?" Harold asked.

"We got an echo in here?" Billy asked. "Because Nando's sister is the brains of the family. She wants to keep the gold a secret." He grinned. "We'll find it and keep our own secret. Get my drift?" Billy's laugh was menacing. "Now, how do I get to his sister's house?"

"Use the GPS," Harold said.

"No. Tell me how to get there." Billy would never leave a computer trace in his car. Harold gave Billy directions.

In the café, Nando asked for a table facing the window. Twisting his pinky ring, he reviewed the details of Victoria's plan while he waited and enjoyed the sweet aroma of croissants and other French pastries. He watched the brightly lit parking lot. When Isabel got out of her car, her sequined sneakers sparkled as she passed under the glaring light from the light pole. Nando sent a text. *Go!*

As soon as she walked in, he waved her over, pulled out her chair, leaned in, and kissed her cheek. "I'm glad you came," he said.

Once their coffee and strawberry croissants were served, he kept the conversation light. "So, your holiday break is almost here. Are you going back to New York?" he asked, already aware that she wasn't.

"I'm looking forward to the break, but my family is coming here for the last *Nutcracker* performance, and they'll stay through Christmas."

"Do you miss New York?"

"Dancers get used to moving around. I miss my family, but that's about it. I do like it here in Austin, though. Have you lived here all your life?"

"Yes. I guess you know my family is often in the news. Did you see Sunday's paper?" he asked. Nando watched a pink glow rise in Isabel's cheeks. He was disappointed. He'd hoped Victoria was wrong about Isabel being the culprit who triggered the newspaper article.

"I saw something about it." She lowered her eyes and fluffed it off. "Are you and your sister close?"

"Like most brothers and sisters, I suppose."

Nando turned the conversation back to Christmas. When he was ready to leave, he kept up the charade. "May I call you? Maybe we can have dinner after the holidays."

Isabel gave him her cell number. "This was nice," she said, reaching over for his hand. "That's an interesting ring. I have a picture of my great-grandfather wearing one that looks just like it."

Nando shrugged. "Interesting," he answered. He walked Isabel to her car. Turning her to face him, her back against the driver's door, his lips brushed hers. "Merry Christmas," he said and walked away.

Isabel was surprised by the kiss. That her heart skipped a beat, surprised her more, but the coffee date revealed nothing. He hadn't even blinked when she mentioned the ring, and now she'd have to change her cell phone number.

# CHAPTER 52

## THANK GOD FOR SEQUINS

Dusk turned to night while Mrs. B. and Father Melvyn sat in her car and watched the window at Café Russ. Nando and Isabel were clearly visible at the window table.

"Oh no," Mrs. B. said, peering through her binoculars.

"What?" Father Melvyn asked.

Mrs. B. thrust the binoculars at the priest. "She's reached for his hand. She's looking at the ring and talking. What is she saying to him? I don't read lips."

Father Melvyn took the binoculars and adjusted them, but too late. Nando and Isabel had gotten up and were walking out of the cafe to Isabel's car.

"Duck," Mrs. B. said. They slid down in their seats. When Father Melvyn peeked over the rim of the car door, Nando was walking toward his car.

Father Melvyn said, "That's a relief."

Frustrated and worried, Mrs. B. said, "I'm calling her. I don't care if she realizes we're spying. What is that girl thinking?"

Mrs. B. dialed. Isabel was still; her head was pressed back on the headrest. She didn't answer.

"What is she doing?" Father Melvyn asked.

Mrs. B. peered through the binoculars. "Oh God," she gasped. "There's someone in the back seat." A figure leaned forward and held something against Isabel's head.

They watched Isabel start her car and drive slowly out of the parking lot.

"Get going," Father Melvyn said. Mrs. B. handed him the binoculars, started her own car, and followed.

Mrs. B. turned the ignition key. "Keep your eyes on her car. It's dark, and I don't want to lose her."

Billy pulled up to the curb in front of the Asturias mansion. "Get out and case the place. I'll drive around. Call me when it's okay to go in."

From the French doors at the back of the house, Harold called his boss. "I can see the alarm pad," he whispered. "The light's green."

Twenty minutes later, dodging in and out of the shrubs, plants, and shadows, Billy joined Harold at the French doors.

Breaking in was easy; finding what they wanted was not. They started upstairs in the bedrooms, carelessly pulling things apart. The average time for burglary was twelve minutes. This would take longer.

They discovered nothing; Billy cursed. "C'mon," he said. He and Harold ran down the back stairs into the kitchen. Billy reached for the freezer door handle. "You start with the pantry."

The sound of the garage door going up stopped them. Scrambling, they flattened themselves against the wall next to the kitchen door that opened in from the garage. The garage door went up then down a second time. "What the hell is going on?" Harold whispered.

Billy put his finger to his lips signaling Harold to be quiet, and gripped his gun, ready to strike. They heard scuffling and a female yelp; then, the door flew open, giving them cover.

"Stop fighting, Isabel," Nando snarled and dragged her into the kitchen. Her wrists were duct-taped behind her back; another piece covered her mouth.

The last person in was a smaller woman dressed in black. She held a roll of duct tape in one hand and a gun in the other.

As soon as the trio was inside, Billy stepped up. He pushed his gun against the armed woman's head.

"Drop it, and turn around," he ordered. She didn't move. He cocked his pistol. "Now!"

She dropped her gun; Billy shoved her. "Hands up," he commanded. Harold stepped forward, picked up the gun, and pointed it. "She's the sister," he said.

"Billy!" Nando gasped.

"Where's the gold?" Billy's tone was icy.

Victoria blurted, "Damn you, Nando."

"Shut up, bitch," Billy snarled as the doorbell started to ring. It rang and rang, repeatedly chiming in the house.

"What the hell?" Billy snarled. "See who that is," he told Harold. "You two," he said, waving the gun at Nando and Victoria. "Don't make a sound." Harold went out through the kitchen door.

They could hear a female voice shouting at the front door. Billy's cell phone rang. "It's a broad. Grab her before someone calls the police."

Billy shoved the trussed Isabel down on the kitchen floor. "Stay there," he snarled. At gunpoint, he pushed Nando and Victoria toward the front door. Holding Victoria's arm, he signaled to Nando to open it.

Nando tore open the door, reached out, grabbed the screaming doorbell ringer, and yanked her inside without realizing who it was. "Laurel!" he exclaimed.

"I want to talk to you—" Laurel's shouts died in her throat when a gun was shoved in her face.

"Shut up or you get it first." Billy pushed her against Nando. He then grabbed Victoria's hair and yanked her head back. "Where's the damn gold?"

At the sound of a scuffle behind them, still holding Victoria by her hair, Billy swung around. Harold was dragging Isabel into the front hall.

"This one was trying to get away."

Billy twisted the handful of Victoria's hair. She gasped. Looking at Nando, he said, "Times-a-wastin," he said. "Tell me where…"

The blare of sirens interrupted his actions. "Shit!" he snapped. "All of you, on the floor." He pushed Victoria down hard.

Harold grabbed the girl already bound and gagged and shoved her down beside Laurel.

Billy cocked the trigger. "All of you, close your eyes or die." The wail of sirens was closing in.

Victoria heard their footsteps going toward the back doors; she dared a look. They were gone. She jumped up. "Let's go!"

Nando started to apologize; she cut him off, all business. "We only have minutes. I'll take this one." She grabbed Isabel by the hair and pulled her to her feet. "Take Laurel and keep her quiet." They dragged the girls through the kitchen. "And take the money," Victoria ordered.

Holding Laurel with one hand, Nando reached into the pantry, shoved cans and bottles out of his way, and pulled out the nylon bag. The sirens were now right in front of the house. Laurel tried to twist free and scream.

Nando slapped her hard. "Do that again, and I'll put your lights out permanently."

Victoria shoved Isabel down the cellar steps. Nando dragged Laurel down behind him.

"There." Father Melvyn said, pointing to the huge house on an unfamiliar street. They watched Isabel's car disappear into a garage. A second car pulled in beside hers.

On her third try and Mrs. B. hissed into her cell phone, "C'mon Jake, pick up." Then, "thank God," she said. "You've got to get here. Isabel has been kidnapped at gunpoint." She gave Jake the address.

After she explained what they'd witnessed, Jake said, "I'm sending squad cars from the nearest precinct, and I'm on my way. Don't do anything!" Jake ordered.

Mrs. B. and Father Melvyn were about to get out of their car when a Prius jerked to a stop on the driveway, where moments earlier, Isabel's car had entered the garage. In the dark, they couldn't identify the woman who jumped out and ran to the front door, pressed her finger on the doorbell, and screamed, "I know you're in there, Nando! Open this door, or I'll scream down the neighborhood!"

The front door opened, a man's arm reached out, grabbed the shouting woman, and yanked her inside. The door slammed shut.

The first squad car arrived, killed its siren, but left the lights flashing. Mrs. B. ran over. "In the house. A girl has been kidnapped."

The policewoman nodded. "We got the call."

A second squad car arrived. The policewoman gave directions. "You two take the back," she told the arriving officers. With their guns drawn, two uniformed officers made their way around back, and the policewoman and her partner went to the front door.

"Police, open up!" she shouted, then stood to the side and waited.

An unmarked car screeched to a halt behind them, followed by two more squad cars. Jake and Marv jumped out and ran toward the house. "Stay here," he shouted to Mrs. B. and the priest. As soon as Jake was gone, Father Melvyn tapped Mrs. B.'s arm and jerked his head toward the shrubs. Unnoticed, they backed up and slipped away.

Staying close to the bushes, they used the trees on the front lawn for cover and reached the front door undetected.

The entry foyer was empty. They crept through the dining room and moved in the direction of the garage.

When they reached the kitchen, Jake spun around at the sound of the footsteps, his gun at the ready. "I told you to wait outside! I could have shot you!" he yelled. "Why are you in here?"

Marv ran down the front steps and into the kitchen. "No one up there, but it's been ransacked."

Jake was about to order them out when Mrs. B. pointed. The door to the garage was ajar.

"Look! That's Isabel's car!"

Father Melvyn was desperate. "Jake, there isn't much time. We won't get in the way. Let us help you search."

Jake snapped, "Arguing with you two is like arguing with a brick wall and wasting time. Stay out of the way."

Marv had opened another door. "Cellar," he said and felt for a light switch. Marv went down, followed by Jake, then the housekeeper, and the priest.

The detectives went deep into the basement, leaving Mrs. B. and Father Melvyn at the foot of the stairs looking around. Father Melvyn aimed his flashlight beam into shadows created by old furniture and junk.

Marv and Jake came back fast. "Nothing. They may have gone out the back," Jake said, heading up the staircase. Father Melvyn made a final sweep of the walls with his flashlight.

"Wait!" Mrs. B. yelled. "Over there." She ran to the shelves on the adjacent wall, where the flashlight beam had reflected off something shiny on the floor. It was partially trapped behind the bookcase. She wrenched it out. "This is Isabel's sneaker."

"Are you sure?" Jake asked.

"Yes. She was wearing these today. I admired the sparkles and flowers." She handed it to Jake. The four looked at each other.

"Where exactly did you find this?" Jake asked.

"Here," she said. "Sticking out from the side of this bookcase."

"How the hell did it get back there?" Marv muttered as the two detectives and the priest tried to pull the case away from the wall; it wouldn't budge. Grunting from the strain, they tried pushing it sideways.

It didn't move.

The detectives ran their hands along the shelves, and Father Melvyn felt the frame from top to bottom. His left hand hit something metal. He pushed down on it. With the loud creak of unoiled hinges, the bookcase swung away from the wall. "Look out!" he shouted. They jumped back.

"What the hell?" Jake sputtered. Shaking his head in disbelief, gun in one hand, flashlight in the other, Jake stepped behind the bookcase and into a tunnel, followed by Marv.

Mrs. B. muttered, "Thank God for sequins," then followed Marv, with Father Melvyn close behind.

# CHAPTER 53

## THE LAST HOARSE SCREAM

"Move," Victoria hissed, shoving Isabel through a rough-hewn tunnel. At a dead-end, Victoria pressed a lever. When the false door swung open, Victoria pushed her through. Isabel was astonished to find herself in the prop room in the Rue de L'Histoire Theatre. She heard scuffling and turned to see Laurel struggling against Nando's grip.

"Enough," Victoria snarled and swung Isabel around. She ripped off a length of the duct tape from Isabel's wrists and handed it to Nando. "Use this and make it tight." Realizing what Victoria had done, Isabel tested the tape on her wrists, but they were still tightly bound.

Victoria handed Nando her gun. "Watch them while I check the theater. There was only one performance today. So there shouldn't be anyone here."

Isabel prayed that someone would find the sneaker she'd managed to get off her foot before Victoria had dragged her behind the bookcase. Isabel looked over at Laurel, whose eyes were wide with fear. Isabel realized Laurel was terrified, but then again, so was she.

Victoria walked back into the prop room. "No one's here," she said and grabbed Isabel's arm. "Let's go."

"Now what?" asked Nando.

"Everyone knows our dear Laurel is obsessed with you and hates Isabel." Victoria stood face to face with Laurel. "You're very pretty but not very bright," she sneered. "I watched you puncture Isabel's tire. Did you really think that would accomplish anything?" Victoria laughed. "I'll tell the police at the right time."

"What about Isabel's car?" Nando asked. "The police must have seen it by now."

"Right," Victoria said. "Let me think." She massaged her temples with her eyes closed for a moment. "Here's the story. You invited Isabel to the house. That's why her car was in the garage. Laurel followed you and created a scene." Victoria looked from Isabel to Laurel and nodded, content with the developing scenario. "Someone called the police, but Laurel, who was—is, insanely jealous, had a gun." Victoria smiled. "Yes. That's it. Laurel is insane, and when she heard the sirens, she kidnapped both of you at gunpoint, forcing you out the back door and through the wooded area, leading across the fields to the theater. I'll make sure she has a key when they find her."

"How'd she know the way?" he asked.

"I don't know!" Victoria snapped. "She'll be dead, so the police won't be able to ask her. We left my car at the mall, remember? So I'm not home, and I don't know anything."

Victoria took a breath. "Moving right along. When you got here, you tried to grab the gun, but she smashed you over the head. Later, I'll hit you so you'll have a scalp injury." Nando made a face; Victoria ignored him. Then, in a sugary-sweet voice, she continued. "Our darling Isabel, here, got free and must have run up the ladder to the catwalk. Laurel, determined to kill her, followed."

Isabel listened. Her fear turned to red-hot anger at Victoria's arrogance and certainty that they could get away with murder. She pulled away, determined not to make it easy.

Victoria grabbed her arm and held her in place.

"And our blackmailer?" Nando asked.

Victoria's laugh was wicked. "What's he going to do? Go to the police? Once we know for sure who this sucker is, we may alter the scene a bit. After all," she laughed, her voice again becoming syrupy, "I'd rather keep all the money. Then again, maybe it's the ghosts." Her high-pitched giggle scared Isabel.

Victoria reached for the coil of rope on the floor. "Here." She made a slipknot, passed the long end through Laurel's arms, and handed it to Nando. She then took another length of rope and made another slipknot.

Isabel squeezed her arms tight against her sides, preventing Victoria from slipping the rope between them. Nando reached over and slapped Isabel with his free hand. She saw the flash of Rafael's ring before it crashed into her cheek. The jolt loosened her arms enough for Victoria to slip the rope through.

Victoria held Isabel in place while Nando started up the steps. Laurel tried to pull back; Nando yanked the rope; Laurel stumbled.

"I'll push her from behind, but you need to pull her."

Isabel heard Nando curse as his foot slipped off a metal step. The leather soles of his designer Italian shoes were not meant for climbing metal rung ladders.

"Hurry up," Victoria ordered. Once on the catwalk, Nando slammed Laurel down and tied the end of her rope around the first bolt he saw. "I'm ready," he called down.

Isabel struggled, dropping to her knees. Victoria grabbed the long end of the rope, wrapped it around Isabel's neck, and threw the loose end to Nando.

Nando pulled. Anything Isabel did to resist made it harder to breathe. Struggling for air and getting dizzy, she involuntarily moved her feet up the steps to keep pressure off her throat. Finally, she reached the catwalk and watched Nando knot the end of her rope on the bolt where he'd tied Laurel's.

A minute later, Victoria was on top of her and tore the duct tape off Isabel's lips, making her cry out as the sticky tape took skin with it.

"You were such a beautiful dancer. You could have had a great future if you'd left well enough alone," Victoria said. "You made me do this." Victoria grabbed Isabel's hair.

Isabel opened her mouth to scream. Nothing came out. Victoria's voice sounded far away, even though her face was close.

"Yell as loud as you like. There's no one to hear you."

Isabel fought to suck in as much air as she could through her constricted throat; she felt her eyes bulge.

"Move Laurel away. I need leverage," Victoria told Nando, relaxing the pressure of the rope on Isabel's throat. Isabel took advantage of the moment, tilted her head back, and gave one hoarse scream.

"Laurel, drop down!"

"Bitch!" Victoria snarled and yanked the rope tighter. Isabel saw Laurel fall to the walkway before black spots danced in front of her eyes. There was a strange beeping in her ears. Isabel fought not to pass out.

Victoria's head snapped up. "Someone's disengaging the alarm!" She hissed at Nando, "Fast. Take out the ghost light." Nando looked around and saw a metal tool on the floor of the walkway to his left. He picked it up and hurled it. The globe broke; the ghost light went out.

Tony arrived at the theater early; he wanted to be ready. Confident that Victoria would pay, he felt his fortunes were turning. Tonight would be the start of the rest of his life. Upset at first that she hadn't delivered the total amount, he realized the delay had helped him.

He'd taken a safe deposit box where he stashed the duffle bag with the first installment, part of which he'd used to open an account in a US Bank Western Union. Later, he'd transfer the monies either to Belize or the Caymans. He also kept copies of the pictures he'd taken of the gold, the skeleton, and the hidden room at the theater.

Whistling softly, Tony disengaged the alarm. He heard a crash and the sound of breaking glass. What happened to the ghost light? He walked toward the sounds of scuffling and footfalls on metal and reached for the overhead light switch.

Jake's and Marv's police issue, LED flashlights, lit the last ten feet of the tunnel as they arrived at the dead end. "This must lead somewhere," Jake said. "Marv, hold your flashlight up." Mrs. B. and Father Melvyn looked over Marv's shoulder while Jake ran both hands over the stones, across the center, and then around the edges.

"Aha!" Jake said, pulling down on a lever. The wall swung open, and they walked through. "Where are we?" Marv whispered.

Mrs. B. walked in. "We are in the Rue de L'Histoire Theatre."

Noise. Brawling. Mrs. B. pushed past the men and ran to the stage, with Father Melvyn on her heels. She looked up toward the sounds above her head.

Father Melvyn yelled, "Up there!"

Voices yelped, cried out, and cursed. Marv pointed his flashlight up at the bodies twisting, turning, and colliding on the narrow walkway.

"That's Isabel," Mrs. B. shouted, pointing to a body almost halfway over the rail. Someone was pushing her.

"It's Victoria Asturias!" Father Melvyn shouted.

Jake and Marv aimed their beams at the two figures. Momentarily blinded by the bright light and shocked to hear her name, Victoria took her hands off Isabel's back.

"Police! Stop!" Jake shouted.

"Help," Isabel's croak was barely audible as she slid down to the walkway.

Pressing their flashlights into Mrs. B's and Father Melvyn's hands, Jake and Marv ran to the catwalk ladder.

Heart thudding in her chest, Mrs. B. held the light steady and watched the battle on the catwalk. She heard Father Melvyn whispering prayers as he, too, kept the beam of his light on the action.

They saw Victoria yank the rope around Isabel's neck, forcing her to stand up. Victoria screamed, "This is all your fault!" She placed both hands on Isabel's chest and pushed her halfway over the rail. Nando tried to reach Victoria, but Laurel scooted back, blocking his path.

"What's that sound?" Mrs. B. asked. The stressed ropes creaked and groaned as they twisted against one another and against the bolt on the metal piping of the catwalk, followed by a screech of metal pulling off metal. Something flew across the narrow catwalk. It thudded into Victoria, hitting her between the shoulder blades, making her cry out and jerk backward.

Her hands came away from Isabel, who once again slid to the floor.

Mrs. B. gulped. "Oh, God."

Jake had reached the walkway and yelled once again. "Police! Stop!"

Ignoring the order, Victoria reached down to grab Isabel's rope, but the dancer was fast. She twisted her body, pulled her legs and feet into her chest, and kicked Victoria hard in the stomach. The impact of her forceful legs lifted Victoria off the catwalk floor and flipped her over the rail. There was one scream, then a sickening crunch as the overhead lights came on.

"Look!" Father Melvyn said. Mrs. B. glanced across the stage to see Tony Volpe, one hand on the light switch, staring up at the catwalk.

Nando leaned over the rail and screamed his sister's name.

Jake reached the girls who were sprawled on the narrow walkway. Nando took off in the opposite direction.

Coming up behind Jake, Marv yelled, "Go!" Jake leaped over the girls and gave chase.

Nando jumped for the metal ladder adjacent to the catwalk, but his leather soles slid off the rungs. Screaming, trying to stop his fall, Nando grasped a rope beside the ladder and clung to it with both hands. The thrust of his body made the rope swing out wide. He twisted, trying to stop it when something above him clanged.

He looked up as a sandbag crashed into his face and snapped his head back. His hands released the rope from the force of the blow. He landed at Tony Volpe's feet.

Emergency vehicles and police cars filled the parking lot of the Rue de L'Histoire Theatre. Father Melvyn and Mrs. B. pulled their coats closed in the cold night air and watched the police and EMS activity swarming in and out of the theater.

"Is Isabel ever coming out?" Mrs. B whispered to Father Melvyn. "I'm terrified for her. She took quite a beating." The priest squeezed her shoulder.

Two officers, with Tony Volpe between them, exited the theater. Jake and Marv followed. They passed in front of Mrs. B. and the priest. She heard Jake say, "Count this again before it goes into evidence."

Medical technicians hurried out with a gurney. It was Nando. Father Melvyn had already placed the prayer stole he always carried in his pocket around his neck. He started toward Nando, but the paramedics lifted the gurney into the ambulance and took off, sirens blaring.

Victoria's gurney was rolled out next. She was unconscious with an oxygen mask strapped to her face, an IV in her arm, and foam blocks immobilizing her head and neck.

Before the paramedics lifted her into the ambulance, Father Melvyn made the sign of the cross on her forehead. He continued his prayers even after the ambulance doors closed.

Another paramedic escorted Isabel and Laurel to a third EMS vehicle.

As soon as Mrs. B. saw Isabel walk out under her own steam, she sighed with relief and ran over. Sitting beside the dancer, Mrs. B. hugged her as the medical technician examined and treated her bruised and bleeding feet. Isabel sobbed and pressed her face into Mrs. B.'s shoulder.

Jake walked over. "How are they?" he asked. The paramedic pointed to Laurel. "She's okay. Looks like minor cuts and bruises, but this one," he said, indicating Isabel, should be examined at the hospital."

Laurel cried, "He said he loved me! I'm sorry. I was jealous. I thought he was leaving me for you."

Isabel lifted her head. "And for that," she said, her voice hoarse, "you drove a nail into my tire and shredded my pointe shoe?"

Laurel clamped her mouth shut.

# CHAPTER 54

## TIME IS NOT ON MY SIDE

Jake and Marv walked into the interrogation room, where Tony Volpe waited to give his statement.

"What were you doing in the theater. There were no performances tonight?" Jake asked.

Tony explained that he'd been spending nights in the theater trying to find out what was going on. He'd returned intending to spend the night hoping to catch the culprits who were pranking the theater–or discover if there was a ghost.

Marv sputtered, "Do you expect us to believe a ghost story?"

"I don't expect you to believe anything," Tony snapped. "You asked me what I was doing there. So I'm telling you."

"Continue," Jake said.

"When I walked in, I heard a commotion coming from the stage area. Before I could turn on the overhead lights, I heard shouting from the other side of the building. Then a body fell from the catwalk. I was shocked," Tony said. "And then another body and a sandbag plummeted to the floor in front of my feet."

"Write it down," Jake said, pushing a pad and pencil across the table.

The detectives walked out of the interrogation room.

"Anything?" their lieutenant asked.

Jake shook his head. "Nothing we can use—yet. There's more to this guy's involvement than meets the eye."

"We accessed his prints from New York," Marv said, "but we have to wait to see if they show up on the duffle bag we found with the money."

"We've searched his office. Nothing suspicious," Jake added.

"Did you put a rush on the prints?" the lieutenant asked.

"We did," Jake answered. "Can't we hold him as a material witness?" he asked, disgusted that Volpe might get away.

"No. He claims not to have seen anything before the bodies fell, and we don't have probable cause for search warrants." The lieutenant shook her head. "Cut him loose and have him watched. Then, if those prints match, pick him up again."

Dressing Wednesday morning, Tony Volpe felt that time was not on his side. He'd need to act fast. He chose one of his bulkiest jackets and left his apartment, grateful to Mother Nature for the cold December air.

At Walmart, he bought shaving cream, shampoo, and a men's compression vest. Then, returning to his car, he threw his purchases in the back seat and muttered, "Got that, fellas?" He was sure the police had a tail on him.

Next stop, the bank. He wouldn't take a bag inside. That would be a red flag.

In the private room for safe deposit-box holders, Tony pulled out the plastic bags and twine he'd stuffed in his pants pockets before leaving his apartment. In record time, he shoved all the money into them, along with the pictures he'd taken at the Rue.

He threaded the cord through the bag handles, tied them around his chest, and then tucked the bottoms into his waistband. When it was all secure, he left the bank and went home.

First part done, he thought, entering his apartment. He knew the police would comb the theater again, and the company might not be able to perform that evening, but that was no longer his concern. At the top of his list was how fast the police might get a search warrant.

Tony pulled on the compression vest, leaving the tabs loose. He stuffed it with the bags of money and tightened the pull-tabs. He then dressed and looked at himself in the mirror. Stiff and uncomfortable, it worked nonetheless. He undressed, removed the shoes that lined the closet floor, then pulled up the carpeting and slid the money and pictures he'd taken out of the bank under it, smoothed and re-tacked the carpet, and returned the shoes to the closet floor. Satisfied, he now had to wait for night— that was the hardest part.

It was midafternoon when the phone rang. "Hi, Tony," said John Bono. "The police finished. We can go on tonight."

"Wow. Much to do," he answered. Lucky break. This was an opportunity. "I'll be right over." He pulled up the freshly tacked carpet, took everything out, and hid it all on his body, under the compression vest, along with his passport. It would be an uncomfortable day, but he'd manage.

At the theater, Tony parked under a light. He wanted his car visible. Inside, he forced his mind on the work necessary to get the stage ready and directed his crew to work fast; there were only a few hours before curtain. Waiting was agony; keeping a neutral, professional air was exhausting.

"You don't look so good," Charlie said. "You okay?"

"Yes. I feel like I'm coming down with something, or maybe the whole episode took its toll."

Time barely moved. Fearing the police would arrive with a warrant, every strange sound made him jump; every time the backstage door opened, his heart flipped.

The performance went well, but he hardly noticed. He oversaw the cleanup and preparations for the next day and waited until everyone, including Charlie, was gone. As they left, his crew told him to feel better, and Charlie said, "Have a Hot Toddy when you get home."

Tony nodded, smiled, and sat behind his desk, finishing paperwork, and waited.

Sweating from his tightly wrapped midsection, he considered making his escape through Victoria's tunnel but thought better of it. Would the police be waiting on the other side? So instead, he went to the costume shop and rummaged around.

Ready, he thought, looking in the mirror. He'd left the light on in his office and the alarm disengaged, and made his way across the darkened auditorium and let himself out.

With his new black wig, eyeglasses, and mustache, he kept his head down and hunched his shoulders.

Then, eyes lowered, he passed a few winos and night-people on his long walk through the old section of the city to the downtown bus station where he boarded the first bus out of Austin.

# CHAPTER 55

## TRUTH IS STRANGER THAN FICTION

Despite the cold, sunlight streamed into the kitchen window at St. Francis de Sales rectory. In five days, it would be Christmas. For the first time in two weeks, Father Melvyn, Mrs. B., and Father Declan enjoyed coffee and rolls together, and LaLa sat in her favorite chair at the table. She wiggled in anticipation and batted her eyes, welcoming them back to normalcy.

"Do you have the full story?" Father Declan asked.

"The police are piecing it together, but there are so many unanswered questions. Fernando Asturias died on the way to the hospital, and his sister, Victoria, hasn't regained consciousness. Who knows if all the facts will ever be known," said Father Melvyn.

"Amazing how truth is often stranger than fiction," Mrs. B. said, refilling their cups.

"Then there's the stage manager who disappeared without a trace," Father Melvyn added.

Father Declan looked at the time. "I'd love to hear this, but I have a funeral mass, so I'm off to the church."

"You can read all about it in the papers. They're covering it non-stop," Father Melvyn said. After Father Declan left, Father Melvyn asked, "What's happening with the company since Volpe's disappearance?"

"A veteran of the crew, a man named Mel, took over as stage manager. It's going fine. John said all the shows since that night have been sold out." She turned the coffee cup in her hands. "Why, Father, do we humans gravitate to tragedy?"

Father Melvyn shook his head. "Another question for the ages. Many psychological studies address this." Rubbing his mustache with his thumb, he added, "Perhaps, in some ways, it's because we know that there but for the Grace of God—" He shook his head. "Is Isabel dancing?"

"She resumes her roles tomorrow. There are only a few performances left. Her family arrives in two days." Mrs. B. looked troubled. "I heard from her last night after her Aunt Marie called her. The story reached the papers in San Angelo."

The doorbell rang twice, intruding on their conversation. "Hold your horses," Mrs. B. muttered, making her way to the front door. "Coming," she called out. Lala ran to her observation perch and growled.

Mrs. B. looked at LaLa and wondered what troubles were coming to their doorstep now?

"Good morning." Jake's greeting was jovial.

"And to you," Mrs. B. answered.

"Got a cup of coffee for a hard-working detective?" He walked past her toward the kitchen, smiling internally at her wide-eyed surprise.

"What's in that case?" Mrs. B. asked, following him.

He didn't answer. LaLa made a peculiar sound, something between a meow and a growl, as if unsure of how to greet him.

"How are you, Jake?" Father Melvyn asked, handing him a steaming cup.

"Under the circumstances, not bad. What a case this turned out to be. Talk about the sins of the father." Jake shook his head. "As you know, Volpe got away. We're still not sure of his involvement, but his disappearance speaks volumes."

"Roll?" Mrs. B. offered.

"Don't mind if I do." Jake reached for the knife and slathered butter on it, making the priest and Sammi wait. He took a bite. "Ummm. Good roll," he said, smiling.

"When we searched the Asturias home, we found journals left by Victoria's and Nando's great-grandfather, Victor. It was through his journals that we learned the how and why of that tunnel."

Almost as an aside, he said, "To dig and build such a tunnel in today's world might not be so easy. But, of course, El Chapo and the Sinaloan Drug Cartel have done an impressive job with their drug and escape tunnels between the U.S. and Mexico." Jake washed another bite of the roll down with coffee and let that sink in. He was enjoying keeping them in suspense.

"Since there are no performances on Mondays, we sent a team into the theater. They found new plasterboard behind a cabinet in the prop room. When we broke through, we found a skeleton. From Victor's journals, we surmised it was Rafael Sanchez." Jake drank more coffee. "Isabel has given us a DNA sample to see they are related." While Jake ate the rest of his roll, the priest and his friend Sammi waited in silence.

"According to one of Victor's journals," Jake continued, "he 'took care' of Rafael Sanchez and stole the gold Sanchez was accumulating. He hid the body and the gold in what was a barn on Sanchez land. He said changing the deed cost him, but he didn't say how much or who he bribed in the land office."

Jake became thoughtful again. "Sometimes vanity makes criminals outsmart themselves. Fearing reprisals from the Italian mob, he chose not to dispose of the body or move the gold. Instead, he left it all in the barn, then built a community theater over it and donated it to the city, but had a secret tunnel constructed from his house to the theater." Jake set the heavy satchel on the table.

"What's in there?" Father Melvyn asked, pointing to the case.

"Open it." They didn't move. "It won't bite," Jake said, chuckling at their reluctance.

LaLa jumped on the table and sniffed the case.

"Oh, this is ridiculous," Mrs. B. said. She reached out and opened the case. She pulled out several smelly old diaries. "What are these?" she asked.

"Victor Asturias's journals," Jake said, noting their shocked faces. "They are not evidence of anything recent, but they go to motive and must be made available to the DA and the Asturias lawyers." Jake fought to control his desire to laugh. He'd never seen them speechless. "Interesting read. Kept me up for two nights."

"What's going to happen to Victoria?" Mrs. B. asked.

"Hard to say. The ADA will file charges against her, but the doctors say Victoria will be a quadriplegic if she survives at all." Jake's eyebrows knit. "I think many questions will go unanswered."

"Such as?" Mrs. B. asked.

Jake became serious. "We don't know if Victoria had anything to do with Adam Leightman's murder since we've never found the weapon used to crush his skull."

Jake scratched his head. "And, according to Victor's journals, there should have been gold stashed in that secret room with the body. Where is it?" Almost to himself, Jake said, "Too bad Nando died in the ambulance after the sandbag snapped his neck. He could have told us a lot."

"Terrible end," Father Melvyn said, crossing himself.

Jake looked at his wristwatch and drained his cup. "I seem to have misplaced my satchel," he said, jutting his chin at the case on the table, "but I'm sure it will turn up in a day or two."

Mrs. B. followed him to the front door. "Jake, to whom would that gold belong if it's found?"

Jake shrugged. "Complicated question. The law says the property owner. If it had been in the theater, it would have been the ballet company, but it's not there. If the DNA proves the skeleton is Rafael Sanchez, Isabel's family might have a claim."

"Could Victoria and Nando have found it and gotten it out? Could it be hidden somewhere in their house?"

Leaning in, Jake whispered, "It's not for publication, but I'm sending another team to the house. They had a secret tunnel in the basement, maybe there's a secret hiding place, but I wonder if finding that gold would unleash more hell. Read Victor's journals. You'll understand."

He added, "Rafael Sanchez was no angel. Ill-gotten gains and all that."

Crossing the threshold, Jake turned back. "Sammi, one of these days, you're going to learn to trust me and give me the information you and the padre ferret out before the crisis. I'll be back when you remind me that I'd forgotten that case here." He winked and waved goodbye.

Two days later, Jake arrived at the rectory to pick up the case, he'd 'forgotten,' Father Melvyn greeted him.

"Thank you, Jake," the priest said. "Mrs. B. and I read them. They explain so much." He shook his head. "They read like a nasty crime novel."

The detective and the priest shook hands. Jake took the case and departed.

# CHAPTER 56

## TRUTH BE TOLD

Isabel peeked out, then yanked open her door. "What are you doing here?"

Her aunt marched past her. "When we spoke on the phone," her aunt began, "I promised we'd keep this whole horrid episode a secret for a few days." Aunt Marie pulled off her coat. "How about a cup of coffee?"

"Did you drive?"

"No. I flew. I must get back home tonight. This, however, cannot wait. I need to know what the hell really happened."

Isabel put up the coffee. Because she wasn't expecting anyone, she hadn't put make-up on her bruised neck. Her aunt reached over and pushed Isabel's hair back. Isabel looked away.

Turning the hot cup in her hand, her aunt began. "As you know, your mother had heart surgery as a child, and the entire family became very protective of her, maybe too much, especially my father. You know you were her miracle baby," her aunt said with a smile. Isabel nodded. "Truth be told, we've always suspected Rafael's mafia connections, but certainly not the details I've read in the papers. I'm not sure your grandfather knew them either. After all, Rafael disappeared, leaving everyone to guess what the truth was." Aunt Marie added more sugar and stirred.

"Your mother was ashamed of this mob thing and spent her life hiding it from you and from your father."

Isabel listened in stony silence.

Marie sighed. "I never agreed with her, but being so much younger and not wanting to stress or upset her, I said nothing. Now it's all out in the open."

"Is there any way we can hide it?"

"Hide it? The story is in every major paper from Midland to Houston, and your name is in the middle of everything."

Isabel covered her face with her hands. What had she done? Would her family, especially her mother, forgive her for dredging up this ugly old history?

Isabel choked off a sob. "I just want to have a great Christmas with all of you and get through the last performance. Can we do that?" Isabel sipped her coffee to control her building emotions. "Besides, these people can't hurt us anymore." In desperation, she added, "I swear, the day after Christmas, I'll tell all of you everything." She looked at her empty cup. Almost to herself, she whispered, "And, I broke my promise."

Her aunt answered: "I know all about that, and there'll be hell to pay."

"Mom and Dad will be here in two days. Maybe the story won't be on the front pages anymore."

"I hope so. But right now, tell it to me."

Isabel swallowed hard and told her aunt everything. "Victoria Asturias was determined to kill me and almost succeeded that night in the theater because she learned that I was looking for proof of my Grandfather's claim. I've never found anything to uphold it, but after the kidnapping and attempt on my life, the police found a skeleton hidden behind a wall in the theater when the story came out. I don't know how they came to the conclusion that it may be Rafael Sanchez, but I've given a DNA sample to test."

"That wasn't in the papers!" Aunt Marie reached for Isabel's hand. "I know how much you loved my father, and he adored you. What you did was for him, and it almost got you killed, but I'm proud of you."

Her aunt's reaction unglued her. Isabel burst into tears.

"Does anyone else know?"

"Yes," Isabel said, swallowing a sob. "My boss's mother, Mrs. B., and the pastor of St. Francis de Sales Church. They saved my life."

"Well, I shall thank them." Aunt Marie looked at her watch. "Stop crying and get your coat. I'm taking you to dinner, and you're taking me to the airport. My flight is at 9:00 p.m."

At the terminal, Isabel hugged her aunt. "I'll be back with my boys in a couple of days," said Aunt Marie. "We'll face my sister together after Christmas."

Isabel watched her aunt walk into the terminal and felt an incredible sense of relief.

She had an ally in the family.

# CHAPTER 57

## THE LAST SHOW

Despite her worries about telling her mother what had happened, on December 23rd, Isabel was thrilled to see her parents. While they checked in at the hotel, she glanced at the newspaper racks. Nothing about the Rue, at least not on the front pages. A small relief.

Her aunt and cousins arrived at the same time. Isabel joined them for a quick snack and entertained them with stories of the production's funny mishaps and the great reviews they'd received, including her own notices; she left out the news about the crimes.

She was overjoyed to have her family there and was sorry to leave them, but it was time to get ready to dance. Handing her dad the tickets she'd arranged, she said, "Great seats. After the performance, we are going to a party at my boss's mother's house. Enjoy the show." She hugged and kissed each one.

"Thank you," she whispered when she hugged her aunt.

Isabel arrived at the theater earlier than usual. The stagehands were hard at work, preparing for the last performance.

In the dressing room, she took out her favorite picture of her grandfather, Oratio, with his father, Rafael, and walked out to the stage.

"Hi, Miss Reardon. Feeling good?" Charlie

"Yes. Thank you. Is the prop room unlocked?" He nodded.

Isabel walked into the little room where the skeleton had been hidden for a hundred years. She'd been in the theatre several times since that terrible night, but tonight was different.

Holding the picture against her heart and closing her eyes, Isabel felt someone behind her. She swung around. Charlie stood in the doorway.

She held out the photograph. "This is a picture of my great-grandfather. It hasn't been confirmed yet, but I believe it was his skeleton they found behind the wall."

Charlie looked at the picture. "You know, Miss Reardon, no one has been able to explain for sure why that bolt pulled out of its housing and hit Victoria in the back." He looked at the picture. "Maybe you had help up there."

Isabel fought back the tears. "Maybe." Charlie smiled. "Warm-up class is about to begin."

Pushing the picture into the pocket of her sweatpants, Isabel joined the company on stage. Everyone was in a good mood. No one talked about what had happened or about Laurel getting fired.

In the dressing room, Isabel tucked the picture of her grandfather and Rafael in the mirror frame while she applied heavy stage makeup to her neck and face. She used it generously on her legs to ensure the bruises wouldn't show through the tights. Her parents hadn't noticed her neck because she'd used it earlier and kept her hair loosened all day.

The lights flashed. Time to start. The plucky first notes of the overture began. Isabel felt a rush of excitement.

Costumed and ready, she made her way to the wings. Orlando was there. As always, in the moments before their entrance music, they held hands, looked into each other's eyes, and synchronized their breathing.

Isabel's eyelids fluttered, as a warmth enveloped her. It was the aroma of her grandfather's favorite pipe. Her mouth pulled into a smile. She felt secure, protected.

The legato strains of the music beckoned the Snow Queen and her Cavalier from the wings into a magical land of beauty. The Snow Scene ended the first act. Isabelle, as the Snow Queen, and Orlando, as her Cavalier, stepped in front of the curtain for their bows.

On the third call, Orlando and Isabel looked at each other as if there was no one else in the world, then turned their radiant smiles to the audience. Orlando bowed deep, and Isabel performed her deepest curtsy with her hands crossed over her heart. Applause rocked the theater.

The final curtain came down on the season's last *Nutcracker*. Isabel and the dancers hugged, wished each other happy holidays, and took off to the dressing rooms.

Mrs. B. opened the door to cries of "Merry Christmas!" Father Melvyn gestured to the happy knot of guests, including Orlando, Isabel, and her family, to precede him.

Isabel kissed Mrs. B. and introduced her family, beginning with her parents, then her aunt and her two cousins.

"Mrs. B., it's lovely of you to do this," said Lizabetta Sanchez-Reardon.

"My pleasure. We are all very fond of your daughter." Mrs. B. hid her apprehension. Isabel had told her about the conversations with her Aunt Marie, who, when introduced, hugged Mrs. B. and winked.

The doorbell rang again, and a mighty cheer greeted Jake and Terri Zayas. Mrs. B. was happy that they'd come. Maybe Jake wasn't going to stay mad that she and Father Melvyn had become involved in another murder.

Watching her guests, Mrs. B. saw they were all mingling, talking, laughing, eating, and enjoying the party. Jake and Terri spoke with John and Lisa, who were beaming, relieved that the ghost stories had been laid to rest.

Isabel's family, too, glowed. This had been a magical night for them, watching Isabel light up the stage.

Once the party was in full swing, Father Melvyn led them in songs and carols with his deep baritone voice.

Isabel's Aunt Marie pulled Mrs. B. aside. "My niece told me how much she owes you and the priest. I want you to know that I took it upon myself to tell Isabel's parents. They were immensely grateful she wasn't killed. We agreed that for Isabel's sake, we wouldn't discuss it until after Christmas."

"I'm glad," Mrs. B. said. "Did you all enjoy the show?"

Aunt Marie beamed. "My sister and brother-in-law cried with joy. Isabel was magnificent. I get goosebumps just thinking about how beautiful she was onstage. And that young man who partnered her. Wow, what a striking couple they made on stage."

The two women looked over at Isabel and Orlando, smiling and talking. They looked at each other, eyes twinkling, "You never know," Mrs. B. said to Aunt Marie.

The party broke up at 2 a.m. Before they left, Isabel hugged and thanked Father Melvyn and Mrs. B. again.

Father Melvyn was the last to leave. "Great party," he whispered. "Tomorrow is Christmas Eve. I think LaLa would like to wish you Merry Christmas."

"Yes, of course. I have a gift for her, too." And you, she thought.

While they said their goodbyes, downtown, at the Zero Club, a mournful sax, accompanied by drums and a guitar played for the last hangers-on.

The music filtered into the office where Billy Slips sat at his desk, reading a newspaper. He dialed. "Mack, you saw the news on the Asturias scandal?"

The sleepy voice yawned and answered, "Yes."

"Looks like they're going to sell the mansion. I want it. Make it happen."

Mack, the head of Billy Slips' Marvel Real-Estate business, didn't ask why. He only said, "Will do."

Billy was satisfied. He'd bet there was more gold hidden in the Asturias home. His plan was a win-win. He'd find the gold then resell the mansion. Even if he didn't find it, the estate would bring in a fortune on resale.

The marquee at the Rue de L'Histoire Theatre was dark. Inside, the final strike had been completed hours earlier, but Mel, the acting stage manager, and Charlie, the longtime custodian and extra stagehand, stayed late to finish the manifest.

While they worked, they talked about the stunning events that had taken place.

"The story is mind-blowing," Mel said. "Now the papers are speculating that Asturias Enterprises is bankrupt, and the mansion will be sold to the highest bidder." He shook his head. "And Tony? Go figure."

"You can never tell about people," Charlie answered. "Any idea why the ropes pulled that bolt off?"

"No. The inspector scratched his head, literally. All he came up with was that the ropes put too much strain on the bolt from the physical struggle going on, and it pulled off the pipe. But—" Mel frowned. "Freaky," he said. "It shouldn't have happened."

"You look exhausted," Charlie said. "Go home. I'll do the lockup and turn on the ghost light." The day after the melee, he'd replaced the bulb and globe that had been broken in the melee.

"Thanks for staying, Charlie. *Nutcracker* is ready for pick up the day after Christmas." Mel grabbed his jacket. "Aren't you glad there are no ghosts?"

Charlie smiled and wished him a happy holiday. After Mel left, he rechecked all the levers, bolts, and locks. Everything was secure. Then he walked into the prop room.

After the police had broken through the wall and found the skeleton, they'd removed it for DNA testing. When they finished their investigation, he'd put up new wallboard, spackled and painted, then sealed the prop room entrance to the Asturias tunnel and pushed the cabinet that had hidden the secret room to the front of what had been the tunnel entrance.

Content that all was well, Charlie grabbed his jacket. On the notice board, he read the schedule. At the end of January, the Bernardi-Bono Ballet Company would present *Giselle*.

He liked the drama of that ballet. Women, jilted by their lovers, die of broken hearts on the eve of their weddings and become Wilis, the vengeful cemetery spirits, haunting the graveyards at night, in the dark, searching for men to dance to death.

Taking a final look at the vignette he'd arranged on stage with chairs and tables in a semi-circle, facing the long pole of the ghost light, he whispered, "Merry Christmas."

Smiling, he engaged the alarm and left.

## CHAPTER 58

### IN THE QUIET OF NIGHT

The silence enveloping the Rue de L'Histoire Theatre was broken only by the soft creaks and groans of the building resetting itself after the day's work.

Air currents gently swayed the backdrops above the stage, creating a faint squeak in the fly-wires holding them. Night creatures, never visible by day, skittered across the floor while the fabric of the wings moved ever so slightly as if brushed by a breeze.

And the ghost light stood tall on its long pole, sending its glow out from center stage.

Fragments of dust, cast white in the light's radiance, floated up from the floor, twisting, turning, and moving like a corps of ghostly Wilis dancing their heartbreak in the quiet of the night.

And the theater waited.

**Thank you for reading** *Catwalk Dead, Murder in the Rue de L'Histoire Theatre.* If you enjoyed the book as much as I enjoyed writing it, please consider leaving a review at https://www.amazon.com › B07ZHK8886

**Sign up** for my monthly newsletter, **HODGEPODGE,** updating you on soon to be released stories, recommendations for more mystery/thriller/suspense books as well as other interesting facts of fiction.

**Go to** http://fdellanotte.com **and email me, with NEWSLETTER ONLY in the subject box.**

**BRACKISH WATERS.**

*In nature when fresh water meets salt water and vigorous turbulence occurs, fresh and salt waters mix, becoming brackish.*

*Welcome to the novel's brackish pool where the turbulence of imagination mixes facts with fiction.*

From the outset in book one of the Housekeeper Mystery Series, the action is in the very real city of Austin, Texas, in a fictitious area of town where the fictitious parish of St. Francis de Sales, is located.

In the first book, *I'm Going to Kill that Cat,* a public fight between two senior parishioners triggered by a mischievous pussycat names LaLa, leaves one woman dead and the other accused of murder. The new team of amateur detectives, Father Melvyn and Mrs. B., find themselves embroiled in a murder that opens old scandalous wounds. Can they unravel this mystery before an innocent ends up in jail and one of them dead?

https://www.amazon.com B079RJL893

**COMING IN AUGUST, 2021:**
*The Church Murders and the Cat's Prey.*

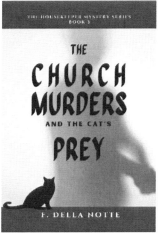

Current events and various international organizations and philosophies inform book three.

The story opens on Easter Sunday with a series of shocking attacks on churches throughout Central Texas, and the attack at St. Francis de Sales is the first in of the shootings and fire-bombings. A far-reaching plot by an international cabal takes shape, but at St. Francis, is there a personal vendetta aat work against Father Melvyn?

Can Mrs. B. and Father Melvyn help Detective Jake Zayas of the Austin police department untangle this web of intrigue and violence, or will they fall victims to hate and corruption?

*FOR CHARACTER BACKSTORIES in the Housekeeper Mystery Series, go to* http://www.fdellanotte.com *Leave your email dress to receive FREE character profile for Mrs. B., Father Melvyn, other characters and even the cats.*

## ACKNOWLEDGEMENTS

My heartfelt thanks go out to family and friends who support and push me to tell yet another story. A special thanks to my friends in the world of theater, especially ballet theater. Their lives, their craft, their beauty, and determination fuel much of my writing.

My critique group in Austin has been invaluable. Without KP, Helen and Kathy, I couldn't have gotten it all down, organized, and making sense. Thank you for your patience and encouragement.

Thank you to Mike Valentino, whose editing was invaluable. Any errors or omissions are my own.

Then there are my treasures. You all know who you are. You give my life balance and depth, and I thank God every day for making you my family.

I will remain ever grateful for everyone and everything He has put in my life – even the hard stuff.

TO MY READERS: *GRAZIE, SPASIBO, MERCI, GRACIAS, TACK.* IN ANY LANGUAGE, I THANK YOU FOR READING MY BOOK AND HOPE YOU WERE ENTERTAINED BY A CAST OF ECCENTRIC AND QUIRKY CHARACTERS.

To learn more about the author and share your thoughts, go to **fdellanotte.com.**

Leave your e-mail address in the comments section for notices of upcoming books, giveaways, and events.

Made in United States
North Haven, CT
01 February 2022

15483890R00233